When Julie Ives wrote her first novel, *Welcome to Welby Island*, she was inspired by her daughter's The Breakfast Club T-shirt, and put pen to the paper as the story flowed from her imagination. After the publication of the first novel, she realized that there was more that her main characters had to say and do, so she began the sequel, *Welcome to Welby Island: The Reunion*, which will continue the readers' journey with Leanne, Devon, Amber, Rosalie, and Leonard.

Julie is married to Howie and mother to Maggie and resides in South Florida where they enjoy all things outdoors.

I dedicate this book to all who read
Welcome to Welby Island and asked for more.

Julie Ives

WELCOME TO WELBY ISLAND: THE REUNION

AUSTIN MACAULEY PUBLISHERS™

LONDON • CAMBRIDGE • NEW YORK • SHARJAH

Ordering Information:
Quantity sales: special discounts are available on quantity purchases by corporations, associations, and others. For details, contact the publisher at the address below.

Publisher's Cataloging-in-Publication data
Ives, Julie
Welcome to Welby Island: The Reunion

ISBN 9781641827621 (Paperback)
ISBN 9781947353923 (ePub e-book)

Library of Congress Control Number: 2020917067

www.austinmacauley.com/us

First Published (2020)
Austin Macauley Publishers LLC
40 Wall Street, 28th Floor
New York, NY 10005
USA

mail-usa@austinmacauley.com
+1 (646) 5125767

I would like to thank all of the people at Austin Macauley Publishers that helped bring *Welcome to Welby Island: The Reunion* to life. From submissions and editing to production and marketing, without your professional support, I would not be an author of two published books.

Chapter 1
Christmas Day

Snuggled on the couch, warmed by the crackling fire, Leanne watched Luke and Lindsey tear into the gazillion presents that were part of Devon's vision of Christmas on Welby Island. It seemed like years had passed, although it had only been six months since the night, she and Devon sat on the beach late in the evening following Leonard and Amber's wedding when he told her what he imagined a family Christmas would be like. Having lost his mother by the brutal hands of his father at the age of sixteen, Devon was basically on his own from then on, with no family to speak of. Leanne looked from the twins to Chet's smiling face and when she landed on Devon, she wondered to herself, how she has been so lucky to have been given a second chance at love, a real love, the kind that comes from deep within the heart, not the same kind of love she had felt for Blake when they had met at college in Santa Clara. She had transferred her junior year from a school in Michigan, Blake had originally been accepted to Cali U, but when both of his parents died in a car accident ten days after his high school graduation, he had no way to pay the tuition, so he commuted back and forth from a small apartment he rented a mile away from Santa Clara College. He was bitter, pissed off, and stunned to learn that the house he grew up in was in full foreclosure, and any money his parents had in the bank, was only enough to bury them. He had an older brother, Brent, who had left home five years earlier, and was, as Blake had told her, "Shacking up with his gay lover somewhere on Maui." When Leanne asked him why he didn't contact his brother, he laughed and said, "He was banished from the family by my 'saintly' Irish father, who apparently had some buried sins of his own. I met three of them at the funeral." Blake never spoke another word about his family during their courtship or years of marriage. Leanne moved in with Blake in the tiny apartment her senior year, by this time Blake was attending law school. Leanne worked three jobs, paying the rent, food, and utility bills. They lived off whatever they could afford to buy and whatever Leanne could scrounge from the restaurant she worked at waitressing three nights a week. She always made sure that Blake had a nice meal on the table to come home to every night after long days of school and studying. Even though she had studies herself and had taken a second job in the college campus store, she spent weekends typing papers for a dozen law students including Blake and never complained. If she mentioned to Blake how tired she was, he would wrap his arms around her and soothingly say, "Babe, this will all pay off in the future when I am a big-time lawyer, I promise." Leanne believed him. But then again, Leanne believed everyone. When she lived in Michigan with her parents, life had been normal: happy. Then the summer before beginning her freshman year of college at Mich. U, her mother was stricken with cancer, it ravaged her fast and furious and she died three months later. Her father promised her that they would be okay, they would move on, and Leanne believed him. That was until he brought home Janice. Janice was 10 years older than Leanne, 16 years younger than her father, and had gold digger written all over her smug face. Janice moved in barely a year after her mother's death. Leanne came home for summer break, after finishing her freshman year, and found that Janice had removed every single thing of her mothers, right down to the curtains. There was not one memory left. Janice gutted the kitchen that Leanne's mother had been so happy in. Leanne had such wonderful memories of being a young girl baking in the kitchen with her mother. They would sing, dance, and laugh as they made muffins or homemade pasta. There would be flour everywhere and her father would come home from work, and say, "Look at my two flour girls," and twirl them both around the kitchen. Leanne spent the summer working at a local camp for kids with special needs when she returned to school for her sophomore year, she buried herself in her studies. She knew at an early age that she wanted to work with kids, so she chose a major in early childhood education, and minored in business. The following summer she decided to transfer to Santa Clara College for her junior and senior year, strictly to get as far away as she could from Janice, and unfortunately, her father. However, when she met Blake, her ambitions took a back seat. She graduated with both degrees, but never fulfilled her dreams. After graduation, she took a full-time job at a local advertising agency to continue supporting them. A year and a half later, Blake graduated from law school and passed the Bar exam. They moved to Los Angeles where Blake accepted a position at a small law firm, Jacoby & Tanner. Leanne was concerned about the move to such a big city, but Blake assured her he was doing this for her, he said he would start small and climb his way up to partner. Leanne believed him. Six months later, Blake proposed to Leanne, telling her that he heard from a colleague that the young married attorneys moved up faster. Leanne believed him. A month after the proposal they were married at City Hall. Leanne had just turned twenty-five. The months flew by Leanne was able to find a job at an advertising agency because of admirable references from her previous job in Santa Clara. Blake did exactly as he said he would, he started moving up in the firm and the money started coming in. They bought a big house in a beautiful neighborhood up in the hills. Two years later, at the age of twenty-seven, Leanne found herself pregnant and unemployed. Blake was thrilled about the pregnancy, and having twins was the icing on the cake. He asked Leanne to quit her job and start volunteering for charities that the wives of Jacoby and Tanner chaired, he told her that it would really help him move up the ladder a lot faster. Leanne believed him. When the twins were born, Leanne was totally consumed with them. Blake would come home bearing gifts for the babies and flowers for Leanne. They had a large group of friends, mostly the other lawyers and their families. Leanne hosted lavish dinner parties and back yard barbecues that were the talk of the town. They travelled with the twins to warm climates for the Christmas holidays. Life was good, just like Blake had told her and she believed. It wasn't until the twins turned three, and Blake made partner, did Leanne feel the tides start to turn. Blake worked longer hours, rarely making it home for dinner. Leanne's days were filled with playdates and charities. As exhausting as it was, she always kept herself well presented in her designer clothes and a smile on her face. It was beginning to take its toll. One night, a very rare night that Blake was home by seven, she put the kids to bed and joined Blake on the couch with a glass of wine. She asked him about his day and listened attentively as he told her about this case and that case. He would always end by swirling the scotch in his glass and say, "I told you, babe, I was going to the top." Leanne would smile and clink glasses with him. However, on this particular night, Leanne needed to be heard. She began to tell Blake about her day, but when he cut her short, claiming he needed to make an important call, Leanne sighed and drank her wine as he left the room. As the months passed by, Leanne became more exhausted. The twins turned four and began pre-school. Classroom volunteering was a must according to the other moms, so Leanne became a room mom. Activities started for the twins, ballet for Lindsey, and soccer for Luke. Then, of course, there were the days of contagious diseases, strep for Luke and ear infections for Lindsey, dentist visits, well check-ups, and growth spurts which required new clothes and dreaded shopping trips. When the twins reached first grade, Leanne was bullied into joining the PTA. As she now reflects back, this may have been when the ice began to crack, with the help of a sledgehammer named Penny Perkins.

"Mommy, Mommy, this one's for you!" Leanne, having been lost in thought, snapped out of it as Luke and Lindsey tugged on her arm. "Mommy this one's special, it's from Devon to you, open it, open it!"

Leanne looked up to see Devon standing beside her, he bent down close to her ear and asked, "What has your mind all gaggled up Queen Bee?"

Leanne laughed and replied, "Nothing." She turned to the twins and said, "Okay, let's see what we have here," she began to un-wrap the small package in her lap. Once the wrapping was off, she stared at the gift in her hand. It was a picture of Claine Cabin with all the words the five, Leanne, Devon, Rosalie, Amber and Leonard, had painted on it. She stared at it for a minute in silence, as she read the words that were photo-shopped onto it, "Will you marry me?" She looked at Devon, who was now down on one knee in front of her, holding a small box with the most beautiful aquamarine and diamond ring in it. The twins were bouncing on their toes telling her to say yes. She looked at Chet standing behind Devon, wearing an ear to ear grin on his face, then looked Devon in the eyes and said, "Yes. Yes, I will marry you."

Chapter 2

The month of January flew bye, February was upon them and Leanne dreaded the thought of having to bring the twins to Los Angeles for Blake's week with them. Since their divorce last July, Blake had only seen the kids once and only because he was in Seattle for the weekend. He called her in October and said he was in Seattle on business and could only spare an hour to see the twins. It infuriated her, but she agreed. Blake wanted to come to the house, but Leanne said no, she would bring them into the city, and he could take them for ice cream. When she arrived at the designated meeting place, she practically turned tail and left. There, sitting at a table was Blake and Allie, the nanny she caught him in bed with. Blake stood up and held out his arms for the twins, but they didn't budge, they clung onto Leanne's legs. When Blake told them to come and sit down, they looked up at Leanne with glassy eyes. Leanne bent down and said, "Go have ice cream with Daddy. I'm going shopping very close by and I will be back in one hour to get you," she kissed them both on top of the head and walked them to the table. Without even acknowledging Allie, she turned to Blake and said, "I will be back in one hour," turned and walked out the door.

She wasn't worried about seeing Blake again, because she knew this time, she would have Devon with her, but the thought of being away from Luke and Lindsey for a week had her stomach in knots. Devon made arrangements for them to stay at a friend's house in LA for the week. The friend happened to be Renay Zimmer, the actress who gave him a place to stay when he arrived from London when he was eighteen. She was out of the country and offered her house to them for as long as they needed it. Rosalie and Harold also invited them to stay at their house, but the idea of a week alone together, for the first time, was a gift waiting to be unwrapped.

When Saturday, February sixteenth arrived, Leanne was as ready as she would ever be. Chet offered to fly them to LA and was going to spend the night with them so they could meet Rosalie and Harold for dinner that night. They loaded the luggage onto Sadie and buckled up. Luke and Lindsey were over the moon with excitement to be flying on Sadie and fought over who would sit up front with Chet, but Leanne told them they had to sit together in the backseats, which did not make either of them happy. Devon saw the opportunity to give Luke and Lindsey the gift he bought for them. He reached into his bag and brought out the box, he turned to the twins and said, "Let's see if we can turn those frowns upside down. I have something for you, but it's not a toy and you have to take very good care of it."

Both kids nodded vigorously and asked, "What is it, what is it?"

Devon opened the box and handed Luke the cell phone he had bought for them, then explained that is was a phone and it was for any time they missed Mommy they could call her. He told them to keep it with them every night so he and Leanne could call them to say goodnight, and then he added, "Oh, and I might have forgotten to mention, that I installed a few games on there."

Luke and Lindsey's eyes lit up, Luke said, "Thanks, Devon! Since I'm two minutes older than Lindsey, I'll be in charge."

"Not fair Luke, I want to be in charge," protested Lindsey.

Leanne saw where this was headed and jumped into the fray, "Okay, okay, you two, this was a gift from Devon, so no fighting. This is how it's going to work, we have a three-hour flight ahead of us, Luke you get to play games on the phone for the first hour and a half and Lindsey you can have it for the next hour and a half. Once you get to your father's house, the phone goes into the suitcase. At night you keep it by your bed, understood?" They both looked at Leanne and nodded.

Devon added, "I put your moms and my phone number in it, and there is a charger in the box, you will need to charge it every night, got it?" Again, both children nodded.

Devon turned back around, looked at Leanne, put his hands in the air, and said, "I should have gotten bloody two of them."

Leanne laughed and said, "One will do, and that was very thoughtful of you. It didn't even cross my mind, but it does make me feel better knowing we can reach them at any time."

Devon reached for Leanne's hand and replied, "Well then, I guess I didn't make a complete muddle of it."

When they landed at SoCal Executive airport, there was a long, sleek black limousine waiting for them. Chet stored Sadie in the hanger, went in, and filed his flight paperwork and then they were off.

*****

Leanne had made previous arrangements with Blake, that she would drop the kids off at twelve noon on Saturday and pick them up the following Saturday at noon, to which he agreed. When the limo pulled up in front of her old house precisely at noon, the one she, Blake and the kids had lived in for six years, she felt nothing, not one pang of regret, not one feeling of longing, however, what she felt was anger, as she watched Blake load his golf clubs into the trunk of his car. She got out of the limo, followed by Devon, Chet, and the twins. She marched up the driveway to where Blake stood and asked, "What are you doing?"

Blake closed the trunk of his car, turned to Leanne, and with a smug look on his face replied, "Hello Leanne, you're early."

Leanne tapped the watch on her wrist and responded, "No we are not early, we are right on time, twelve noon as planned. So again, I ask you, what are you doing loading golf clubs into the trunk of your car?"

"Well, if you must know, I am going to play a round of golf with a client," Blake replied, by this time Devon had approached and was standing at Leanne's side.

Leanne the locomotive came out of retirement and started her engine, "The hell you are Blake. This is your week with Luke and Lindsey, and I better not find out you ditched them with your pop tart."

Just then Allie emerged from the house and walked over to the three of them. When she caught sight of Devon, she went wide-eyed, "Oh my God, you're Devon Davis. I can't believe it. I have all of your CD's!"

All three of them looked at her, but Devon being Devon, reached out his hand and said, "And you must be Allie. I have heard a lot about you." Allie just stood there star struck.

Annoyed, Blake said to Allie, "Take the kids inside and get them settled." Allie didn't speak, she just nodded with her eyes glued to Devon, then walked over to the twins, who were clinging to Chet's legs.

Leanne rounded on Blake and growled, "Don't let me find out you were not with those kids all week. If I do, you will find yourself in front of the judge faster than you can say 'fore,' got it?"

Blake smirked and retorted, "Don't forget Leanne, I'm a lawyer, a very good lawyer."

Leanne took a step closer to Blake, and replied, "And don't you forget, I'm a mother, a very good one, just ask the judge who awarded me full custody of OUR children," and with that said she turned and walked back to the kids.

Devon turned to Blake and said, "Apparently everything I have heard about you is accurate, so let me say this, you mess with Leanne and those kids, you mess with me, got it?" Devon turned and walked away, leaving a stunned Blake in his wake.

Once back in the limo, Leanne let loose, "Can you believe that asshole? He was going to play golf, probably hoping to be gone before we got here. If he leaves the kids with that tart all week, there will be hell to pay."

Chet patted Leanne's knee and said, "Don't you worry any Leanne, I think you put the fear of the Almighty in him, and if the look on his face when we left is any indication, so did Devon."

Devon smiled at Chet, put his arm around Leanne, and said, "Well he is a complete and utter ass, but I think he'll do right by the kids, and remember they have the phone, they can call us at any time to come and get them."

Leanne took a deep breath, reached out for Chet and Devon's hands, and said, "Thank you. I don't know what I would do without either of you."

Chapter 3

Renay Zimmer's house sat high in the Hollywood hills, it wasn't as big as the house on Welby Island, but it was situated on a cliff with the most amazing view of the Pacific Ocean. The interior had an open chef's kitchen with a breakfast nook, a quaint dining room, a huge living room with floor to ceiling sliding glass doors that opened to a gorgeous slate patio with a kidney shape pool, a built-in fire pit and a seven-seat teak bar. Upstairs had four ensuite bedrooms, each with their own balcony. Leanne walked through the first floor of the house looking at all the pictures hanging on the walls of Renay and other celebrities, posters of movies she had been in, and red-carpet appearances. She didn't hear Devon walk up behind her as she stood in front of a picture of Renay and Guy Grant. Devon wrapped his arms around Leanne's waist, rested his chin on her shoulder, and said, "I'm going to ask Renay for an autographed copy for Amber."

Leanne smiled and replied, "That would be really nice."

Devon laughed and said, "Well, my intent is, to bring her down a few notches before she meets them in person at our wedding."

Leanne turned to face Devon, and said, "Um, well, I know we haven't talked much about the wedding, but I was thinking, and only if you are okay with it, but I thought maybe we could have a small private ceremony on the beach of the big house, you, me, the twins with Chet officiating, and then throw a big party Labor Day weekend, like a reunion from Amber and Leonard's wedding, but with Chet's cronies and your friends added."

Devon said, "That sounds like a splendid idea. However, I would love to see how you will put that one past Amber and Rosalie."

Leanne sighed and replied, "Hmm…that might be a problem."

Devon cupped her face with his hands, kissed her lips, and said, "Let's give it some thought. However, I do love your vision of our wedding day, and I love you."

They kissed tenderly and then with more passion, Devon took a breath and pointed out the fact that they had six hours before they were to meet Rosalie and Harold for dinner. He suggested that they move to the bedroom, but Leanne was hesitant because Chet was with them and said so. Devon smiled and said, "No need to worry there, our man Chet is on his way with Jorge, the limo driver, to Hollywood Studios. I got him a tour pass and I don't expect we'll see him for a few hours."

Astonished, Leanne poked Devon in the chest and said, "Hey, I would have done that with him. I would love to see the behind the scenes of Hollywood."

Devon laughed and said, "I have us booked for Tuesday, but for now, why don't we go upstairs, take off all of our clothes, and I'll call 'action.'"

Leanne smiled slyly, and said, "The first one up the stairs wins," and took off running.

*****

Chet and Devon were in the living room waiting for Leanne to come downstairs. A few minutes later she emerged wearing an aqua colored pantsuit with pencil leg pants and a long tuxedo-style jacket, which not only matched the color of her eyes, but also the engagement ring Devon had given her at Christmas.

Chet whistled and said, "Well don't you look mighty pretty, Leanne."

Leanne smiled and replied, "Thank you Chet, and I must say you are looking mighty handsome yourself."

Chet straightened the collar of his navy-blue blazer, which he wore over a light blue button-down oxford shirt with pressed khakis and black loafers, replied, "Well, thank you, Leanne. I'm not used to wearing such fancy duds, but Devon dragged me into one of those men's stores in Seattle and made me buy them for tonight."

Devon laughed and said, "You can wear them more than once, you know. Maybe you could ask out Frieda from the bakery you visit so often. I'm pretty sure she fancy's you."

Leanne's eyebrows shot up as she said, "Really now? Do tell Chet."

Feeling a tad bit uncomfortable, Chet shuffled from one foot to another, and replied, "Ain't nothing to tell. Devon here is just making up stories."

23

Devon snorted and said, "Ha! I think not. Every day you come home with a bag of those jelly donuts you fancy."

"Never mind that, you should be focusing your attention on your own gal," Chet retorted.

Devon laughed and patted Chet on the shoulder as he walked over to Leanne, put his hands on her cheeks, and said, "You look stunning," and kissed her lips.

Leanne replied, "Thank you. And you look ridiculously handsome. Now if you two children are done bickering, I think we should get a move on it, Rosalie will be bent seven ways to Sunday if we are a minute late. She is so excited to see us, she texted me three times, making sure we would be there on time." With that said, they headed out the door to a waiting Jorge and the limo.

*****

The reservation was for eight o'clock at Cagney's on Wilshire. Rosalie and Harold chose the restaurant because they are regulars there, and the clientele is a mix of the rich and famous, which would make it easier for Devon to blend in. Once inside they gave the hostess Rosalie's name and were told that she had not yet arrived, but she would seat them at the table to wait. Once seated, Leanne said, "What the hell? She texted me three times today, making sure we would be here on time, and she's not even here."

Ten minutes later, Leanne looked up to see Rosalie rushing toward the table with Harold in tow and following close behind were Leonard and a very pregnant Amber. Her hands flew to her mouth and tears filled her eyes.

Rosalie reached the table and was talking a million miles a minute, "Oh my God, I'm so sorry we are late, who would think a pregnant woman would have to pee so much, here we were heading out the door, and country girls gotta go—"

Leanne cut her off by standing up and rushing around the table to hug Rosalie and Harold, then took a few steps forward and grabbed Amber in a momma bear hug, with tears streaming down her face, she backed up to take in all of Amber, from her bulging belly to her sparkling blue eyes, "Amber, look at you, oh my God, you're pregnant!"

Not able to hold back, Rosalie said, "Ya think? Can you imagine my shock when, she and Boy Wonder here, showed up on our doorstep this morning? I was keeping them coming, a surprise for you, and BAM! I'm mowed over by our country girl six months pregnant and with twins nonetheless."

Absolutely speechless, Leanne just stood there taking in the sight before her. Devon and Chet were on their feet, hugging everyone, it wasn't until Leonard tapped Leanne on the shoulder, did she break her trance, she turned to Leonard and said, "Oh my God Leonard," and wrapped her arms around him, hugging him tightly. "I just can't believe this, what a wonderful surprise." She turned to Rosalie and said, "And here I was thinking you were texting me like a crazy lady so we wouldn't be late. Thank you, Rosalie, what a fabulous surprise."

After all the hugging and OMG's were done, the seven of them sat down at the table, and the questions shot rapid-fire from Leanne. When they got to the part about the pregnancy, and the when, since they knew the how, it was

Rosalie who said, in typical Rosalie fashion, "Yeah, so it looks like Country Girl and Boy Wonder got the hang of the 'you know what' pretty fast."

Amber, being Amber, replied, "Oh we sure did, and let me tell you Leanne, yours and Devon's little escapade on the cabin floor, doesn't hold a candle to what we christened inside and outside of that cabin," Leonard coughed and took a sip of his water. Amber kicked him under the table.

The four men shot their eyes to Leanne. Devon's eyebrows went up like an umbrella, and he said to Leanne, "Ah, so you are the kiss and tell kind of girl, are you?"

Flustered, Leanne replied, "No, well yes, but I only told these two the night before Ambers wedding, when we went down to the beach, but that's not the point here, is it?" Leanne turned back to Amber and asked, "So does this mean you conceived on your honeymoon?"

Shoving a garlic roll in her mouth, Amber mumbled, "Apparently."

"Why didn't you tell us sooner?" asked Leanne.

"Well," said Amber, "We wanted to wait at least three months to make sure everything was okay with the babies, then Rosalie called us a few months ago and asked us to come to visit when you were here, so Leonard and I thought it would be fun to surprise you." ."

Leanne laughed and said, "Well that you did. I'm so happy for you two."

Rosalie was eyeing Leanne, and once she figured it out, she said to Leanne, "I have a funny feeling that's not the only surprise of the night. Give me your hand," Leanne looked at Rosalie and put out her right hand, "Not that hand Locomotive, the left hand." Leanne raised her left hand off her lap and pointed it and her gorgeous engagement ring at Rosalie, "I knew it!" shouted Rosalie, "I could see it written all over your face."

Amber, always a little slow to catch on, asked Leanne, "Oh my word, are you and Devon engaged?" Leanne nodded. Amber tried twice to jump out of her chair to get to Leanne but couldn't manage to get her bulk out of the chair.

Amused, Devon said, "Well aren't we all a basket of surprises," and congratulations were passed around the table.

Chapter 4

Devon and Leanne woke to a glorious Thursday morning. Devon had a meeting with his manager, Gordy Little, downtown at noon and Rosalie was picking Leanne up to go shopping. But before they started their day, Devon and Leanne lingered in bed a little while longer. Devon had told her about meeting with Gordy, but not the details, so Leanne asked, "So what is your meeting about?"

Devon turned to face her, propped his head on his hand, and replied, "Well, I've finished the last song for the album, so all we have to do now is come up with a title for it."

Leanne adjusted to a sitting position and said, "Well, that should be easy enough."

Devon laughed, and said, "One would think, but I just can't seem to come up with one."

Leanne reached for his hand and said, "I've heard most of your songs, except for the last one you just finished, but I would say this album is different than the others, it's softer, more personal. If I had to use one word to describe it, I would say…enlightenment."

Devon let go of Leanne's hand and sat up, he looked at her and said, "Bloody hell, that's it. I just couldn't put my finger on the word or feeling that I felt while writing the songs, but I wrote most of them during or after my stint at Claine Cabin. Enlightenment, yes, you are bloody brilliant."

Amused, Leanne said, "Your welcome."

Devon kissed her and said, "And for that, Queen Bee, you are getting breakfast in bed," he pulled on his jeans and dashed out of the room.

*****

Rosalie insisted on picking up Leanne for their day of shopping. She was as curious as a cat to see the inside of Renay Zimmer's house and would have her realtor beacon on high. She arrived promptly at noon, and Leanne took her on a tour of the house. Most of it Leanne had seen herself, but the zinger was the massive home theatre; it could hold a hundred people.

Rosalie's professional opinion was, that is wasn't a pretentious house, it felt more subdued, comfortable and the view was the star. Rosalie figured she could get nine million for it, and as if reading her mind, Leanne told Rosalie, "Forget whatever you're thinking, the house isn't up for sale."

Rosalie scoffed and replied, "It may be one day, and Devon is going to make sure I get the listing."

Leanne laughed and said, "I saw that coming a mile away. Come on let's go buy those baby clothes for Amber and Leonard's babies."

*****

Leanne and Rosalie spent an hour store hopping and then decided to have lunch at a sidewalk café. Leanne had noticed something about Rosalie as they shopped. She was always looking behind her. When they placed their order for Cobb salads and a glass of chardonnay, Leanne broached the subject, "Rosalie, can I ask you a question?"

"Sure, what's on your mind?" replied Rosalie.

"Well, that's pretty much what I was going to ask you. You seem, um, well a bit jumpy. No, that's not the word, maybe more like distracted, like you are expecting to see someone," said Leanne.

Rosalie sighed, and said, "Okay, you're right, but I can't actually put it into words, it's more like a feeling."

Concerned, Leanne asked, "What kind of feeling?"

"I'm not sure, it's been nagging at me for about a month now. I feel like someone is watching me. I know it sounds crazy, but every once in a while something happens that makes the hairs on my neck tingle," said Rosalie.

Confused, Leanne asked, "Why would you think that? Has anything happened?"

"No, not really," replied Rosalie, "Except, a month ago, I got a call from a guy that wanted to see one of my properties I have listed. It's a small bungalow down by the marina, the house is nothing special, but the property the house sits on is massive and in a great location."

"Why would that make your neck tingle? You deal with people looking for houses every day," Leanne asked.

"Normally it wouldn't, but he set up the appointment to meet at the house the following day at two, but he never showed up. I waited an hour and nothing, not even a phone call to reschedule, and when I tried to reach him on the number he gave me, it was for the diner over on Wildwood," replied Rosalie.

Leanne, feeling a slight tingle on her neck, said, "Huh, that's odd. But you know what, it was probably someone looking outside their price range, just looking for information, or better yet, it could be one of your competitors being an asshole."

Rosalie gave that some thought and said, "You're right. I'm just reading into it," their salads arrived, and the subject was changed.

Chapter 5

Chet had arrived yesterday, and they went to Rosalie's and Harold's house for a barbecue. Leanne was expecting take out, but to her amazement, Rosalie had put together fabulous arrangements of hors d'oeuvres and salads, and Harold manned the grill with steaks and lobster tails. They chatted the night away and were surprised to find it was midnight when they said their goodbyes.

Today, Leanne was like a butterfly fluttering from flower to flower, as she packed her suitcase. She was beyond excited to pick up Luke and Lindsey. They spoke every night at bedtime and the twins told her stories of what they did, a lot of them began with "and Allie took us here, and Allie did this," but Leanne wasn't going to dwell on that right now. Once she found out the true facts of the week that is when she would deal with Blake. But today, the most important thing is that her babies will be in her arms in less than an hour.

Devon walked into the room and asked Leanne, "Are you all set up here?"

Leanne closed her suitcase and replied, "Just about, let me take one more look around, and then you can take the suitcases downstairs."

Devon sat on the edge of the bed watching Leanne, when she came out from the bathroom, he told her to sit down next to him. He took her hand and said, "This has been a fabulous week, but I have to admit, I'm really looking forward to seeing the tickle terrors."

Leanne smiled at him and said, "It really has been wonderful. Having some time alone with you has been such a gift, and the time we got to spend with Rosalie and Harold was an added bonus, but I really miss my babies."

Devon kissed her hand, stood up, and said, "Well, let's go get them."

Chet and Jorge were sitting in the living room, Jorge got up and took the suitcases from Devon and left the house, Chet stood up and said, "What the devil took you so long Leanne? Don't you know those youngins will be running around in circles waiting for us?"

Leanne laughed and replied, "I know they will, and I can't wait to see them."

Devon said to Leanne, "Looks like Chet missed them as much as us."

Chet said, "Well it was too dang quiet in that house all week. Bella and Blaze whined and moped all day long, so let's get a move on it," they locked up the house and headed for the limo.

*****

They arrived at Blake's at five of noon, and true to Chet's words, Luke and Lindsey were literally running in circles on the front lawn. Their suitcases were on the porch and the front door was open, but there was no sign of

Blake or Allie. When Leanne, Devon, and Chet got out of the car, Luke and Lindsey came running towards them, straight into Leanne's open arms. She hugged them with all her might, kissing them all over their faces. Once she let go, Luke and Lindsey ran over to Chet and Devon, and it turned into one big group hug. Jorge retrieved the suitcases from the front porch and loaded them into the trunk. By this time Allie had opened the door and was standing on the porch. Leanne turned to Devon and Chet and said, "Can you get the kids buckled up in the car? I need a minute with Allie."

Leanne walked across the lawn to the porch and asked Allie, "Where is Blake?"

Nervous as a cat, Allie replied, "Um, well, he had to go to the office this morning, and hasn't returned."

Leanne took off her sunglasses, silently counted to ten, and then said, "Is that so?"

"He said he would be back by noon. I just called him, but he didn't answer," replied Allie.

Leanne gave that a thought for a moment. She didn't want to unleash her anger on Allie, so she took a deep breath and said, "Okay, well then I have two things to say to you. First, I would like to thank you for taking care of Luke and Lindsey this past week, and second, pack your bags and run for the hills. I can tell you right now that Blake is not at the office, and if true to form, he is out conquering his latest plaything." Leanne put her sunglasses back on, turned, and headed across the lawn, leaving Allie looking like a deer in headlights.

*****

34

The twins talked non-stop the whole flight home. They told stories of having gone to the beach with Allie, to the zoo with Allie, and to the farmer's market with Allie, where they got to feed the chickens, which they now want as pets. When they finally stopped for a breath, Leanne said, "Well that sounds like you had a great time with Allie, but you didn't mention all the fun things you did with Daddy."

Luke and Lindsey looked at each other, finally Luke reached into his pocket and pulled out a hundred-dollar bill, held it up and said, "Daddy asked us to keep a secret. He said to tell you he was with us all week when really he was at work."

"He had really important meetings," added Lindsey.

Leanne didn't know if it was a good thing she was on a plane or a bad thing, because the locomotive was starting her engine. Devon saw that familiar look on her face, grabbed her hand, and pulled her to the front of the plane out of little ears hearing range and said very cautiously, "Leanne, look at me. Leanne, you need to count to ten and take a deep breath."

Leanne took a deep breath and counted to ten, twice, then looked Devon in the eyes and said very quietly, "He paid our kids one hundred dollars to lie to me. He abandoned them all week with his twenty-six-year-old girlfriend, whom you can bet sure as shit, he's cheating on as we speak. But to think he can get away with this, with money, that's just so low, even for him."

With a firm grip on Leanne's shoulders, Devon very calmly said, "Leanne, we will take care of this when we get home, right now you need to go back there and reassure Luke and Lindsey that they did nothing wrong by taking the money and tell them not keeping the secret was the right thing to do."

Leanne nodded, "You're right. I'm okay. I'm calmer, but when we get home, I am going after him like a bat out of hell."

Devon kissed the top of her head and said, "That's my girl."

Chapter 6

They arrived back on Welby Island at four o'clock. After
unloading the suitcases from Sadie, Leanne set out to see
what she could whip up for dinner. When she opened the
refrigerator, she saw that it was fully stocked and there
was a pot of homemade sauce sitting front and center,
"Well, that was easy. Pasta it is," she said out loud to
herself.

Just then Devon walked into the kitchen and asked
Leanne, "Are you talking to the refrigerator?"

Leanne turned and replied, "No. Well, yes. But I
wasn't talking to the refrigerator, I was talking to myself. I
was wondering what to make for dinner, and when I
opened the fridge, there sat a pot of homemade sauce, so
pasta it is."

Devon walked over to Leanne, wrapped his arms
around her and she instantly molded into his embrace. He
kissed her head and said, "I fondly recall when you wore
your chef's hat at the cabin, sometimes it was for pleasure,
other times to calm yourself. So, I'm going to take a guess
and say that you were looking to do a bit of chopping on
the butcher block."

Leanne didn't budge from Devon's warm embrace, but she answered with a tinge of leftover anger, "Yup, I was going to put a slab of meat on there and picture it was Blake's head, then pound the shit out of it. But since we are having pasta, I'll have to settle for chopping up carrots for the salad, and I'll use my imagination as to which body part I am chopping up."

Devon released his hold on Leanne and said, "Ouch, that poor carrot. However, I think I might have something to cheer you up. I was sorting through the mail and found this," he pulled an envelope out of his back pocket and handed it to Leanne.

Leanne walked over to the island, sat down, and opened the envelope, which was addressed by Kate Quinn, and then she squealed with delight. Devon was pouring them each a glass of wine. Startled by Leanne, he asked, "What's the matter?"

"Oh, nothing's wrong, come see," replied Leanne. "It's an invitation to Amber and Leonard's baby shower. It's going to be a country hoe-down on the farm."

Confused, Devon looked at Leanne and asked, "A hoe-down. What the bloody hell is that? It sounds frightening."

Leanne laughed and said, "No it's not. A hoe-down is a dance in a barn. It's a country thing."

Still confused, Devon said, "Who in their right mind would want to dance in a barn?"

Amused, Leanne replied, "Oh never mind. Just think of it as a big party on a farm."

Devon took a sip of his wine and said, "Ah, well that certainly clears it up, it should be a ton of fun."

Leanne stood up and kissed Devon and said, "It will be. I'm going to get dinner started. Do you know where the twins are?"

Devon stood and replied, "Yup, they are out front with Chet and the dogs. I think I'll go see what they are up to," he grabbed a beer from the fridge for Chet, picked up his wine glass, and headed outside.

*****

At six o'clock, Leanne walked out onto the front porch, what she saw made her heart swell. Devon, Chet, Luke, and the dogs were sitting in a circle on the lawn and Lindsey was running around them yelling, "Duck, duck, duck, goose." Lindsey tapped Bella's head and the dog got up and chased her in a circle. Leanne laughed and called out to them, "Okay gang, dinner is ready."

Leanne set a bowl of pasta, the salad, and a loaf of her famous focaccia bread on the table poured milk into the twin's glasses and took her seat. She loaded pasta and salad onto Luke and Lindsey's plates, while Chet and Devon helped themselves. Once everyone was settled, she turned to Chet and asked, "Did Devon tell you about the invitation we received from Kate?"

Chet reached for a piece of bread, and replied, "Nope. What's it for?"

Before Leanne had a chance to reply, Devon said, "A dance in a barn."

Leanne smirked and said, "Actually, it's a baby shower for Leonard and Amber. It's going to be a country hoe-down."

"Well that sounds mighty fun," said Chet.

Devon looked at Chet in astonishment, and asked, "You actually know what a hoe-down is? It sounds quite odd to me, a bunch of people dancing in a barn."

Chet laughed and said, "Son, me and my Annie used to attend our church hoe-downs every Friday night. We would dosey-doe and two-step the night away."

Devon, wide-eyed, asked, "What the bloody hell are a dosey-doe and two-step?"

This time it was Lindsey who answered, "I can show you. Stand up."

Devon looked at her, then at Leanne and Chet, who were both obviously amused, then back to Lindsey and said, "Okay pint-size, show me what you got."

Devon stood and Lindsey grabbed his hand and lead him into the middle of the kitchen, and said, "Okay, now we have to hook our arms together like this, then when the song comes on we do this, and when the man tells you to switch partners, you dosey-doe over to the girl on your right, it's easy."

Devon, still not convinced, said, "So what you're saying is, we hook arms, dance in a circle, then move onto other people?"

Pleased, Lindsey said, "Exactly! But we need more people," she turned to Leanne, Chet, and Luke and said, "Come on, let's all show him."

Luke, shoveling pasta into his mouth said, "Unt uh, no way. Mimi Goodwin asked me to dance with her in the school play, and I said no."

Chet laughed and said to Leanne, "Come on, let's show them how it's done."

Leanne got up from the table, joined Chet, standing face to face, took a bow, hooked arms, and began dosey-doeing around the kitchen. When it came time to switch partners, Leanne hooked arms with Devon, and Chet and Lindsey paired up and they danced until they fell down laughing. When they were all done, they returned to the table and Devon said, "Well that was fun. However, I think I'll need a bit more practice."

Lindsey smiled proudly and said, "Don't you worry Devon, I got you covered," and that set the table into a fit of laughter.

Chet finished his pasta, turned to Leanne, and asked, "So when is this shindig happening?"

"Friday, May tenth. I'll call Kate tomorrow and find out more details," replied Leanne.

Chet said, "I can fly us all there on Sadie if you can find out where the nearest airport is."

Devon had an idea of his own and said, "Why don't we make a road trip out of it? We can rent a camper and stop and see some sights along the way."

Chet, liking the sound of Devon's idea, added, "Me and my Annie had a camper when we first got married, I'd hitch it to my truck, and we would pack it up and go north to Canada or east to Yellowstone Park or wherever the open road took us."

Luke and Lindsey were both on board, and let it be known, "Way cool," they both said at the same time.

Leanne, on the other hand, was not as fond of the idea, and said, "Um, so you want to rent a camper and hitch it to Chet's truck and drive to Oklahoma?"

Devon laughed and said, "Well that's not quite what I had in mind. I was thinking maybe something more in line with my tour bus."

Leanne raised an eyebrow and said, "Oh, so we're taking your tour bus?"

Feeling a tad frustrated, Devon replied, "No, but there are campers that look like tour buses, but are equipped like a house, with a kitchen, bedroom, and a bathroom."

Chet knew what Devon was talking about and said, "You're talking about a Winnebago."

"Exactly, a Winnebago," replied Devon, pleased to know someone understood what he was talking about.

Leanne, still skeptical asked, "And exactly how long would it take to get from Seattle to Oklahoma in a Winnebago?"

Devon smiled at her and answered, "Well, I'm not quite sure. But I can find out easily enough. Where is the invitation, it must have their address on it?"

Leanne got up, walked over to the refrigerator, removed the invitation, and handed it to him. Devon looked at the address, typed it into his phone, and said cheerily, "Twenty-four hours. It is 1,728 miles to be precise."

Stunned, Leanne said, "Are you kidding me? You want to drive twenty-four hours with two kids, are you crazy? Did you not just experience three hours on an airplane with them?"

Amused, Devon replied, "Well, we will have Blaze and Bella to keep them company, Chet and I will take turns driving, and we'll spend three nights at campgrounds along the way. According to this map, we'll travel through, Oregon, Idaho, Utah, and Colorado, before we get to Oklahoma."

Still not convinced, Leanne sarcastically said, "Idaho? What are we going to do there, pick potatoes?"

"Possibly, but the point is, we will see places we've never seen before along the way. And, once we arrive at the farm, we can park there, and will have all the comforts of a hotel room," replied Devon.

Giving this some thought, Leanne looked around the table to see four pairs of eyes pleading with her. Outnumbered, she reluctantly said, "Okay, I'll run it by Kate tomorrow. If she agrees we can park on the farm, then I guess it will work." Hoorays, hoots, and hollers came from around the table. Leanne wondered what the heck she just signed up for.

*****

The next morning, they had a leisurely Sunday breakfast. After the kitchen was cleaned up and the kids were off crabbing with Chet, Leanne told Devon that she was going to throw a load of laundry in the washer, then call Kate.

Leanne dialed the number on the invitation, it rang three times until Kate answered, "Good morning, Quinn's Bakery."

Leanne said, "Kate, is that you? It's me, Leanne."

"Oh, Leanne sweetie, it's so nice to hear your voice," replied Kate.

Leanne asked, "Am I catching you at a bad time? It sounds like you might be busy. I didn't know I would be calling the bakery, but it was the number on the invitation."

Kate cheerily said, "No, no this is perfect. I put the bakery number on the invitations because I'm trying to keep it a surprise for Amber. Leonard knows, and let me tell you, that baby girl of mine is curious as a cat, but I don't think she's caught on yet."

Leanne laughed and said, "When Amber sets her mind to something, she latches on and doesn't let go, so I'm sure you would know if she knew."

"That is very true," agreed Kate.

Leanne said, "Well, I'm calling to tell you that we will be there. We wouldn't miss it for the world. But I have a few things I wanted to run by you. Devon came up with this crazy idea that we should rent a Winnebago and drive there. We would spend a few nights camping and sightseeing on our way. We would arrive at the farm on Thursday, and I was wondering if it would be possible for us to park somewhere on the farm?"

Excitedly, Kate replied, "That sounds like a wonderful idea! Absolutely, we have a hundred acres, so you can park anywhere you like."

Astonished, Leanne said, "A hundred acres!"

Kate laughed, and said, "Well, in Oklahoma, you go big or go home. The nearest motel is 30 miles away, so having the camper will make it much more convenient. It's a wonderful idea."

Leanne and Kate talked a few minutes more and then said goodbye. Leanne went downstairs to find Devon to tell him about her conversation with Kate. The house is so damn big, it took her a half hour to find him in the north wing in his recording studio. He was on the phone with Gordy when she walked in and raised a finger to signal he would be off shortly. Leanne walked around the room, surveying all of the equipment. She had only been in this room once before, and that was the day they confronted the guru's and Devon bought the house. She can remember it like it was yesterday, the pure and utter shock, she, Leonard, Amber, and Chet felt when Devon told Blair and Micah, he wanted to buy the house for two point five million dollars. A number Rosalie had given him since apparently, she was in on the plan. Devon hung up the phone, turned to Leanne, and said, "Hello beautiful. What brings you to this side of the house?"

Leanne sat on the couch and tucked her legs up underneath her, and said, "Well, it took me thirty minutes to find you in this ginormous house, but I wanted to tell you that I spoke to Kate, and she thinks us driving a Winnebago to Oklahoma is a wonderful idea. She said that there is plenty of room to park on their one-hundred-acre farm."

Astonished, as was Leanne, Devon said, "One hundred acres? That's not a farm, it's a bloody town."

Leanne laughed and replied, "Right. Anyway, it looks like we will be going on a family road trip."

Devon smiled at her, got up, and went to sit next to her, put his arm around her and said, "I love the sound of that, family road trip. It has a nice ring to it. And since we are on the subject, when might we make this family thing official?"

Leanne smiled at him and said, "Well, I have been giving that some thought."

Devon raised an eyebrow and asked, "And?"

Leanne replied, "I'll let you know after our 'family road trip,' that is if you don't run for the hills," she kissed him, got up, and sauntered out of the room.

*****

Later that night at dinner, Devon's cell phone rang. Usually, he wouldn't answer it while eating, but he looked at the number and saw that it was Rosalie calling, so he answered, "Well, hello Rosalie, what a nice surprise."

Chet and Leanne could hear Rosalie yelling, "What the hell is wrong with you Rock Star? Do you have rocks in your head? What were you thinking about calling Harold and planting the idea of renting a camper to drive to Oklahoma? Are you nuts?"

Amused, Devon replied, "Well Rosalie, I thought it would be fun…"

Rosalie cut him off, "Fun! Are you kidding me? Now you have Harold all excited, talking about this camper, that camper. When I get my hands on you, I am going to throttle you."

Leanne told Devon to give her the phone, he handed the phone to her, and Leanne said, "Listen, Rosalie, I wasn't too pleased about the idea either, but then I talked to Kate this morning and she said the nearest motel is 30 miles away. So, having our campers parked on the farm will be more convenient."

Rosalie, not buying what Leanne was selling, replied, "It's bad enough the party is a hoe-down in a barn, but trekking across three states in a camper and parking on a farm is just ludicrous!"

Leanne, not wanting to drag this out said, "Rosalie, we are doing this for Leonard and Amber. It will be fun."

Rosalie scoffed and said, "Fun, ha! Its nuts, is what it is. Tell Rock Star if anything goes wrong, I'm coming after him," and she hung up.

Leanne handed the phone back to Devon, and said, "Well that went well. Nice going Rock Star."

Devon put his hands in the air and said, "Well Harold thought it was a dandy idea. Who knew Rosalie would not agree?"

Leanne replied, "Have you not met Rosalie?"

Chet, not able to hold it in any longer, burst out laughing, which in turn got Leanne going. Devon looked at the two of them and said, "I should have thought that through a tad more perhaps."

Leanne, wiping the tears of laughter from her cheeks replied, "Ya think?"

Chapter 7

March breezed in with a few surprises. The weather had turned unusually springy, flowers were popping up from the saturated earth, and trees were budding with every ray of sunshine. It was a gorgeous Saturday, so Leanne took advantage and opened the windows in the house, while Devon and Chet cleared the leaves from the patio, which signaled fun for the twins and hounds, as they played in them rather than bagging them as Devon had asked. By two o'clock, they were done with all of their house chores. Devon, Leanne, and Chet sat on the front porch with a pitcher of cold tea and watched the kids and dogs run around on the lawn, racing back and forth from the frigid water. Out of nowhere, the dogs started barking like crazy. Concerned, the adults got up and went to see what all the excitement was about. As they reached the dock, they saw a caravan of small boats heading their way. Chet shaded his eyes from the reflecting sun off the water, and said, "What the heck? That looks like Leroy and Stan."

Devon asked, "Why are they coming out here? Do you and the cronies have plans?"

Chet replied, "Beats me. We ain't supposed to go fishing until tomorrow afternoon."

Leanne looked out as the boats got closer to the dock and said, "Um, that looks like a lot more people than just Leroy and Stan."

Confused, Chet said, "That second boat there has Henry, Pete, and Eloise, and my lord, is that Frieda?"

The boats were just about at the dock. Devon, Leanne, and Chet walked to the end of the dock to help secure the lines. When all eight boats were secure, the chaos began. "What the blazing tarnation's are ya'll up to?" Chet asked Leroy.

Leroy laughed and said, "Well since you didn't come to the mainland today, we had to bring the surprise out to you."

Curious, Devon asked, "And what surprise might that be, Leroy?"

Stan stepped forward and answered, "You mean to tell me that this old coot didn't tell you that today's his birthday?"

Astonished, Leanne turned to Chet and said, "Todays your birthday? Why didn't you tell us?"

Chet replied, "Ain't no need to be celebrating. I've had enough of them. I've lost count."

That's when Henry piped in, "Well, this one's a big one, the big seven-oh."

Devon reeled towards Chet and said, "Your 70th birthday? Are you kidding me? And you never told us?"

"Well, ya never asked, and there ain't any need for you to know. If Leanne had caught wind of it, she would have been planning some big hoopla," replied a slightly embarrassed Chet.

Leanne, still registering that Chet was turning 70, when he didn't look a day over 60, said, "You got that right."

Henry walked up to Devon and Leanne and said, "I hope it's no inconvenience, but when Chet didn't show up on the mainland, we reckoned he was trying to avoid us, so we brought the party out here, if ya'll don't mind us setting up here?"

Pete wheeled a big red cooler down the dock to where they stood and said, "I got a cooler here packed to the rim with some steaks, burgers, sausage, and marinated chicken, and my wife Eloise made her prize-winning potato salad. Maryjane, Denny's wife has been cooking for three days straight. So, we got all the fixings for a barbecue."

Leanne turned to the crowd on the dock, and said, "Absolutely, you are all more than welcome. What a wonderful surprise for Chet."

Chet mumbled under his breath, "Say's you."

Devon laughed, put his arm around Chet, and said, "Happy birthday, Old Man."

Just then, as the crowd on the dock began to unload their boats and carry their bags up to the house, this petite woman, with her hair the color of a copper pot, braided in twists on top of her head, and the most beautiful round brown eyes, walked up to Chet, holding a large bakery box, and said with a slight accent, "Happy birthday Chet. I made your favorite, German Chocolate cake with buttercream frosting."

Flustered, Chet took off his hat, ran his fingers through his snow-white hair, shifted from foot to foot, and said,

"Um, well, that was mighty nice of you Frieda. No need for you to go to all that trouble."

"Frieda!" Devon and Leanne said at the same time.

Frieda turned to them and said, "Well, yes, I'm Frieda. I own the bakery in town,"

Amused, Devon replied, "Yes, so we've heard."

Chet, wanting this conversation to derail, said to Frieda, "Here, let me take that box from you. I'll show you to the kitchen," and off they went down the dock.

Devon and Leanne were the last ones standing on the dock. Devon swung his arm around Leanne's shoulders, and said, "Well, it looks like our man Chet has kept a few secrets from us, time to go celebrate with 30 of his closest friends."

Leanne laughed and said, "He is a man of mystery," and they walked down the dock towards the house.

*****

The party was in full swing by five o'clock. Pete was manning the grill, the cronies were gathered on the patio telling stories of adventures they've had with Chet, and at least ten women were bustling around the kitchen. Leanne and Devon mingled within the crowd, happy to meet everyone. At eight o'clock, well after the sun had gone down, everyone gathered in the kitchen, and Frieda presented her amazingly beautiful cake. They sang happy birthday and Chet blew out the candles, all seventy of them. Benny, from Benny's Bar and Grill, the Monday night gathering place for Chet and the cronies to watch sports, slapped Chet on the back and said, "I thought we might be needing the fire department to put out that blaze," which brought the room to roaring laughter.

*****

After the last boat was loaded and all of the good-byes were said, the caravan made its way back to the mainland. Chet, Devon, and Leanne waved to them until they turned the bend, then they began to walk down the dock. Leanne hooked arms with Chet and said, "You have a wonderful group of friends. Tonight, was a lot of fun."

Chet patted her hand and replied, "They've kept me going since I lost my Annie, but you, Devon, and those kiddo's, ya'll have filled a void in me."

Leanne looked at him and said, "I know what you mean, we're family. And by the way, I really like Frieda."

Chet, with misty eyes, looked at her and said, "Me too, I know my Annie would have liked her too," they walked the rest of the way to the house in silence.

Chapter 8

April was filled with a flurry of activities, including numerous school functions for the twins, which Chet was running them to and from the mainland for. Devon had to fly to Los Angeles to put the finishing touches on the album and work on the Enlightenment tour schedule, so Leanne found a few hours to walk through town. She had been meaning to stop by a couple of the shops and thank Chet's friends for the wonderful surprise party, but her first stop was spontaneous: A-Plus Reality. She and the kids had been spending every night on the island since Christmas, and she knew to keep the house she bought was a waste of money, so she decided to sell it. The bells on the door rang as she entered the office, the receptionist was a perky blonde, maybe twenty years old, Leanne told her that she was looking to list her house, and the receptionist called out, "Momma, someone's here to see you."

A few minutes later a woman came around the corner, looked at Leanne, clapped her hands together, and said, "Well Leanne, what a nice surprise."

Leanne was taken back to see Adele, a friend of Chet's that came to the island for the birthday party, "Adele, what a coincidence. I just happened upon your office and spontaneously decided to sell my house over on Cove Lane."

Adele was thrilled to see Leanne and was more than eager to help her. She asked Leanne which house was hers, and Leanne replied, "Number twenty-four, the slate blue house with the white wrap-around porch."

Adele looked at her and said, "Well isn't that a coincidence. I had a lady in here just last week asking about that very house. Said she thought it was adorable and she was very interested in seeing the inside, but I told her it wasn't on the market. I offered to show her some other houses, but she said no, and walked out."

Curious, Leanne asked, "Well that's odd, why my house?"

Giving it a moment's thought, Adele replied, "Well honey, I don't quite know. But how about you take me over there, and we have a look around and then I can give you a price and we can write up a contract?"

Leanne shrugged off the tingle on the back of her neck and said, "If you have time, that would be great."

Adele smiled and said, "Absolutely. Let me get my purse and we'll head right over there."

*****

Leanne and Adele spent an hour going over the details for the sale of the house. Leanne left Adele's office with a signed contract and a smile on her face. The next stop she made was at Frieda's bakery. She opened the door and was welcomed by the sweet aroma of baked goods. For an instant, she was transported back to her childhood, when she would come home from school and walk into the same wonderful smell, and the warm embrace of her mother. She shook off the memory and walked up to the counter where Frieda was loading assorted baked goods into the glass case. Frieda looked up, her face and beautiful brown eyes lit up, "Oh my goodness Leanne, what a nice surprise."

Leanne took in that lovely face and said, "Hi Frieda. I was in town running some errands and I wanted to stop by and thank you for the wonderful party you all arranged for Chet."

Frieda smiled, wiped her hands on her apron, and replied, "Oh sweetie, it was our pleasure. We are all very fond of Chet."

Leanne, reading between the lines, smiled and said, "Well, I believe the feeling is mutual," which resulted in a slight blush on Frieda's cheeks. However, not wanting to stick her nose in where it didn't belong, Leanne changed the subject to small talk about the bakery and the weather.

Leanne left Frieda's, but not empty-handed. Frieda insisted she take a bag of jelly donuts home with her, which just so happen to be Chet's favorite. Next, Leanne headed to Pete's Meat Market. She wanted to thank Pete and Eloise for all the food they brought to the party, and also to pick up some pork chops for dinner.

After chatting with Pete and Eloise for a half-hour, she headed back to the dock where she would ask Henry for a ride back to the island. She had made arrangements with Chet when he dropped her off in the morning, to bring the twins home after school since he would be back from fishing with Leroy and Stan around the same time school let out. When she arrived at the dock it was buzzing with activity. She caught sight of Henry and another man standing by a small boat, she walked over to them and said, "Hi Henry."

Henry turned to her and said cheerily, "Well hello there Leanne. How are you this fine day?"

Leanne smiled and replied, "I'm great, thank you for asking. This weather is definitely a gift from Mother Nature. Henry, I was wondering, would it be possible to get a ride back to the island?"

Happy to oblige, Henry said, "Sure thing Leanne. I want you to meet Jeff, he's a new hire. With spring coming right around the corner, we're busier than a pack of squirrels looking for acorns. Hey Jeff, would you mind running Leanne out to Welby Island?"

Jeff tipped his baseball cap up, looked at Leanne through his mirrored sunglasses, and replied, "Sure thing, nice to meet you, ma'am."

Leanne reached out her hand and said, "Nice to meet you, Jeff. I appreciate the ride."

Leanne and Jeff got into the small boat. Henry untied the lines and sent them on their way. On the ride to the island, Leanne asked Jeff where he was from and his reply was, "A little bit of here, a little bit of there." Apparently, Jeff was a man of few words. Leanne gauged him to be about 30 years old but didn't dare ask, so they motored on with no conversation that was until they turned the bend and the big house came into view.

Jeff whistled and asked, "Is that your house?"

Leanne laughed and said, "Yup."

Jeff said, "Well you must have a big family."

Leanne replied, "Actually, my fiancé bought it last May. I have two children from my previous marriage and Chet lives with us too. Have you met him yet? He was at the dock earlier this morning picking up his friends to go fishing."

Jeff snickered, "You mean the four old geezers?"

Taken back by his reference, Leanne replied, "Well, I wouldn't call them old geezers, but yes, that was Chet, Leroy, Stan, and Frank."

Jeff didn't respond, he docked the boat and tied a line to the hook, then jumped out of the boat and held out a hand to Leanne and helped her off the boat. As she was gathering her packages, Jeff asked, "Want some help carrying those up to the house? I wouldn't mind getting a look around."

For some reason, the hair on the back of Leanne's neck tingled, she answered, "Um, no I'm good. Thanks for the ride," and headed down the dock. When she reached the lawn, she turned to see Jeff still standing there, looking at the house. Jeff caught sight of her looking at him, so he untied the line, pushed off the dock, and headed back to the marina.

Chapter 9

It was May second, the Friday night before their family road trip to Leonard and Amber's baby shower in Oklahoma. Leanne was at the stove stirring a pot, while Chet sat at the kitchen island reading the newspaper. Devon walked into the kitchen, his nose on high alert, asked, "What is that fabulous aroma I smell?"

Without turning around, Leanne replied, "I believe I heard that question a lot from you at the cabin. But to answer you, that fabulous aroma would be chicken chili."

Devon walked over to her, wrapped his arms around her waist, and asked, "Might you need a taste tester? I would be happy to sign up?"

Leanne wiggled out of his arms and replied, "No thank you. It needs a little more time."

Disappointed, Devon reached for a piece of the cornbread cooling on the rack. Leanne smacked his hand. Devon drew back and looked at a Leanne. He smiled at her and said, "Well, there's a bout of déjà vu."

Leanne laughed and replied, "Yes, I remember vividly."

Chet looked up from his newspaper and said, "What's with you two? You sound like you're talking in code or something."

Devon swiped a piece of bread, went and sat next to Chet and replied, "Just a little reminiscing from our days at the cabin. Oh wow, Queen Bee, this is really good. I hope you made two pans."

Leanne put her hands on her hips, and looking directly at Chet, she said, "That is the second pan. Apparently, Chet and the twins helped themselves to the first pan." Chet quickly brought the newspaper to his face, avoiding Leanne's glare.

Devon opened the laptop he brought into the kitchen and said to Leanne, "Come sit a minute. I want to show you and Chet what I've mapped out for our journey."

Leanne wiped her hands on a dishtowel, grabbed the two bowls of sliced carrots she made for the twins' snack, and said, "Let me bring the kids their snack, and then you'll have my full attention.

A few minutes later, Leanne returned to the kitchen to see Chet and Devon hovered over the laptop. She squeezed in between them and said, "What the heck is that?"

Devon looked up at her and said proudly, "That is our first stop, Pendleton, Oregon, where I have purchased our tickets to a rodeo."

"A rodeo?" said Chet and Leanne at the same time.

"Yes, a rodeo," Devon continued, "I have mapped out all of our stops and researched fun things to do. I chose Pendleton and the rodeo because it's only a four-hour drive and I thought we would keep the first day's drive short, to get a feel for the camper, which by the way, I think you will be very pleased with."

Leanne still not one hundred percent on board with the whole driving to Oklahoma in a camper idea, replied, "Hmmm."

Devon ignored her skepticism and moved on to the second stop. "From there, we'll drive about seven hours to Idaho Falls, Idaho…"

Leanne interrupted him and said, "And this is this where we'll pick potatoes?"

Devon looked at her and said, "No Miss Sarcastic, this is where we land at the Grand Teton's National Park. They have a zoo, seven acres of zoo to be exact, and approximately four hundred animals."

Leanne sat down next to Chet and said, "Okay, that sounds interesting. The kids will love that."

Pleased to see Leanne's interest piqued, Devon continued, "Well, that was my thought. Then our next stop will be Bryce Canyon in Utah, where we will visit the hoodoos…"

This time it was Chet who interrupted, "The hoo what's?"

Leanne added, "Is that the male version of the hoo-ha's?" which brought her and Chet to a fit of laughter.

Confused and slightly annoyed, Devon asked, "And what might a hoo-ha be?" which made them laugh even harder.

Once composed, Leanne replied, "Never mind. Continue. Tell us what a hoodoo is," which unleashed another round of laughter from Chet and Leanne.

Devon, even more annoyed, said, "Aren't you two a barrel of laughs. As to avoid another round of laughter by saying the word, I will show you instead," he turned the laptop toward them. Leanne gasped and Chet let out a slow whistle. Very pleased with their reaction, Devon continued, "And, these, funny ones, are the hoodoo's. They date back millions of years and are full of myths and mystery. I thought it would be an educational experience for the twins. I have us signed up for a one and half mile hike down into the canyon with a tour guide, and then that evening we will go to an area called Sunset Point, to see one of the most amazing sunsets ever, so says the website."

Stunned, Leanne said, "Oh Devon, they are breath-taking. The colors of the rock formations, the red, pink, and yellow, make it like looking into a volcano."

Chet added, "I ain't ever seen nothing like that in all my life. It looks like another planet."

Very pleased with himself, Devon replied, "Well then, I'm glad you approve. Now onto the last stop. I have chosen Denver, Colorado, specifically, the Ritz Carlton."

Leanne looked at him with wide eyes and said, "A hotel, with big beds and even bigger bathrooms. After traveling in the camper for four days, that is a gift for sure. You really have thought of everything."

Chet, looking confused, said, "Why do we need to stay in a fancy hotel when we got the camper?"

Devon laughed and replied, "Well, I thought it would be nice to have one night out of the camper, where we could do some shopping in the city and have a meal in a nice restaurant before we go to the farm and spend three more nights in the camper."

Leanne looked at Chet and sternly said, "Don't you argue with him. I want the Ritz Carlton."

Chet sat up straight and said, "Yes ma'am."

Devon laughed and said, "Okay, so I have arranged for us to pick up the camper Sunday morning at ten a.m. Leanne, we'll load up your SUV and drive to the rental place and leave it in the lot. We should be able to hit the road by 11 a.m. Sound good?"

Chet and Leanne nodded.

Chapter 10

Leanne was up at the crack of dawn on Sunday morning. After what Devon had laid out to her and Chet Friday night, she had to admit, she was really excited about the trip. She made a pot of coffee and started on the pancake batter. Just as she was getting ready to crack an egg, her phone dinged. She wiped her hands on the dishtowel, picked up her phone, and saw the text was from Rosalie, "Getting ready to leave. Tell your fiancé, if anything goes wrong, I'm coming after him."

Leanne laughed and texted back, "You should see the places Devon has mapped out for us to stop. I have to tell you, I'm really excited."

A few minutes later Rosalie responded, "Ha! I keep asking Harold where we are going and all he says is, 'on an adventure.' This has disaster written all over it. See you Thursday."

Leanne typed back, "Sit back and enjoy the ride. Can't wait to hear all about it," adding a smile emoji.

Rosalie sent back a not so smiling emoji.

*****

They were all packed and ready to go. Chet and Devon carried the luggage and coolers down to the dock, with Luke, Lindsey, and the dogs in tow, and loaded the boat. Leanne made one last trip through the house, turning off lights and unplugging the coffee pot. She grabbed her purse and jacket, headed for the front door, set the alarm system, closed and locked the doors walked down the front stairs, and headed for the dock. Devon had brought her car to the marina yesterday, so all they had to do was load it up and be on their way.

*****

With the light Sunday morning traffic, it took them less than thirty minutes to get to the Winnebago rental place. Devon went inside to check-in, while Chet, Leanne, and the kids unloaded the car. Ten minutes later, Devon came out of the office and walked across the gravel parking lot to them, and said, "They're bringing it around now." A minute later this gigantic bus looking thing motored up to them. The twins were jumping up and down with excitement and the dogs were wagging their tails frantically. Chet let out a whistle and said, "Ain't reckon I've seen a camper that big. That's twice the size of the one we test drove." Leanne just stood there with her mouth open, but nothing came out.

Devon greeted the man that came out of the camper, then turned to them and said, "Okay gang, let's load her up."

Leanne struggling to comprehend what was in front of her, slowly moved forward. Devon took the suitcase from her and asked, "So what do you think? Will this do for our family road trip? Leanne nodded, "Wait until you see the inside," Devon added.

Leanne climbed the three stairs to the inside of the camper and stopped dead in her tracks. It looked like the inside of a hotel suite. The living room had two large sofas, a fifty-five-inch TV hanging on the wall above an electric fireplace, a few feet further in was the kitchen with a banquet-style dining table. Past the kitchen on the left was a half bath, right before the entrance to a large bedroom with a king-size bed and another TV hanging on the wall. At the very end of the bedroom, was a full-size bathroom with double vanities, a large walk-in shower, and a long double door closet. Leanne was trying to absorb all of it when Devon came up behind her, she turned to him and said, "Wow, I have to tell you, I had my doubts, but you truly have thought of everything. This, this is incredible. It has all the comforts of home."

Devon kissed the top of her head and said, "It will be a splendid trip, I promise you. I was thinking it would be best to set you and the twins up in here. Chet and I will take the pull-out sofa's upfront. This way we can get early starts in the morning without waking the three of you."

Leanne couldn't argue with his logic, so she agreed and said, "Can I ask you a question?"

Devon smiled and said, "Sure."

Totally serious, and a bit concerned, Leanne asked, "Do you and Chet know how to drive this thing?"

Devon quickly replied, "Haven't got a clue. But we'll figure it out as we go."

The look on Leanne's face was priceless. Devon laughed and said, "I'm kidding. Remember last Tuesday when I went to the mainland with Chet and we were gone for five hours? We actually came out here for a driving class. And I'm happy to report, we both passed with flying colors."

Relieved, Leanne replied, "Good to know," and they headed upfront to get the show on the road.

Chapter 11

It took them a little under the four hours they anticipated it would take to get to their first stop, Pendleton Oregon. They arrived at the campsite and found their assigned parking spot. Once settled, Chet took the dogs for a walk while Devon made arrangements to have the shuttle take them over to the rodeo within the hour.

*****

Being the first time at a rodeo for all of them, they were overwhelmed with the size of the arena and all there was to see and do. They caught the last half hour of the rodeo that was in progress when they arrived. After that, they walked around and came across a cow milking contest, which had the twins squealing with joy. Leanne peaked into some of the shops. She was thinking it would fun if they all wore cowboy boots to the hoe-down. The last store she went into, she hit the jackpot. The walls and floor were lined with boots. She walked around until she found exactly what she was looking for, a pair of turquoise boots with black stitching. She brought them to the counter and asked the shop keeper if they had them in a size seven.

When he brought them out and Leanne tried them on, they fit perfectly and were surprisingly comfortable. She went to the door and called out to Devon, Chet, and the kids to come into the store. Devon walked in first, took one look at Leanne with the boots on, and said, "Well, it looks like you found something you fancy. And, I must say, they suit you."

Pleased, Leanne looked down at her boots and said, "I love them. I think we should all get a pair."

Chet stepped forward and said, "I wouldn't mind taking a look around. I had a pair way back yonder when I was a youngster. I wore them every day for two years straight, until my toes got scrunched and the heels fell off. Then my momma threw them in the trash. Ain't had a pair since."

Excitedly, Lindsey said, "I want a pink pair!"

Leanne smiled at her and said, "Come with me, sweetie. I saw the perfect pair for you." Hand in hand they walked to the back of the store.

Devon looked down at Luke. Luke looked up at Devon, shrugged, and said, "I'm game if you are?"

Devon laughed and said, "Is that right? Okay then, let's go find us a pair of cowboy boots."

A half-hour later, all five of them left the store wearing their new boots and headed over to barrel races.

Chapter 12

The next morning, they were on the road bright and early. The sun had barely peeked over the horizon. They had been driving nearly an hour before Leanne emerged from the bedroom. She moved to the front of the camper and sat on the couch behind the driver's seat, where Chet was at the wheel with Bella and Blaze at his feet. Devon looked over at her from the passenger's seat and said, "Well, good morning Sunshine. Sleep well?"

Leanne laughed and replied, "Apparently. When did we leave the campsite?"

Devon got up, walked to the kitchen, and poured her a cup of coffee. He handed her the cup, sat down next to her, and answered, "Just short of an hour ago, I'd say."

Astonished, Leanne said, "Really? I never heard or felt a thing. How did you and Chet sleep out here last night?"

Devon stretched and replied, "Actually quite well. The couches pull out, so they were roomy enough, except my bed felt rather empty, that was until Blaze joined me."

Leanne put down her coffee, leaned over, gave Devon a kiss, and said, "Well, I would be happy to switch places with you. Sleeping with the twins is like having an octopus on each side of me. I literally had to detangle myself to get out of the bed."

Devon laughed and said, "No thanks. I'll leave the tickle terrors to you."

Leanne stood up and said, "I'm going to make some breakfast, any requests?"

Devon gave that a moment's thought and replied, "I wouldn't turn down one of those scones I smelled baking last week."

Leanne laughed and said, "Well your nose always knows. I actually made them for the trip and froze them. Give me a few minutes to warm them up."

Devon stood, kissed Leanne, and replied, "Chet and I are switching off every two hours, so I'll eat first, and then he can come to have his."

*****

By noon they had driven six hours with an estimated hour left to get to their next stop, Idaho Falls, Idaho. The twins, Bella and Blaze have been good as gold. They stopped once to let the dogs do their business. When they finally arrived at the campsite, they were all eager to exit the camper. Luke, Lindsey, and the dogs were the first ones out, the dogs jumping and barking. Chet stood up and said, "I'm gonna take the kids, all four of them, for a walk down by the river. What time you reckon we'll head to the zoo?"

Devon looked at his watch and replied, "It is one o'clock now, let's say, two-thirty, according to Zeke in the office, the zoo is three miles away, and they have a shuttle service to and from."

Chet nodded and said, "Sounds like a plan," and headed off in the direction of the kids.

Leanne went to the refrigerator and brought out a pitcher of cold tea, grabbed two glasses from the cabinet, and poured some for her and Devon. When she turned to hand Devon his glass, he was gone. She walked to the front and went down the stairs of the camper. She walked around to the other side and a slow smile crept across her face. Devon had neglected to show her all the bells and whistles that the camper was equipped with, but there he stood, under a large retractable awning, opening up a couple of folding lawn chairs, each having their own side table attached. Leanne walked over and handed him a glass of tea and sat down in one of the chairs. She took a deep breath, looking out at the gorgeous view of the river and mountains behind it, and said, "This is just beautiful. I've never been any place like it. How did you find this place?"

Devon took a seat next to her, sipped his tea and replied, "Well, actually, I had a little help from modern technology. I used an app called Campsite Finder."

Leanne looked at him with loving eyes, and said, "Thank you, Devon. You really put a lot of thought into this trip."

"Well, you have to remember, I use a tour bus to travel around the country, but that involves multiple hotel stops, with no time in between concerts to actually sit back and enjoy the scenery. It's something I had hoped to do one day," replied Devon."

Leanne gave that some thought before responding. She didn't want to upset Devon, but she was curious as to how he felt, so she asked, "Devon, do you ever miss England?"

Devon looked off into the distance and replied, "No. Never once have I longed to go back. However, years ago, maybe ten, Gordy came to me with a European tour schedule, and London was on it. I told him no. He pushed me, not knowing the reason why I did not want to go back there, and I told him, if he kept pushing, I would fire him. He never mentioned it again."

Leanne reached for Devon's hand and quietly said, "I'm sorry I asked that question. It was insensitive of me."

Devon turned to her and said, "Don't be sorry. That is in the past, but if you were to tell me you wanted to go to England, then I would take you."

Leanne leaned back and said with a smile, "No thank you. But I wouldn't mind seeing Italy."

Devon looked at her with a raised eyebrow, and asked, "Perhaps for a honeymoon?"

Leanne lifted her glass, took a sip, and replied with amusement in her voice, "Perhaps."

When Chet and the kids got back to the campsite, they set off to find Zeke and the shuttle. Leanne turned to Chet and asked, "Will Bella and Blaze be okay alone in the camper?"

Chet laughed and said, "The way they ran up and down that riverbank, I'd say they'll sleep the whole time we're gone."

Devon added, "I don't believe we'll be gone more than a few hours. I was thinking we might barbecue those steaks you packed Leanne. Zeke told me that a lot of the campers gather up at the pavilion where there are grills and a huge fire pit."

"Well good thing we are in Idaho, home of the potato, maybe we can dig some up at the zoo," said an amused Leanne.

Devon laughed and said, "Oh aren't you a funny girl."

Chet piped in and said, "Don't you worry Leanne, I packed potatoes and salad fixings. I can't be eating my meat without a potato."

*****

They spent two hours at the zoo. The twins didn't know which way to turn. To the sloths, or the lions, or the penguins or the peacocks which apparently roamed freely around the grounds. Once they got to the petting zoo, it was all about the baby goats for Lindsey. Luke got a kick out of the talking donkey. If you asked the donkey a question, he would answer you with a braying sound, which translated to hee-haw, which just cracked Luke up.

Once they had seen everything there was to see, including the Native American exhibit, they called Zeke for a ride back to camp. It had been a beautiful early spring day, sixty-five degrees, and full of sunshine. They arrived back at camp to find a family with four kids, all around the twin's age, and two dogs, parked next to them. Chet let Bella and Blaze out of the camper and along with the twins, ran into the fray of fun the other family was having. A football was being tossed around, bubbles were being blown and laughter filled the air. Leanne went inside to prep the steaks and potato's when she came out a half-hour

73

later with a glass of wine in her hand, she found Chet and Devon sitting over at the neighbors, each holding a beer in their hand. When she approached the group, a beautiful woman with hair the color of gold, jumped up out of her chair, grabbed a chair for Leanne, and said, "And you must be Leanne. I'm Katie-Lee and this is my husband Bo."

Leanne smiled warmly, shook both of their hands, and said, "It's so nice to meet you Katie-Lee and Bo. I see you have met Chet and Devon."

This time it was Bo who spoke, "Yes ma'am. We called them over to join us, didn't have to twist their arm when I offered them a beer."

Leanne laughed and said, "Oh I bet you didn't."

"Well we just spent two bloody hours petting goats, so I would say we earned it," said Devon.

Leanne, having sat down next to Katie-Lee, felt her touch Leanne's arm and quietly say, "Do you not swoon every time that man opens his mouth?"

Leanne laughed and replied, "And then some," hoping that Katie-Lee had no idea of exactly who Devon was: the famous rock star.

The adults chatted for an hour or so, then ultimately decided that they would all head over to the pavilion for a potluck dinner, combining their meal plans. The icing on the cake was Katie-Lee having all the fixings to make s'mores.

The pavilion was filled with another dozen families. Everyone mingled, shared food and the conversation flowed non-stop, with the s'mores being the hit of the night. At nine o'clock good-byes were said, kids were gathered, and everyone headed to their camper.

Chapter 13

The trip from Idaho Falls to Bryce Canyon in Utah was a straight shot down Route 15. The traffic was light, and they were making good time. After seeing billboard after billboard advertising the 'Happiest City in the USA,' being Provo, they decided to stop and have lunch there. Devon guided the camper into a roadside gas station to fill up. Everyone exited the camper to stretch and Chet walked the dogs over to a grassy spot to let Bella and Blaze do their business. As Devon was heading over to the front door of the gas station, a man came out and greeted him and said, "Hola Senor. I'm assuming you are in need of some gas?"

Devon replied, "Yes sir, and we would be grateful if you could recommend a place for lunch."

The man wiped his brow with the bandana in his hand and replied, "Well, if you are favorable to tacos, my wife Carla has a small restaurant on the other side of the building. She makes the best tacos this side of Mexico."

Devon raised an eyebrow and said, "Is that what I smell? It smells amazing."

The man laughed and said, "Si Senor. Best homemade salsa you'll ever taste. Why don't you go see my Carla around back, I will fill you up here, then we can settle up when you've finished your meal, Si Senor?"

Devon thanked the man and walked over to where Chet, Leanne, and the kids were standing, and said, "Well it looks like we found our spot for lunch. Apparently, the owner's wife has a restaurant right around back, which he claims has the best tacos this side of Mexico."

Chet and Leanne turned their heads in the direction of the gas station. Leanne looked back at Devon and said, "Seriously? You want to eat tacos from behind a gas station?"

Devon replied, "Yup."

Chet turned to Leanne and said, "Let me tell you something Leanne, you find some of the best food in some of the oddest places. When I was stationed in Korea, we would be in a small town and the locals would feed us out in the street. Best dang barbeque I've ever had."

Still skeptical, Leanne replied to both Chet and Devon, "Well you do know we still have three more hours to drive and only two bathrooms?"

Devon laughed and said, "Come on Queen Bee, where is your sense of adventure?"

Leanne quickly replied, "Not in my stomach."

Devon swung his arm around her shoulders and said, "If I can dance in a barn, you can eat a taco from behind a gas station."

Leanne groaned, and they all headed around to the back of the gas station, where they were greeted by a heavyset woman with long black braids, and a smile as wide as her girth, "Welcome, my name is Carla, please come sit," she said as she guided them to a lone picnic table under a huge shade tree. Once they were seated, she handed them each a small piece of paper with five items written on them, Tacos-beef or chicken, Taquitos-beef or chicken, Burrito-beef or chicken, Enchiladas-beef or chicken and combination platter of all four.

Leanne was scared. She was looking at the menu for her safest option when Carla appeared with two baskets of warm chips, a clay bowl filled with homemade salsa, and another with guacamole. Leanne figured her safest bet was to just eat the chips, until Devon spoke up and said, "Senora Carla, we will have two orders of the combination platters and five sweet teas."

The round woman smiled a big open mouth grin at Devon and said, "Si Senor," and scurried away.

Leanne looked at Devon with concern and asked, "Are you sure?"

Devon laughed and picked up a chip, dipped it in salsa, and fed it to Leanne. He watched as she chewed. She closed her eyes and moaned. When she opened her eyes, she said in sheer euphoria, "Oh my God, that is the best salsa I have ever tasted. And these chips, my lord."

While she was still savoring the tastes, Devon dipped another chip into the guacamole and fed it to her. Again, she closed her eyes and moaned. Amused, Devon leaned over to her and quietly asked, "Do you need a minute to yourself, or perhaps a cigarette?" Leanne just moaned.

Ten minutes later, Carla arrived with their order, set it down in the middle of the table, passed around paper plates, napkins, with plastic utensils, and retreated back to the shack she emerged from. The five of them ate in silence. Leanne couldn't decide what she liked best, but after fifteen minutes the two platters were empty, and everyone agreed it was the best Mexican food they ever had. Carla came out and over to their table and asked if everything was to their liking. Leanne could only moan, so Chet said, "That was the best Mexican food I've ever had, thank you kindly, ma'am."

Carla was thrilled and kept repeating, "Gracias, gracias." She handed Devon the check, cleared the table, and headed back inside.

Devon looked at the check and said with surprise, "This can't be right."

Leanne snatched the check from his hand and read the written amount out loud, "Ten dollars and seventy-five cents. Are you kidding me?"

Devon took the check back from her and told the others that he was going to pay for the gas and lunch and would meet them back at the camper. He walked to the front of the gas station and met the man that had greeted them when they arrived, "Ah, Senor, so what did you think of your lunch? Was I right about the salsa?"

Devon asked the man, "May I ask what your name is?"

"Si Senor, my name is Luis," he replied.

"Well, Luis, I must say, and my family concurs, it was the best Mexican food we have ever had. Thank you very much for the recommendation," said Devon.

"You are most welcome Senor. I have filled your camper, so you are set to be on your way," said Luis.

"What do I owe you for the gas?" asked Devon.

"That will be fifty-two dollars, Senor," replied Luis.

Devon removed two hundred-dollar bills from his wallet and handed it to Luis. Luis looked at the money in his hand and exclaimed, "This is too much money for gas and the lunch, Senor."

Devon smiled and patted Luis on the shoulder and said, "That is a tip for your lovely wife and her fabulous food."

Luis looked from the money to Devon and asked, "For real?"

Devon laughed and said, "Yes, for real Luis. Please pass along our gratitude to Carla."

Nodding like a bobblehead, Luis replied, "Si Senor, gracias, gracias," and shook Devon's hand.

When Devon returned to the camper, he asked Chet where Leanne was. Chet shrugged and said, "Not sure, she just hurried out of here and said she'd be right back."

Leanne returned a few minutes later, Devon said to her, "For the love of the Queen, please don't tell me you were in the bathroom."

Leanne laughed and replied, "Nope, I just went to place an order with Carla for two dozen of everything we ate, plus two containers each of salsa and guacamole. I told her we would pick it up on our way back, so she is going to freeze it for us to take home."

Devon smiled a long, slow smile and said, "So I'm gathering you fancied our gas station lunch?"

Leanne replied, "You bet your British butt I did."

As they pulled out of the gas station, Leanne looked out the window to see Carla and Luis waving frantically. Carla crying tears of joy, which probably had something to do with the five hundred dollars Leanne slipped her with the promise that Carla would get a proper sign out front and updated menus. Leanne knew bringing her 'trip disaster fund' would come in handy.

*****

They arrived at Bryce Canyon at three p.m. Leanne and the twins had slept the three hours it took for them to get there, mostly due to their full bellies. Once the camper was parked at the campsite, all five got out and stretched. Chet said he was going to take the dogs for a walk and the twins tagged along.

Devon and Leanne took a walk around the grounds and checked in at the office. They were scheduled to go on a mile and a half hike down into the canyon at four p.m., which was surely needed after the lunch they had. When Chet and the kids got back, they changed into their jeans and hiking boots and headed out to meet their tour guide. It turned out that there was a last-minute booking of five college girls, and the guide asked Devon if his group minded if they joined them. Devon had no problem with that until the girls joined them and went into hysterics. One of the girls screamed, "OH MY GOD! You are Devon Davis," which set off a frenzy from the other four. After numerous selfies and autographs, the guide cleared his throat and said, "Okay, that's enough. Mr. Davis and his family are here to enjoy the hike. If you girls can't dial it down, then you are going to have to stay behind, understood?" All five girls nodded. The ten of them headed down the trail into the canyon, with the tour guide leading, followed by Chet, the twins, and the pack of giggling girls, leaving Leanne and Devon bringing up the rear. Devon, not wanting to get tangled up with the girls, reached for Leanne's hand and slowed her down. Leanne looked at him, then laughed out loud and said, "What's the matter Romeo, not a fan of the groupies?"

Devon looked over at her and said, "Those days are over Queen Bee. The only female I want going gaga over me is you."

Leanne smiled and said, "Sorry to tell you this, but I am way past the gaga stage. I'm more at the luckiest girl in the world stage."

Devon stopped, turned to Leanne, and replied, "Really now? Isn't that a coincidence, because I just so happen to be the luckiest guy in the world," then bent down and kissed her.

The hike down into the canyon was spectacular, the colors of the rock formations were stunning, and from the bottom of the trail, looking up, it was magical. The tour guide told them stories of myths and legends buried within the hoodoos. He told them that they could each take one loose rock from the trail, which legend says, will bring you good luck, but any more than that would bring fury from the hoodoos. Devon and Leanne were skeptical, but Chet, the twins, and the college girls, stared at him wide-eyed.

The hike back up the canyon trail was more difficult than going down. When they reached the top, they collapsed on the ground. Leanne's legs burned and felt wobbly. Chet rubbing his back said, "What the heck were you thinking Devon? Are you trying to put me in an early grave?"

Rubbing his own back, Devon replied, "How the bloody hell was I supposed to know it would be that difficult. The website said, 'a leisurely hike down a path.'"

The tour guide said, "You should have asked for the donkey package."

Devon asked, "What the bloody hell is the donkey package?"

This time it was one of the giggling college girls that answered, "Oh, we read about that. You ride a donkey down into the canyon. We wanted to do it, but they were all out of donkeys."

Devon looked at her like she had just landed from Mars, and said, "Well lucky for us. I'm happy to use my own two feet, thank you very much." All five girls swooned at his British accent. Leanne rolled her eyes.

The tour guide wanted to move things along, so he cleared his throat to get their attention and said, "Okay gang, let's head over to Sunset Point for happy hour and the sunset barbeque."

Chet said, "That's music to my ears. Lead the way, young man."

Leanne groaned and asked, "Exactly how far of a walk is it to Sunset Point?"

The tour guide laughed and replied, "No worries ma'am, we have a shuttle to take ya'll up to the point. Let me tell you, this is one sunset you do not want to miss. It's the most gorgeous sunset you will ever see, so let's get a move on."

When they arrived at the Point, they were pleasantly surprised to see numerous red and white check blankets spread amongst the green grass. The air was filled with the aroma of grilled chicken, ribs, burgers, and hot dogs, and there were a dozen or more people lounging around, drinking cocktails with little umbrella's in them, ice-cold beers and bless the hoodoo's, wine. Leanne didn't so much want a drink as much as she wanted to stick her aching feet into the cooler holding the beers. Leanne and Luke walked over to a vacant blanket and plopped down, while Devon, Chet, and Lindsey went to get beverages. Luke turned to Leanne and said, "Mommy, this was a great day. Aren't you glad Devon thought of a road trip?"

Leanne looked at his sweet little face, looking more grown-up every day, and replied, "I am sweetie. But what makes me happiest, is that you and Lindsey are having a great time," just then Lindsey came running over with two bottles of lemonade, followed closely by Chet with a beer in each hand, and Devon, bless his cotton socks, with a beer in one hand and a glass of wine in the other.

Devon handed Leanne her glass of wine and sat down next to Chet on the blanket. Luke and Lindsey asked if they could go play catch with the other kids across the lawn. Leanne agreed but told them, "Remember, if you can't see me, I can't see you, so stay where I can see you." Both kids said, "Okay," and ran off to play.

Chet turned to Devon and said, "I gotta tell you son, you done well. Those two kids are happier than ducks in the water, and I might add, I've never felt younger or more energized since ya'll come into my life. The two of you have been the answer to my prayers since losing my Annie."

Leanne got on her knees and hugged Chet. Devon needed a minute to gather his words and finally replied,

"Sir, you have not only been a friend and father -figure, but also an answer to my prayers to one day be the kind of man I always wanted to be. You have filled a place in my heart that has been empty for a very long time. So, thank you for being not only an inspiration but an example of what a good man is."

Leanne turned to Devon and Chet and raised her glass in a toast, "Here is to the best two men who have ever crossed my path. I am so thankful to have both of you and for the way you love me and my children, our children. I love you both very much."

With glassy eyes, Chet said, "Aww, now look what I've gone and done. Gone and gotten all mushy. What do you say we go get us some of that barbeque?"

Leanne stood and replied, "Lordy, I didn't think I could eat for three days after that lunch today, but that hike has me starving."

Devon stood and held out a hand to Chet and helped him up off the blanket, and the three of them headed for the grills.

*****

The sun set at exactly six fifty-eight. The crowd was gathered at the edge of the Point to watch it slowly descend behind the hoodoos. The bright orange ball set the hoodoos on fire. They turned a fiery red and orange mixing with the yellow and magenta colors of the sky. It was breath-taking, Leanne, still in awe as the sun set into the horizon, said, "Wow. I thought we had the most beautiful sunsets on Welby Island, but this is mind-blowing. The colors that reflected off of the hoodoos, meeting with the colors of the sky, were like a painting forming right before our eyes."

Devon, with his arm around Leanne's shoulder, kissed her head and agreed, "It's the simplest things we take for granted. But this image, this I will remember for a lifetime," as he looked over at Chet and the twins staring wide-eyed and mouths gaped open watching the final remnants of the setting sun.

After the sun set and the chill began to pierce the air, they headed back to the campsite for the evening, taking with them a very memorable day.

Chapter 14

The next morning, they set out at the early hour of five a.m. for Denver and the Ritz Carlton. After yesterday's hike at the hoodoos, Leanne was looking forward to getting there and taking a nice long, hot bubble bath to soak her aching body. Denver was approximately a nine-hour drive. They had been on the road for five hours when the camper jolted violently. Chet was at the wheel and asked Devon, as he slowed the camper down, "What the heck was that?"

Not knowing the answer to the question, Devon replied, "I'm not sure. Pullover to that dirt spot on the right and we'll take a look."

Chet guided the camper over to the right and parked. All five, followed by the hounds, got out to take a look. As they rounded the rear of the camper, they saw that both tires were flat. Concerned, Lindsey asked, "What happen to the tires? They're not round anymore."

Chet replied, "You got that right. They are flat as pancakes."

Leanne, seeing the concern on Lindsey's face, said, "Don't worry sweetie, I'm sure there is a spare tire somewhere on the camper."

Chet looked at her and said, "Leanne, even if we got two spare tires, it ain't gonna fix this. This ain't a car. This camper weighs a whole lot of pounds and will need to go on a lift to change those tires."

Devon looked at the group and said, "Okay, no worries. I have the number of road service that comes with the rental. I'll just give them a call and someone from a nearby town will come and help us," four pairs of eyes turned to him, two had hope, two were questioning. Devon went back into the camper, five minutes later he came out and said, "Well the good news is, help is on the way. The bad news is, the nearest town is an hour away."

All four mouths said, "What!"

Devon, trying to keep them calm said, "No worries, we'll be back on the road soon enough. Once the truck gets here, fixes the tires, we'll be on our merry way."

Leanne, not wanting the kids to worry, said, "Okay, why don't we take this time to straighten up the inside of the camper, then I'll make us something to eat and we can sit outside under the awning and wait for the truck to get here, sound good?" All heads nodded, but no one spoke.

*****

Two hours later, not one car had passed them. None the less, the roadside service truck that was due an hour ago. Luke was throwing stones out into the barren field where they had parked, he turned to the others and said, "I've been doing some thinking, and I have a question. Did any of you take more than one rock from the hoodoos?"

Everyone looked over at him, then Chet responded, "Well I sure didn't, the tour guide told us we could each have one, and that's all I took."

Lindsey nodded and said, "Me too. I didn't want to make the hoodoos mad."

Leanne, not having bought the tour guides spiel, said to Lindsey, "Honey, I'm pretty sure that was a made-up tale. But to answer Luke's question, I only took one."

After a few minutes of silence, Luke turned to Devon and asked, "How about you Devon, how many did you take?"

Devon, who had been standing by the side of the road looking for the roadside service truck, turned to see all of them staring at him. He stuck his hands in his pockets, shuffled his feet in the dirt and said, "Um, well, I may have accidentally put three in my pocket."

Astounded, Chet said, "Three! Did you not hear that man? We were each allowed one. What the blazing tarnation were you thinking?"

Devon looked at them and said, "Oh come on now, you don't really believe that those silly rocks can cause a curse?"

Leanne, Chet, Luke, and Lindsey all turned their heads in the direction of the two flat tires. Luke turned back to Devon and said, "Oh boy, the hoodoos sure are mad at you."

Just then, far down the deserted road, appeared what looked like a tow truck. As it approached, Devon cheerily said, "See, all's well. Help has arrived."

Once the tow truck pulled off to the side of the road and stopped, the driver hopped out of the cab and walked over to the group and said, "Howdy ya'll. I'm guessing you'd be the ones that called in for help." He reached out his hand to Devon and introduced himself, "I'm Ray, pleased to meet you."

Devon shook his hand and said, "Yes, that would be us. However, when I called for assistance, whoever answered the phone said the closest town was an hour away. We've been waiting sometime past that."

Ray took off his cap and ran his fingers through his curly mop of red hair and replied, "Yup, that be Dirk, but he didn't have a rig big enough to haul you in, so he called me. I had to come from Forks Junction, which is an hour south of Piedmont where you called."

This time it was Leanne who spoke, "Haul us in? You can't just change the tires out here?"

Ray looked over at the huge camper and said, "No ma'am. A big ride like this has to go on a lift, and I'm betting that if there is a spare, there only be one, and considering you got two flat, that isn't gonna do you no good."

Frustrated, Devon asked, "Okay, so where exactly will you tow us to?"

Ray adjusted his cap and replied, "Well, I can take you to Piedmont, Dirk's got a lift there, but he doesn't have those tires. He would have to order them and that would be about two days. I can tow you to Forks Junction, call in the size on the way, and have them for tomorrow."

Leanne the Locomotive started her engine, "Tomorrow!" No, that's not going to work. I have a bubble bath at the Ritz Carlton in Denver waiting for me."

Confused, Ray looked at her and said, "Well ma'am, we haven't got a Ritz Carlton in Forks Junction, and most likely no bubble bath, but we got a motel for you to rest your head, and two restaurants to fill your belly. My choice would be Estelle's Diner, best fried chicken, biscuits, and gravy this side of the Alamo."

Leanne shot daggers at Devon. Devon turned to Ray and asked, "Can we ride in the camper while you tow us?"

Ray shook his head and said, "No sir. But I've got enough room in my truck to get ya'll there."

With no other option, they agreed. As they were all piling into Ray's truck, including the hounds, Luke turned to Devon and said, "The curse of the hoodoos," and shook his head.

Devon muttered under his breath, "Oh bloody hell."

*****

They arrived in Forks Junction two hours later, grumpy and hungry. Ray dropped them off at the Dew Drop Inn. The manager of the motel was a perky woman by the name of Doreen. She cheerily told them that they didn't have Wi-Fi, but they had free HBO. She showed them to their rooms, one for Chet, Devon and the dogs, and one for Leanne and the twins, then told them, "Estelle's Diner is just a block behind the motel, best fried chicken, biscuits, and gravy ya'll will ever eat," and left them to settle in.

Leanne grabbed her suitcase, shot eye daggers at Devon, turned, and entered her room, with the twins following her.

*****

An hour later, they were all sitting at a table at Estelle's Diner. Chet, trying to cut the tension, cleared his throat and said, "Um, well since Ray and Doreen both gave thumbs up to the fried chicken, biscuits and gravy, guess that's what I'll be having." Leanne and Devon both grunted.

A few minutes later their waitress came over to the table, she wore a short pink dress with Estelle's written across the pocket, she pulled out her pad from the pocket and a pencil from behind her ear, and cheerily said, "Welcome ya'll, my name's Lucy and I'll be takin' your order. What can I get ya'll?" All five ordered the fried chicken with biscuits and gravy along with sweet teas. Lucy nodded and said, "Good choice, Estelle makes..."

Before Lucy could finish her sentence, a grumpy Leanne said, "Best fried chicken, biscuits and gravy, we know." Lucy smiled at her and turned toward the kitchen.

Devon looked over at Leanne and said, "Well, it looks like someone has her Bitch-O-Meter on high."

Leanne glared at him for three seconds and replied, "Well, it looks like someone doesn't know how to count, or listen. Three rocks, seriously?"

Devon raised an eyebrow and replied, "You don't really believe in that hogwash the guide was saying?"

Leanne scoffed, "Hogwash, ha! I believe him now."

Luke looked back and forth at both of them and said, "Okay, I have been doing some more thinking, and I bet Devon can break the curse."

All eyes turned to Luke, then Devon said, "Oh do you now? And how might I break the curse, as you call it?"

"Well," said Luke, "The guide told us we could each take one, and that it would bring us luck, but since you took three, you got cursed. But if you give the other two away, then the curse won't follow you."

Chet laughed and said, "I think the boy is onto something. Why don't you give Lucy one and then find someone else to give the other one?"

Lindsey added, "Yeah, you could give the other one to someone who could use some good luck."

Devon looked at all three of them, and then at Leanne who was smirking, and replied, "Okay, I can do that. But I still don't believe in the curse."

Luke smiled at Devon and said, "Better safe than sorry. That's what Mommy always says."

Just then, Lucy arrived with their order, and they ate in silence. Once finished, Devon asked Lucy for the check. Lucy wrote it out at the table, tore it off her pad and handed it to Devon, and began gathering the dishes. Chet pushed back from the table and said to Lucy, "That was one mighty fine meal, Lucy. You weren't wrong about it being the best fried chicken. And those biscuits and gravy, well I could have eaten six more."

Lucy smiled and replied, "Well thank you kindly, sir. I will pass that along to Estelle."

Devon took sixty dollars out of his wallet and handed it to Lucy and told her to keep the change. Luke kicked Devon under the table. Devon turned to Luke and asked, "What was that for?"

Luke replied, "Um, you forgot to do the other thing."

Devon looked around the table and all eyes were on him. He shifted in his seat, reached into his pocket, pulled out the three hoodoo rocks, and said, "She's going to think I've lost my mind."

"Well, you better do it, or we might get two more flat tires," said Luke.

Amused, Leanne added, "And if we don't get to the farm by tomorrow, you'll face a worse fate, called Amber."

Defeated, Devon said, "Fine. When Lucy comes back by, I'll give it to her."

A few minutes later Lucy came out of the kitchen with a brown bag, walked over to their table and handed Chet the bag, and said, "Estelle asked me to give these to you."

Chet opened the bag, looked inside, and saw six piping hot biscuits. He looked at Lucy and said, "Well that was mighty nice of her."

Lucy replied, "She peeked through the kitchen window, and when her eyes landed on you, she got all pink in the cheeks. I'm thinking she might be crushing on you. That's why she wouldn't come out of the kitchen to give them to you herself."

Devon and Leanne looked at Chet with raised eyebrows. Feeling slightly embarrassed, Chet said to Lucy, "Well, you tell Estelle, I thank her kindly."

Just as Lucy was turning back toward the kitchen, Leanne spoke up, "Lucy, Devon has a little something for you."

Lucy turned to Devon, feeling ridiculous, Devon fiddled with the rocks in his hand and started, "Um, well, you see, Luke here has the notion that these rocks I

93

pocketed from the hoodoos are cursed, well, not cursed, but..."

Luke cut in before Devon could continue, "The tour guide told us we could each take one for good luck, any more than that, and the hoodoos would get real mad. Devon took three and we got two flat tires, so I told him to give the other two away. So, if you take one, it will bring you good luck."

Lucy, not quite sure she was buying what this clan was selling, but she decided to play along, she turned to Luke and pinched his cheek and said, "Well, aren't you the cutest. I would be happy to accept the rock. Lord knows I could use a bout of good luck."

Devon handed Lucy the rock and said, "Well, now that we have that settled, we'll be on our way. Thank you for a wonderful meal, Lucy," they got up to leave, Leanne glanced back at Lucy and found her fanning herself with a menu, her eyes following Devon out the diner door. Leanne rolled her eyes.

The town only consisted of four blocks, but Leanne wanted to take a look around, so she told the others she would meet them back at the motel in an hour or so. Chet was all for that, he and the kids were going to take the dogs for a nice long walk, and Devon said he was going to give Ray a call and check on the status of the tires. Leanne walked across the street and peeked in a few windows, as she rounded the corner, she saw what looked like an open-air market. Intrigued, she walked toward it. There were several stalls set up with jewelry, Mexican blankets, and a few with pottery and clay pots, but what caught her eye was the old man sitting under the shade tree, displaying a variety of cowboy hats. She crossed over to him, and asked to try one on, the old man smiled a toothless grin, reached across the table and picked up a black one with turquoise beads sewn around the brim, and said, "Si Senora, it matches the color of your eyes."

Leanne took the hat from him and tried it on, the man handed her a small mirror, and said, "Si Senora, it was made for you." Leanne agreed. She spent another fifteen minutes picking out hats for Devon, Chet, Luke, and Lindsey. After paying for the hats she decided to head back to the motel.

When she reached the motel parking lot, she ran into Doreen, "Well howdy Leanne. Looks like you met Fernando."

Confused, Leanne asked, "Fernando?"

Doreen laughed, pointed at the hats, and said, "The hats. Fernando sells them down at the market. Best hat maker for a hundred miles."

Understanding now, that the old man under the tree was named Fernando, Leanne said, "Yes, I stumbled upon the market and was thrilled to find hats for all of us." Leanne went on to tell Doreen about the hoe-down baby shower for Amber and Leonard. She explained that they were heading there tomorrow.

"Well, isn't that exciting?" exclaimed Doreen, "Ya know what ya'll should do? You should go to Round-Up tonight. It's right down the street, and on Wednesday nights they have line dancing classes for the whole family. It would be a hoot!"

Leanne agreed, thanked Doreen for the recommendation, and hurried across the parking lot to her room, excited to tell the others about the Round-Up. She knocked on Devon's door and Luke opened it, Leanne bounced into the room and excitedly began talking a million miles a minute, "Look what I found!" she said as she handed out the hats to each of them. Lindsey was thrilled with her pink hat, as was Chet with the one Leanne had chosen to match his brown boots, Devon and Luke, not so much. Leanne turned to both of them and said, "They're for the hoe-down. Luke put yours on. You are going to look so cute! And Devon, well you will be the hottest British cowboy ever!" Devon and Luke looked at each other and proceeded to put their hats on. Leanne clapped her hands together and said, "And I haven't told you the best part yet. I ran into Doreen in the parking lot, and she told me that Wednesday nights at the Round-Up, they have line dancing lessons for the whole family! Isn't that awesome?"

Chet tipped his hat back and replied, "I'm in Leanne. Sounds like a good time."

Jumping up and down, Lindsey said, "Me too! I can't wait to wear my boots and hat."

Smiling ear to ear, Leanne turned to Devon and Luke and asked, "What about you two, you on-board?"

Devon knew better than to challenge Leanne on this one, considering the two flat tires, and no Ritz Carlton. He smiled and said, "Absolutely. I can use all the practice I can get."

Leanne looked at Luke who replied, "I guess."

Thrilled that everyone was on-board, Leanne, "Great! I'm going to take a shower and get dressed. Oh,

I'm so excited!" and with that, she left the room, with Lindsey following right behind her.

Luke turned to Devon and said, "You better hurry up and get rid of that other rock. Our luck is running out," then he plopped down on the bed and put his hat over his face.

Devon looked at Chet and Chet said, "Don't look at me son. I only took one rock," and burst out laughing.

*****

They arrived at the Round-Up at six-thirty and were surprised to see how crowded it was. Kids were running around playing, while adults were gathered around the horseshoe-shaped bar. Devon announced, "I think I need an ice-cold glass of liquid courage, Leanne why don't you grab the table over there, and I'll get us some drinks. Chet, can you give me a hand?"

Leanne and the twins walked over to the table and looked around. The place was all she imagined it would be, from the sawdust floors, the wagon wheel tables, and the best part was the mechanical bull off in the corner. Luke and Lindsey spotted it too and asked Leanne if they could go look at it, which she agreed to, and off they ran. Chet and Devon returned to the table, with, as Devon had referred to it, liquid courage.

Leanne was so excited she could barely sit still. She sipped her wine and said, "Isn't this amazing? It's exactly like I imagined."

Devon sipped his beer and said, "Well, it certainly is wild west-ish."

Leanne nudged him with her elbow and said, "It's authentic, I think. Do we even know what state we are in?"

Chet answered, "I'm guessing Colorado, but hard to say, being crammed into that tow truck."

Devon looked at her and said, "You know, that's a good question. Ray never mentioned where we were headed. Anyway, speaking of Ray…" and as if saying his name magically made him appear, Ray walked into the Round-Up, with a petite dark-haired girl on his arm.

He spotted them and smiled as he walked over to their table, and said, "Howdy ya'll. I see you're getting to know our fine town." He turned to the girl on his arm and said, "Lana, these are the folks I was telling you about. Had to go retrieve them off the side of the road out by the state line, Devon, Chet, Leanne this is my girl Lana."

Lana smiled and said, "Nice to meet ya'll. Glad to hear that Ray was able to help ya'll out."

While on the subject, Devon asked Ray, "Speaking of us breaking down, did you get my message earlier about the status of the tires?"

Ray tipped his hat back, and replied, "Yes sir. I tried to call you back, but I got no answer, so I left you a message. Tires got here right before I closed up the shop. Sam, my night guy on duty is going to put them on and you should be good to go first thing in the morning."

Leanne interrupted and said to Ray, "Ray, we were just trying to figure out what state we are in. None of us paid attention to where we were on the ride here."

"Well ma'am, you broke down about three hundred miles over the Utah-Colorado state line. But being that Piedmont took the call and sent it to me, we traveled south about a hundred and twenty miles here to Fork Junction, Colorado," replied Ray.

Concerned, Devon said, "Ray, we were heading east on route 70, but now that we have detoured two hours south, might there be a different way to get to Oklahoma?"

"Whereabouts are you heading?" asked Ray.

"Sweetwater, it's quite near the border of Colorado and New Mexico," replied Devon.

Ray laughed and said, "Yes sir, I know it well. I have kin out that way. You can take county road 50 straight out of town, heading east as far as Lamar, then hop on county road 287, and you'll glide right into Sweetwater. Take ya'll about seven and a half hours to get there."

Chet, being from Oklahoma when he was a youngster, asked Ray, "What's your kin's name? I have some myself, not far from Sweetwater, over in Derby."

Ray smiled and said, "Is that right? Well now, my kin are on my daddy's side. He has eight brothers, and the one being in Sweetwater, is Uncle Lee Quinn."

Leanne gasped and said, "Oh my goodness, we're heading to the Quinn farm. Our friends Amber and her husband Leonard are having a baby, well actually two, they're having twins, and Kate and Lee are throwing them a hoe-down baby shower."

Surprised, Ray said, "Well I'll be, ain't that a coincidence, mighty small world. However, Momma and Daddy moved to Phoenix six years ago, and I haven't kept up with the family tree. So many of them spread out all over this country, but let me tell you, growing up, our family reunions were so big we had to rent out a whole campsite down in Durango. Us Quinn kids, we raised all sorts of trouble. Long stories, but when ya'll see Bailey Jr, you ask him, he'll tell ya'll. And baby Amber, she was just a little tyke back then. Ya'll send my congratulations, will you please?"

Devon shook Ray's hand and said, "We certainly will."

Just then a man came up to the microphone and made an announcement that the line dancing lessons were about to begin, then the music was cranked up really loud. Leanne grabbed Chet and Devon's hands and said, "Let's go, its show-time," and they joined Luke and Lindsey and the rest of the crowd on the dance floor.

*****

The next morning at seven a.m., they were all packed and ready to go. Ray knocked on the door an hour earlier, handed Devon the keys, and told him that the camper was parked out front. Devon thanked him and asked, "How much do I owe you?"

"Not a nickel, the insurance covered the tow and the repairs," replied Ray.

Surprised, Devon said to Ray, "Hang on a minute, I'll be right back," he turned back into the room, grabbed his wallet and pulled out three hundred-dollar bills and walked back to where Ray was waiting, handed him the bills.

Ray looked at the money and said, "No sir, you don't owe me a penny."

Devon reached out and shook Ray's hand and replied, "It's a token of our gratitude, which I'll ask you to accept."

Ray smiled widely and said, "Wow, that's right kind of you Devon, and greatly appreciated. Thank you kindly."

As Ray was turning to leave, Leanne came out of her room next door, she spotted Ray and said, "Good morning Ray."

"Morning, Leanne. Did ya'll have a good time last night?" asked Ray.

Leanne beamed and said, "We sure did. I don't know the last time I danced that much. I was just coming over to tell Devon that I think we should grab some breakfast at Estelle's before we hit the road. I woke up starving."

Ray responded, "That two-stepping will do that to you. And trust me, you don't want to be leaving town until ya'll have had a stack of Estelle's maple-bacon flapjacks. Best this side of New Orleans."

Leanne laughed and said, "I believe I heard that about her fried chicken with biscuits and gravy, and they truly were the best ever."

Ray smiled and replied, "Yes ma'am, that's the truth. Ya'll have a safe trip to Oklahoma and be sure to tell my Quinn relations I send my regards."

"Will do," Devon replied.

Ten minutes later, the clan loaded their bags into the camper and set off on foot for Estelle's. They were crossing the street in front of the diner, when Lucy came flying out the front door, running full steam ahead directly at Devon. Everything happened so quickly. Leanne, Chet, and the kids just stared wide-eyed at the scene unfolding in front of them. Lucy had jumped on Devon, wrapping her legs around his waist and hanging on tight as a cobra around his neck, kissing him all over his face. Devon quickly worked to detach her from his body, placed her on her two feet, and said, "What the bloody hell was that all about? You came running at me like a bull in an arena."

As the others looked on, excitedly, Lucy began to explain, "I'm really, really sorry Devon, but when I saw you coming, I just lost all my senses. Okay, so remember yesterday when you gave me that silly rock? And sweet little man over there," pointing at Luke, "said it would bring me good luck. Well, last night when I got home after my shift, my honey, Jimmy, had the whole house lit with candles, and Lordy, maybe a hundred rose petals spread all over the floor. I walked in thinking maybe I was in the wrong house. But no, there was my Jimmy, dressed in his Sunday best, holding two glasses of bubbly, smiling like a cat that ate the canary. I just looked at him like he was crazier than a tick hound, and asked him 'What exactly are you up to Jimmy?' And do you know what he did? Well, of course you don't, but anyhow, he got down on one knee and said, 'Lucy, I've been in love with you since the first day I saw you in sixth grade. And now, I know that's some years back,' and I scoffed, "Yeah like twenty," and he says, "Well Lucy, I think it's time we got married. So, what'd you say, will you marry me?" Well let me tell you, I have been waiting ten years to hear those words, and now its official, me and Jimmy are getting married! And it's all because of that rock you gave me yesterday!" sticking out her left hand to show them the diamond ring on her finger.

Devon took a few steps backward for his own safety, and said, "Lucy, you don't truly believe the rock had anything to do with Jimmy asking you to marry him, do you?"

"Oh yes, I do. I have been waiting ten years for this day. And here ya'll come to town, give me a rock, and BAM, I am an engaged woman!" replied Lucy, then she turned to Luke and said, "And you sweetie pie, are my favorite little man forever. You knew those rocks held magic and you insisted Devon give me one," Lucy moved forward and grabbed Luke in a bear hug and was covering his cheeks with kisses.

Once she let go, Luke used the collar of his shirt to wipe off the bright pink lipstick that Lucy left behind. Not knowing what to say, but being raised with good manners, he said, for a lack of other words, "Um, you're welcome Ms. Lucy."

Amused by the whole scene that unfolded in front of him, Chet said, "Well I guess this is cause for a celebration. What do you say we do that over some breakfast? I'm starving."

Leanne hooked arms with him and said, "Me too," and they all headed into Estelle's Diner.

The news of Lucy's engagement had apparently spread like wildfire because the whole diner was packed wall to wall with locals. The story of the rock was told over and over as the food from the kitchen flowed to the tables. Just as Devon, Leanne, Chet, and the kids were finishing up platters of flapjacks, home fries, bacon, and of course, biscuits with gravy, Estelle emerged from the kitchen and walked over to their table. Lucy was clearing the plates, turned to the group, and said, "Well, ain't ya'll special. Estelle doesn't come out of the kitchen for nobody."

Estelle, looking nervous as a cat on a hot tin roof, said, "Oh you hush girl, I just wanted to thank these fine folks for coming in here and turning your luck around, and mine for that matter. I've never seen this place so full."

Luke was pulling on Devon's arm. Devon turned to him and said, "Why are you trying to pull my arm off? You do know I only have two of them?"

Luke pulled Devon closer and whispered in his ear. Devon looked at him and said, "Oh for the love of the Queen, you don't believe in that hogwash, do you?" Nodding, Luke replied, "I sure do. Lucy is living proof. Now just do it."

Exasperated, Devon reached into his pocket, took out the third rock, cleared his throat, and said, "Um, Estelle, breakfast was great. I really fancied the flapjacks and…"

Luke elbowed him and said, "Do it."

Devon sneered at Luke, then turned back to Estelle and said, "I would be very pleased if you would accept this rock as a form of gratitude for your fabulous cooking and warm hospitality."

Estelle stared at Devon in disbelief, as he reached out to hand her the rock, she put her hand to her heart as her eyes teared up and finally said, "For me? No one has ever given me anything except back talk and grief, and here you want to give me a lucky rock. I just don't know what to say."

Devon started to reply. "Well, I'm not actually convinced…" but Luke elbowed him again, so Devon changed course and said, "Um, well then, I hope what you wish for comes true Estelle."

Estelle accepted the rock, and said, "Well, I'm going to start wishing for that new griddle I saw in the appliance magazine, straight up. Thank you, and you fine folks are welcomed here anytime," with that said, she turned to Chet and handed him the pastry box she was holding, and said, "I hope you like lemon meringue pie," and with cheeks the color of apples, she turned back towards the kitchen.

They asked Lucy for the check, but she told them, breakfast was on her and wouldn't let them pay. Leanne shot Devon a look and he got the message. He took his wallet out of his pocket, pulled five one hundred bills, and said, "That is very nice of you. However, we would like to give you an early wedding present," and handed her the five hundred dollars.

Astonished, Lucy asked, "Seriously? But this is so much money. It could pay for my whole wedding."

Devon got up and gave her a hug, and replied, "Congratulations. And tell your Jimmy, I said he is a lucky man."

Lucy wiped away a tear and said, "Thank you. Thank you so much."

Hugs and goodbyes were said all around the diner, then the five of them left feeling happy and full. Luke turned to Devon and said, "You done good Devon, real good."

Devon laughed, swung his arm around Luke's shoulder, and replied, "You, young man, are smarter beyond your years," and they headed for the motel and the waiting camper.

Everyone loaded into the camper, Devon stayed behind, saying that he was going to settle up with Doreen. He walked over to the office, and found Doreen behind the counter, and said, "Good morning Doreen. We are set to hit the road," and handed her the room keys.

Doreen stood and went to the printer to retrieve a copy of his bill, which he paid by credit card. After signing the slip, Devon said to Doreen, "I need a little assistance, and I was wondering if you could help me."

Doreen smiled and said, "Sure, what's on your mind, Devon?"

"Well, I've heard that Estelle might be in need of a new griddle at the diner, and I was wondering if you could do some snooping of sorts, to find out what she is looking at in that appliance catalogue of hers," said Devon.

Doreen laughed, and said, "Estelle carries that catalogue around like a bible. Always saying, one day she's gonna get a new griddle, new refrigerator, new pots, and pans. She's been in business for thirty years and her kitchen is the same as it was on day one."

Devon raised an eyebrow in surprise and said, "Thirty years? Well, it just might be time for an upgrade. Do you think you could talk to Lucy and get an idea of what she is looking for, and then contact me?"

Doreen eyed him suspiciously and asked, "What are you up to Devon?"

Devon smiled slyly, and said, "Here's my cell number. Find out what she wants from the catalogue, then text me a list and the catalogue information. Will you please?"

Doreen looked at him and said, "Okay. I can do that."

Devon said, "Thank you," and turned to leave.

Just as he reached the door, Doreen called out, "Oh, by the way, Devon, I love your music, I'm a huge fan."

Devon turned, smiled at her then headed out the door.

Chapter 15
The Farm

The trip from Fork Junction to Sweetwater, Oklahoma took eight hours, and the occupants of the camper were ready to get out. They pulled up to the Quinn farm at five p.m. to the sight of at least a dozen people scurrying around. When all five of them exited the camper, Devon shaded his eyes and said, "Wow, this place is massive. There is nothing but land for miles and miles."

Leanne stretched and said, "From the way Amber talked about the farm, I thought it was going to be a lot smaller," as her eyes glided over the white clapboard house with dark green shutters and a huge front porch. Just then, the front door swung open and Kate came out and down the stairs, heading straight for them.

"My goodness, you're finally here. I was starting to get worried about you," said Kate as she pulled Leanne into a hug.

"Hi Kate, I'm sorry we are later than expected, we had to take a slight detour," replied Leanne as she gave Devon a stink eye glance.

Kate made her rounds, hugging Devon, Chet, and the twins and said, "Well, I sure hope it wasn't anything serious. The main thing is you are here now, safe and sound."

Chet turned to Kate and said, "Kate this is quite the spread you have here, and it looks like you have all hands on deck."

Kate laughed and said, "We have been hustling our buns to get this place ready for the festivities, most of the people are neighbors lending a helping hand."

Surprised, Devon said, "Neighbors? There is barely another house in sight, outside of the one up on the hill."

"That's Bailey Jr. and Jenna's house. Hannah and Clay live a mile down the road, and Amber and Leonard are building a house on the back of the land. Bless his heart. Leonard has been working around the clock, hoping to have it finished before the babies arrive. But I don't think that's going to happen. Amber looks ready to burst any minute," said Kate.

Just then, Leonard came around the side of the house. Catching sight of Devon, Leanne, Chet, and the twins, he picked up his pace to a slight jog and called out, "Hey, you guys made it. Wow! It's great to see all of you."

Leanne, Devon, and Chet looked at each other, then back to Leonard. Leanne asked, "Leonard, is that you?"

Leonard laughed and said, "Yup. It's a long story. But let's just say, Hanna and Jenna felt I needed a 'Daddy' makeover," he walked to Leanne and gave her a hug, turned to Devon and Chet and shook hands.

Still stunned by Leonard's transformation, Chet said, "Son, we just saw you three months ago, and well, let's just say you didn't look like that."

Kate hooked her arm through Leonard's and said, "Well, this city boy has had a good dose of country air and I think it agrees with him. He's fit right into this family like a saddle on a horse. Speaking of family, we best get inside before Amber tries to waddle her way out here. And let me just forewarn you, Amber may be a sight of glowing beauty nine months pregnant with twins, but she has hormones raging like wild horses. Let's just say, she can be a force to be reckoned with. She scared poor Leonard into spilling the beans about the baby shower, so she knows all about it."

Devon looked at Leonard and asked, "She scared you?"

"To the bone," replied Leonard. Devon laughed and put his arm around Leonard's shoulder and walked into the house.

Like a lot of homes, the kitchen is family central and the Quinn's kitchen was just that. Hannah was at the stove stirring a pot, Jenna and five kids were scooping cookie dough onto baking sheets. There were three other women working at the counter peeling potatoes and shucking corn, and Amber was feeding baby Claire, who was sitting in her highchair. When Leanne, Devon, Chet, and the twins entered the kitchen, chaos erupted. The youngsters remembered each other from last summer and began to squeal with delight. Amber turned halfway in her chair and screamed, "Leanne!" She tried three times unsuccessfully to get up out of her chair, but her bulging belly was stuck under the highchair tray. She scared the begeebees out of baby Claire, who was now wailing. Hannah walked over, helped Amber out of her chair, and picked up Claire.

Amber waddle-ran over to Leanne and hugged her and started to cry, "Oh my Lord, look at me crying all over you. These hormones are just out of control. Oh, I'm so happy to see you." Then she spotted Chet and lunged at him hugging him tightly, telling him how much she missed him. Then she turned to Devon, who had backed up a few paces, grabbed his arm and pulled him into her bulging belly, wrapped her arms around him, and said, "I've missed ya'll so much."

Devon pried her arms from his neck, stepped back a safe distance, and said, "Amber, you are a vision. Apparently, pregnancy agrees with you."

Amber wiped her nose on her hand and said, "Devon you are absolutely no good at lying. I am as big as a whale."

Kate walked over and put her arm around Amber and said, "Sweetie, it will all be worth it once the babies arrive."

Amber wiped away her tears and said, "I know Momma, you keep telling me that, but I want these little acrobats out, and soon. I swear they are doing flips in there."

Leanne laughed and said, "Oh, I know exactly what you mean. I've been there, done that. But when you hold those two beautiful babies in your arms, you'll forget all about the pregnancy part."

Amber hugged Leanne and said, "I know, you're right. Anyway, ya'll are here and I couldn't be happier. Do you have any idea when Rosalie and Harold will get here?"

"Well, she texted me a few hours ago and said they should be here by five," replied Leanne. And no sooner had the words left Leanne's mouth, when a commotion of horn honking began out front.

The group moved from the kitchen to the front porch, watching as Harold drove up the driveway. Once parked, Rosalie jumped out from the passenger side of the camper and started talking a million miles a minute, "Oh my God, I have so much to tell you. I cannot believe I just drove through three states in a camper."

Astonished at the sight of Rosalie arriving in a camper, the size of a short yellow school bus, Amber said, "Rosalie you drove here in a camper?"

Rosalie, still trying to catch her breath replied, "Yup. And it was fabulous."

Devon raised an eyebrow and said, "So I gather you're not going to do me any bodily harm?"

Rosalie walked over to Devon, grabbed him by the cheeks and pulled him in for a lip-smacking kiss, then said, "You are brilliant Rock Star. This idea of yours was the best. Harold and I had so much fun, and get this, we stopped in Vegas and Harold won $300,000 at the roulette table. And better yet, the hotel comped us a free night in the Presidential Suite."

All eyes turned to Harold as he made his way up the porch stair's, he laughed and said, "No way to lose when I've got my good luck lady with me," and wrapped his arm around Rosalie.

Rosalie and Harold worked their way through the group with hugs and handshakes. When Rosalie caught sight of Leonard, she had to do a double-take. She looked at him long and hard and asked, "Leonard is that you?"

Leonard laughed and replied, "Apparently so."

Shocked, Rosalie asked, "What happened to you? Your hair is all slicked back, you're not wearing glasses and you look like Popeye after he ate the spinach with all those arm muscles."

Kate stepped forward and said to Rosalie, "As I told Leanne, our city boy has turned country."

"Well, I'd say so. He looks like he has been roping cattle," replied Rosalie.

That brought a round of laughter from the group. Leanne linked arms with Rosalie and said, "He looks hot, right?"

Rosalie nodded and said, "It's like looking at Clark Kent turning into Superman."

*****

Kate had set up a family-style table out back under a huge oak tree, which Lee and Bailey Jr. had strung with little white lights. Platters of fried chicken, macaroni and cheese, shrimp and grits, buttermilk biscuits and fried green tomatoes were passed around the table as the chatter continued, and stories of their road trips were told. Once everyone was finished eating, the kids ran off to catch lightning bugs in mason jars, while Leanne, Rosalie, and Jenna cleared the table, telling Kate and Hannah to stay put since they did all the cooking. Once the table was cleared of dinner, the women brought out dessert, consisting of four different pies that Kate had baked, and a tub of homemade vanilla ice cream, which turns out was made by Petey.

Chet, not able to eat another bite after having a slice of apple pie and pecan pie, pushed back from the table, and said, "That was one mighty fine meal, Kate and Hannah. Between our stops on the road and this meal tonight, I think I've gained 50 pounds."

Lee Quinn laughed and said, "Welcome to my world, Chet. Kate's desserts are just too good to pass up. But don't you worry there will be plenty to do tomorrow to help shed those pounds."

Chet rubbed his belly and said, "Sign me up."

Devon added, "I wouldn't mind working off a few pounds myself." All eyes turned to him. He looked around the table, and asked, "What?"

Of course, Rosalie was the first to answer, "You do know that would require you getting your hands dirty, Rock Star?"

Devon looked at her and replied, "I'll have you know, I have gotten my hands dirty plenty of times."

Before Rosalie could volley back with a witty retort, Leonard said, "Devon, I could use a hand installing some doors up at the house."

Devon smirked at Rosalie and then said to Leonard, "I'd be happy to help."

Amber yawned and said, "I'm sorry ya'll, but I have got to call it a night. My back is aching and these two," rubbing her belly, "are kicking up a storm. So, I'm gonna head up to bed, and pray I only pee six times during the night." Leonard got up from the table, helped Amber out of her chair, and walked her into the house."

Leanne watched them go into the house and said, "Oh, I remember those days. You feel like aliens have taken over your body."

Kate laughed and said, "Well I did it one at a time, five times, and that was no picnic. And being her momma, I got instincts that are telling me that those babies aren't going to wait three more weeks to make their arrival."

Hannah rose from the table and said, "Well let's just hope she makes it through the baby shower tomorrow. I'm going to go gather my brood and head on home. Clay, can you round up the kids while I get Claire cleaned up from this piece of pie she's wearing?"

Everyone helped clear the table and headed inside. Devon turned to Lee and asked, "Where would be the best place to park the camper?"

"I'd say over in the field on the right. That way it won't be in the way of all the cars parking here tomorrow. Come on, I'll show you and Harold where."

Leanne put her arm around Rosalie and said, "I'm going to round up the twins and get them to bed. Why don't you and Harold come over for a glass of wine and we can catch up. I want to hear all about your trip."

"Sounds good," replied Rosalie. "I'm going to help Kate finish cleaning up, then go change into something comfy and we'll be over."

*****

Leanne came out of the camper to find Devon, Chet, Rosalie, and Harold sitting in chairs set up a few feet from the camper. Devon poured Leanne a glass of wine and

114

handed it to her as she sat down next to Rosalie. Leanne thanked him and said, "Those two were out for the count in a minute. All the running around in this country air wore them out."

Rosalie took a sip of wine and said, "I can't believe how big they got."

Chet piped in and added, "And they're both smart as whippersnappers. That Luke, he showed Devon here a thing or two on our trip."

Intrigued, Rosalie asked, "Is that so? Do tell Rock Star," giving Devon a curious glance.

Devon shifted in his seat and replied, "Nothing to tell," giving Chet the evil eye.

Leanne scoffed and said, "Oh yes there is," and she began telling Rosalie and Harold the story of the hoodoo rocks.

When Leanne finished, Rosalie with suspicion, said, "Oh come on now, you don't believe those rocks were cursed just because Devon took more than one?"

"Not at first I didn't, but when we got two flat tires in the middle of nowhere, yeah I believed," Leanne replied.

Chet added, "That boy, he was onto something and he wasn't gonna let Devon here off the hook until he gave away those other two rocks. That's how Lucy got engaged to her fella."

"Well I believe in good and bad luck," said Harold, "When Rosalie flew the coop, my golf game went down the toilet. Couldn't make a putt to save my life, and now here on our road trip, I win 300 big ones at the roulette table. She's my good luck charm for sure."

Rosalie reached for his hand, smiled at him, and said, "Harold, your golf game has always been in the toilet." That brought a round of laughter from the group.

After chatting and catching up for another hour, the five of them said their goodnights and headed off to bed.

Chapter 16

Leanne woke the following morning to find the twins wrapped around her. She detangled herself from them and headed for the bathroom. Once dressed in sweats and a sweatshirt, she quietly left the room on her way to the kitchen. She wasn't sure what time it was, but if Devon and Chet were still sleeping, she would skip making coffee and head up to the house. However, when she stepped into the kitchen, she saw that both Devon and Chet's beds were folded up, and both men and the dogs were gone. She walked over to the coffee pot and found a note from Devon, *"Good morning beautiful. Chet and I woke early to go lend a hand to Lee and Leonard. Kate asked me to tell you and the kids to come up to the house for breakfast when you are ready. Well, I'm off to get my hands dirty. I'm over the moon about you...xo Devon."* Leanne smiled at the note in her hand. She started to assemble the makings for coffee but then heard the twins laughing. She poked her head into the bedroom and found them both wide awake watching cartoons. She walked over to the window and raised the shade, turned to the twins, and said, "Good morning my sweet babies."

Lindsey, the feistier of the twins, said, "Mommy, we are not babies anymore. We are almost eight."

Leanne laughed, bent over and kissed their heads and replied, "You will always be my babies, even when you are 88."

Lindsey laughed and said, "You're silly Mommy." Luke, absorbed in the cartoon he was watching, didn't respond.

Leanne clapped her hands together and said, "Okay you two, time for a quick shower, and then we are heading up to the house for breakfast. Lindsey, you go first."

Excitedly, Lindsey scooted off the bed, and said, "I can't wait to see the kids. They are way cool," and headed for the bathroom.

Laughing, Leanne, tussled Luke's hair and said, "You're next."

Without taking his eyes off the TV, Luke replied, "Okay Mommy."

When Lindsey came out of the bathroom, Luke shut off the TV and jumped off the bed and headed for the shower. Leanne picked out a pair of shorts and T-shirt for Lindsey to wear, however, Lindsey had another outfit in mind, "I want to wear my pink shorts, my white T-shirt with the unicorn on it and my cowgirl boots, after all, we are on a farm, Mommy."

Leanne raised an eyebrow at her daughter and said, "Well, in that case, you can pick out your own outfit, dress yourself and make the bed. Once Luke is out of the bathroom, I'll take a quick shower and we'll head up to the house."

Lindsey liked the idea of picking out her own clothes and getting dressed by herself, but not so much for making the bed, but she replied, "Okay."

*****

A half-hour later the three of them walked into the Quinn kitchen, Kate turned to Leanne and said, "Good morning Leanne. Coffee is in the pot."

Leanne helped herself to a cup of coffee, turned to Amber, and said, "Good morning Amber. Did you sleep okay?"

Amber huffed, rubbed her belly, and replied, "Fat chance of that with these two doing gymnastics all night."

Leanne laughed and said, "I remember those nights. And the only place they would get comfortable and settle down was on my bladder. So Amber, when is your actual due date?"

Amber shifted her bulk and replied, "Well at first, Audrey, she's my midwife, said the beginning of June, but at my appointment last week, she just patted my hand and said, 'You're getting there dear.' Seriously, like I don't already know that. Look at me. I'm huge and ready to pop like a balloon!"

Leanne raised an eyebrow at Amber's testy reply, then cautiously she asked, "Amber, are you feeling any twinges in your back?"

Amber scoffed and said, "Leanne, I am way past twinges. It's more like, Daffodil, our pet goat, gave me a swift kick."

Concerned, Leanne looked at Kate, and as if reading her mind, Kate said to Amber, "Then Baby Girl, you need to stay off your feet until the party. Why don't you take a few magazines and go sit in the rocker on the front porch?"

Leanne put down her coffee, and held out a hand to Amber and said, "Come on Country Girl, let me help you up. I'll prop up some pillows and bring you a cup of mint tea."

Yikes! That might not have been a wise choice of words. Before Amber could hoist her bulk out of the chair, she plopped back down and began bawling her eyes out. Just then, Rosalie walked into the kitchen. She surveyed the room, looking from Kate to Leanne, who was bent over hugging Amber, and asked, "What's going on? Amber, are you okay?"

Barely decipherable through the tears, Amber blurted out, "Leanne's going to make me mint tea...just like she did at the cabin," which set off another bout of sobbing.

Leanne tried to hoist Amber up and out of the chair. Failing miserably, she turned to Rosalie and said, "Rosalie, can you give me a hand here?"

Rosalie, not sure what was going on, said, "Sure. Where are we rolling her to?"

Leanne looked at Rosalie, who honestly looked baffled, and just couldn't contain herself. She plopped Amber back down in the chair, laid her head on top of Ambers, as she shook with laughter. Kate, trying to hold it together herself, put the dish towel she was holding over her face, as her shoulders bounced with laughter.

Rosalie looked at Kate and Leanne and said, "It's a legitimate question," which set them off into another fit of laughter.

Amber was too busy sobbing to realize what was happening around her. Leanne pulled herself together and said to Rosalie, "Just help me get her out of the chair. She's going to the front porch to sit in a rocking chair and put her feet up."

They both hoisted Amber up and out of the chair. Kate grabbed a pile of magazines and a few pillows from the living room couch and followed them out the front door. Once they got her settled, the three women went back to the kitchen. Rosalie looked at Leanne and asked, "What's going on with Country Girl?"

Kate handed Rosalie a cup of coffee as they sat down at the kitchen table. Leanne looked at Kate and said, "Kate, she is not going to make it another three weeks. She's having Braxton – Hicks."

Kate nodded and said, "I know. Audrey said the same thing to me the other day."

Rosalie looked back and forth as Leanne and Kate talked. It took her a few minutes, but the light bulb finally turned on, "Wait. Are you two saying that Amber is ready to have those babies now? Don't you think we should get her to a hospital?"

Kate patted Rosalie's hand and replied, "Yes, she's getting real close to having those babies, but she has the best midwife in the county. She'll be at the party and plans on coming prepared, just in case."

Looking like a deer in headlights, Rosalie asked, "In case of what? Oh my God. Amber is having those babies here at the farm!

Kate nodded and said, "Yup. That's how the Quinn women have been doing it for centuries."

Astonished, Rosalie looked at Kate and said, "Sweet baby Jesus. We better get the manger ready."

Chapter 17

By five o'clock the baby shower hoe-down was revving up. People arrived by the carloads, arms filled with gifts for Amber and Leonard's babies. The barn was magically transformed into a country-western dance hall with little white lights hanging from the wood beams, sawdust covered the floor, hay bales were scattered around for seating. Over to the left, there were fifty feet of buffet tables lining the wall whereupon sat dozens of potluck dishes brought by each guest, enough to feed the whole town of Sweetwater. The Massey brothers, a local country band, were set up on a constructed stage, and off to the right was a decorated queen's chair made especially for the momma-to-be, surrounded by a mountain of baby gifts, all wrapped in pastel shades of pink, blue, yellow and green. Amber and Leonard didn't want to know the gender of the babies before they were born, so it was anyone's guess.

Leanne, Devon, the twins, Chet, Rosalie, and Harold walked into the barn. Although Chet helped Lee and a group of neighbors move things this way and that way, put things here and there, he looked around at the finish results and declared, "Well, I'll be. I never imagined it would turn out looking like this when all was said and done."

Devon, in his pressed blue jeans, crisp white button-down shirt, black cowboy boots, and hat, looking like he just stepped out of a western movie, replied, "Well this certainly isn't what I pictured when Leanne explained what a hoe-down was. This place is magical."

Rosalie, who is well known for her occasion appropriate outfits, said to Devon, "Ha, I got this one right, Rock Star."

Devon looked at her from head to toe and replied, "Well Rosalie, from the looks of your denim skirt, red and white check blouse, and your white tennies I'd say you blend in quite well with the table coverings."

Rosalie looked down at her outfit, then over to the tables, realizing she did look like a tablecloth, turned to Devon, and said, "Bite me Rock Star," which set the group off in a bout of laughter.

Harold, dressed in black jeans, black long-sleeved button-down shirt, a turquoise bolero at his collar, with matching belt and black cowboy boots, said, "Don't you listen to him Sweet Rosalie, you are my Daisy Duke. Let's go get us some of that moonshine punch." And off they went.

Chet stepped forward and said, "I could use a little something to wet my whistle. What do you say we follow them?" The twins had run off when they first got there, so they followed behind Rosalie and Harold.

Once Amber and Leonard arrived, the party got into full swing. People were eating, dancing, and chatting with each other. At eight o'clock the band stopped playing and announced it was time to surround the momma and daddy-to-be for the opening of the presents. Amber was seated in the chair, like a queen on her throne, with Hanna and Jenna at her side handing her presents to open. She had only opened ten presents when she doubled over and wailed like a wild hog. The room went dead silent until the next wail came and set them in motion. Controlled chaos took over, orders being shouted from every direction. Audrey, the mid-wife was front and center, calmly talking to Amber, she turned and requested that all the menfolk gather the hay bales and put them together like a bed. She asked Kate to go to the house and get blankets and towels, she sent Clara, her assistant to the car to retrieve her medical bag. She turned to a shell-shocked Leonard and asked him to get two pots of boiling water. When he didn't move, Leanne told Devon to get him seated and she and Rosalie ran to the house to get the water. By the time they returned, the barn had emptied out, leaving only Kate, holding Amber's hand, and Devon and Chet sitting next to Leonard, who was now at Amber's side wiping her forehead with a cool cloth. They placed the pots of water on the table next to Audrey and started to back up toward the door, Chet and Devon standing up to go with them. Amber shot them a look and shouted, "Stop right there! Where do you think you're going?" Then another contraction was upon her and she let out a primal scream, once it passed, panting, Amber said to the three of them, "Sorry, I didn't mean to yell, but we're family now, I want you here. I need you here." Devon and Chet backed up a few paces toward the door looking for the nearest escape route, but Amber looked at them and growled, "Stay right where you are," as another contraction took over her body.

Leanne, seeing the complete terror on Devon and Chet's faces, took them by the arm and lead them to the chairs next to Leonard. Rosalie, not sure what to do and a bit unsettled herself, turned to Leonard and said, "Hey Boy Wonder, it looks like you're going to be a dad real soon. Better get ready for those diaper changes." Leonard looked at her in horror.

Leanne grabbed Rosalie by the arm and said, "Go sit down," but Amber growled at them so Rosalie walked over and took her other hand, while Leanne went and stood by Amber's head, taking the cloth from Leonard and wiped Amber's forehead, while Leonard kept telling her to breathe.

Audrey popped her head out from under the sheet covering Amber's hoo-ha, and said, "Okay Amber, looks like you're ready to push...one-two-three push," and so she did and to everyone's amazement out popped baby number one, a girl. Clara took the baby over to the bathing bin, but five seconds later, Audrey yelled to Rosalie, "Come here, now!"

Rosalie did as she was told, and Audrey told her to grab a towel, and two seconds later handed her baby number two. Clara handed Leanne baby number one and took baby number two from Rosalie. At that moment, Leonard laid his face on Amber's and together they wept tears of joy. Devon stood, cleared his throat, and announced, "I believe now would be a good time for Chet and me to step out." Leanne smiled at them, with tears running down her cheeks, and nodded. Devon and Chet made a hasty exit for the door.

An hour later, to a cheering crowd, Leonard emerged carrying Amber followed by Lee and Kate each holding a baby. Audrey followed them into the house and up to the bedroom. Amber was settled into bed, Leonard by her side as they each held one of their daughters. Audrey gave Kate instructions and told Amber to follow them as she left. Kate and Lee stayed a few minutes longer. As they were leaving, Amber asked them to send up Leanne, Rosalie, Chet, and Devon, a visit that Audrey had approved.

Ten minutes later, Leanne softly knocked on the door of Amber and Leonard's room, when Amber said, "Come in," they slowly entered. The sight before them took their breath away. There, snuggled on the bed were Amber, Leonard, and their baby girls. Amber waved them over and said, "Can you believe it ya'll, two girls." Leanne moved closer to the bed and Amber held up a baby for her to hold, then turned to Rosalie and said, "Come here Rosalie." A little hesitant, Rosalie moved to the side of the bed and Leonard handed her the baby he was holding. Amber told Leanne, "You are holding Annie and Rosalie, you are holding Rose." Not a word was said as the two women gazed at the two beautiful babies they were holding in their arms. Tears filled their eyes as love filled their hearts. They spent a half-hour with Amber, Leonard and the babies, both Devon and Chet took turns holding the babies, a moment neither of them will ever forget.

Chapter 18

The following morning, Leanne, Devon, Chet, the twins, Rosalie and Harold joined the entire Quinn family for breakfast. Hannah, Kate, and Jenna were scurrying around the kitchen, preparing a huge buffet-style breakfast. When Leanne asked what she could do to help, Kate gladly handed over the spatula she was holding and said, "Leanne, honey, if you wouldn't mind taking over making the pancakes, I'd like to go check up on Amber, Leonard, and my grandbabies."

"Absolutely Kate," replied Leanne, "And when you come back, I want you to sit and get off your feet,"

Kate untied her apron, smiled, kissed Leanne's cheek, and as she was leaving the kitchen, she poked Devon on the arm and said, "You've got a keeper there Devon. You are a lucky man."

Devon walked over to Leanne and wrapped his arms around her from behind, rested his chin on her shoulder, and asked, "Do you need any help? I've been known to make a pretty good Mickey Mouse pancake."

Leanne laughed and nudged him back with her elbow and replied, "No thank you, but if you wouldn't mind, could you go see where the kids are and let them know breakfast will be ready shortly?"

"That I can do," replied Devon, he kissed her neck and went to find the twins.

Leanne turned to see Hannah fanning herself with a dishtowel, while her eyes followed Devon out of the kitchen. She caught Leanne smirking at her and said, "How in the world do you control yourself around that man?"

Leanne laughed and replied, "It's not easy. But you, my friend, have quite the hunk of a husband yourself, and he better not catch you making gaga eyes at Devon."

Hannah threw the dishtowel over her shoulder and said, "Oh don't you worry about Clay, he already knows I would pack my bags and run away with Devon, but you're in my way, so no chance of that happening. Anyway, that man only has eyes for you. He is smitten and twice bitten."

Leanne laughed and said, "You are one of a kind, Hannah Quinn Thorton. I am so blessed to have you and your whole family in my life."

Hannah walked over to Leanne and hugged her and said, "We're sisters now, so I won't go trying to steal your man." They both laughed and hugged a tad bit tighter.

*****

A half-hour later the huge clan was seated out back at the long table Lee and Bailey Jr. had set up under the big oak tree. Platters of food were passed around family-style. Amber and Leonard joined them, with the twins sleeping close by in their bassinets. Kate sat at one end of the table and Lee at the other, the chatter was non-stop. Once the kids finished their breakfast, they ran off to play.

Amber asked Leanne and Rosalie if they could stay another day. Rosalie replied, "Nope, sorry Country Girl, Harold and I are going to take another week and travel the open road. When we leave here today, we are heading to Denver, then after that, it's wherever the wind blows us."

Devon, fluffing his feathers said to Rosalie, "Well then, I gather my idea of a road trip worked out better than you expected, considering when Harold first told you about it, you threatened to do me bodily harm."

Rosalie, not one to easily admit when she is wrong, shifted in her seat and said, "Yeah, yeah, okay Rock Star, I'll give you credit for having a good idea. But don't keep filling Harold's head with crazy ideas or you'll have to answer to me."

Devon raised his hands in the air and said, "I wouldn't dream of it. I have once or twice been on your bad side, and I do not intend to go there again."

Harold laughed and said, "Aw, don't you worry Devon, her bark is worse than her bite. She's come a long way since being on that island with you, Leanne, Amber, and Leonard. I got my Sweet Rosalie back and for that, I am truly grateful," he reached over and gave Rosalie a kiss on her cheek.

Rosalie, not one for public displays of affection, took Harold's hand in hers and said, with humor, "Well I'm still boss, don't you forget that."

Harold squeezed her hand and replied, "Yes ma'am," which brought a round of laughter from the table.

Amber turned to Leanne, and asked, "Can you guys stay another day?"

"We would love too, but we have to be back for school on Monday. Plus, we need to make a quick stop in Utah on the way back, and then it is straight through to Seattle," replied Leanne.

Seeing the disappointment on Amber's face, Devon cheerily said, "However, it won't be long before we see you all again. We are hoping you will be able to join us on Welby Island Labor Day weekend for a reunion of sorts, one year later from the day Amber and Leonard were married."

Always quick on her toes, Rosalie asked, "Speaking of weddings, when do you two plan on tying the knot?"

Devon raised an eyebrow and looked at Leanne, prompting the others to look at her too. She squirmed in her chair and said," Um, well, we haven't set a date yet."

Lee Quinn piped up and said, "Then, why don't ya'll do it Labor Day weekend since we'll all be there?"

Leanne looked at Devon, and he knew exactly what she was thinking so he decided to rescue her, "Well, actually we were thinking…"

Before he finished, Leanne cut him off and said, "Yes, we were thinking that would be the perfect time to get married, surrounded by all of you."

Devon shot her a look but didn't say anything. Apparently, the wheels had now been set in motion for a Labor Day reunion on Welby Island, and the wedding of Leanne and Devon."

Chapter 19

By noon all of the hugs and goodbyes were said and done. Rosalie, Harold, Devon, Leanne, Chet, Bella, Blaze, and the twins, were on their way. Harold and Rosalie were headed north toward Denver. Devon and his crew were heading west toward Utah. The plan was to stop in Provo to pick up the food Carla had prepared for them to take home then drive straight through to Seattle. Devon said he would drive the first four hours, which he got no argument from Chet, who said he was going to take a nap after that huge country breakfast. Since the twins were up at the crack of dawn, she told them to go with Chet to the bedroom and take a nap. Bella and Blaze followed right behind. Leanne went to the kitchen and poured two glasses of sweet tea and brought them upfront and sat in the passenger seat next to Devon. They drove in silence for a bit. Devon turned to Leanne and asked, "So what has your mind all gaggled up Queen Bee?"

Leanne sighed and said, "I was just thinking how nice it was to be with the Quinn's. From the moment I met them last summer, I knew they would be an important part of our lives. But after these past few days, and the birth of the babies, I feel like they are family. I haven't felt such a strong family connection since my mom died."

Devon smiled over at her, and said, "I know exactly how you are feeling. I personally have very little experience with family bonding. I loved my mum very much, but I never actually had a family. Between the Quinn's, Rosalie and Harold, I am starting to understand what it means to be part of a large family. However, with that said, you, Chet, and the twins are my life. My every breath is consumed by the love I have for you. Leanne, you made me whole again. The person you met on the plane to Welby Island and the weeks that passed at Claine cabin, was a broken man, just an armored shell that I walked about with, not letting anyone in, only to protect myself, never knowing if I was capable of feeling love, or giving it. But you Leanne, you are my moon, my stars, my sunlight, my every reason to breathe. I will never quite understand how I got so lucky to have you in my life, and I will not for one day ever take you for granted. I am truly blessed by you, the twins and Chet."

Leanne wiped away the stray tears that were sliding down her cheeks, she looked over at him and said, "Devon, when we were sitting at the table this morning, and all of those eyes were on me, they weren't questioning or criticizing, they were eyes of pure love for me, for us. I couldn't deny them the pleasure of being with us when we take our vows to becoming husband and wife."

Devon smiled at her and said, "So basically, you caved."

Leanne laughed, "Oh yeah, folded like a house of cards."

Knowing what Leanne's vision was for their wedding day, he suggested, "Well, you know, we could make a small compromise. We could get married on the beach with Chet and the twins, in a private ceremony, and come Labor Day weekend, we'll just do it again. None would be the wiser."

"Oh no, no, no," said Leanne, "That would never work. Did you see how fast Lindsey told you about Blake banging the nanny? That child would throw both of us right under the bus."

Devon laughed and replied, "That she would. So Labor Day weekend it is then?"

"Labor Day weekend it is," replied Leanne. "I'm thinking of a Hawaiian Luau theme. Flower leis, Hulu dancers, fire eaters, limbo contest, pig roast and inviting everyone we know and love from near and far, to share in our forever moment."

Devon smiled and said, "I like the way you think Queen Bee."

*****

They drove for an hour in peaceful silence. As they approached the turn off for Route 50 heading west toward Provo, co-pilot Leanne told Devon that the exit was coming up. Devon smiled at her and passed the exit continuing north. Confused, Leanne quickly said, "You just missed the exit."

Cheekily, Devon replied, "I was thinking we would take a little detour."

Leanne eyed him suspiciously and asked, "A detour? Where are we detouring to?"

"Well," said Devon, "I was thinking we might swing by the Ritz-Carlton in Denver, for a quick bubble bath and a meal."

Stunned, Leanne looked at him and said, "Are you serious? You're not kidding, are you? Because if you are that would be really, really mean."

Devon laughed and said, "No, I'm not kidding. I talked to Rosalie and Harold this morning, and since they were heading there, I decided we should join them for the night."

Leanne smiled widely and said, "Well let me forewarn you now, once I get in that bubble bath, I may never get out."

Devon laughed, even though he knew she was dead serious, and replied, "Oh no worries there, Rosalie said the same thing. However, Harold and I thought it might be fun to have a pajama party of sorts. We called ahead and booked adjoining suites. We also added the luxury spa package for you and Rosalie. I spoke with the concierge and he said there is a kids club and tonight is a pizza party and movie poolside, which I think the twins would enjoy. And while the kiddies are being entertained, we adults will be having a room service dinner. I think all of us could use a night out of the camper."

Staring at him wide-eyed, Leanne said, "Oh my God. That sounds heavenly! I'm calling Rosalie right now."

Devon listened as Leanne and Rosalie prattled on like schoolgirls. When Leanne finally hung up, he asked, "So I gather Rosalie is on board."

"Absolutely! How long will it take us to get there?" Leanne asked.

"Approximately four and a half hours give or take," replied Devon.

Leanne sighed and sunk back in her seat. After a few minutes of daydreaming, she snapped out of it and sat straight up and asked Devon, "Wait, what about Bella and Blaze. They can't sleep in the camper by themselves all night."

Surprised that Leanne would even think about the dogs in her state of euphoria, he said, "They actually have a pet-friendly policy and a doggie park on the premises."

Relieved, Leanne smiled at Devon and said, "You really do think of everything."

"Well, I try. Oh, and I may have left out the best part," replied Devon.

Leanne couldn't imagine how it could get much better than a luxury spa package, fluffy white robes, and room service, but she asked anyway, "How is that possible?"

Devon laughed and said, "It's a three-bedroom suite. No tangling with the octopus's tonight."

After sleeping with the twins for six nights, those three words were music to her ears. Three-bedroom suite, she looked over at Devon and playfully said, "Oh, so you're going to sleep with them?"

Devon replied, "Not a chance. Tonight, I'm going to be your octopus."

*****

They arrived at the Denver Ritz Carlton at six p.m. Leanne grabbed her suitcase and was the first one out of the camper, yelling at those behind her, "Come on, hurry it up, people. I have a spa calling my name."

Lindsey, dragging her suitcase, trying to catch up to Leanne asked, "Why is a spy calling your name?"

Keeping her pace, Leanne replied, "Not a spy sweetie, a spa. It's a place you go to get pampered."

Still, confused Lindsey asked, "Pampered? Like baby diapers? Mommy do you need diapers?"

Exasperated, Leanne stopped and turned to Lindsey and began to explain, but Devon stepped up and said, "No, Lindsey, Mommy is going to get a massage and relax for an hour."

Understanding, Lindsey excitedly said, "Oh that sounds fun. Can I come?"

Leanne, shooting daggers at Devon as she tapped her watch, had Devon thinking quick on his feet. "Um, well you could if you want. But I had something a little more fun in mind for you and Luke."

Excited, Lindsey said, "Like what?"

"Well," said Devon, "I heard they have an amazing kids club here. You get to go on a scavenger hunt, have pizza for dinner, and watch a movie outside by the pool, and you get to make s'mores. And the best part is, no parents allowed."

Luke, standing close by taking it all in, said, "Way cool. Can we go now?"

Devon, pleased with the twins' reaction said, "Yes, but let's get checked in first."

They headed inside to the front desk, as Devon was checking in Rosalie came running through the lobby dressed in a white fluffy robe. She grabbed Leanne by the arm and said, "Let's go Locomotive, our date with Hans and Franz is in ten minutes," handing Leanne a white fluffy robe.

Leanne looked and Devon. He laughed and said, "Run along. I'll get the kids situated and see you back in the room in an hour. Rosalie has a key. With that said Leanne dropped her suitcase and took off across the lobby with Rosalie.

*****

An hour and a half later, Rosalie and Leanne, literally drifted into the suite. They were so relaxed they thought they were floating. Harold, Devon, and Chet were sitting in the living room, Bella and Blaze at Chet's feet. They looked at the two women and Harold asked, "Well girls, did you like the spa treatment?" They plopped down on the couch and sighed in unison.

Leanne put her head back and replied, "That was pure heaven." Rosalie nodded.

Devon got up, walked over to Leanne, kissed her head, and said, "And very much deserved."

Leanne sat up and asked Devon, "How did the kids make out? Are they happy with the kids club?"

Chet laughed and said, "I'd say so, Leanne. The camp director Jenny came to get them, and they were happier than fleas on a cat."

Devon added, "They will be back at ten p.m. Room service will be here in 20 minutes with dinner, so if you want to freshen up you better hurry." It was a struggle, but

Rosalie and Leanne got up off the couch and headed for the shower.

Leanne came out first. She didn't bother to dry her hair and was wearing comfy sweats and sweatshirt. Five minutes later, Rosalie entered the room wearing a leopard print silk pajama set, and her hair was wrapped in a matching turban.

Devon took one look at her and the words just flew out of his mouth, "Rosalie, what the devil is that on your head?"

Rosalie lifted her hand to her head and replied, "It's a turban. I didn't have time to dry and style my hair, so I wrapped it."

Devon, almost at a loss for words, said, "Oh, I thought perhaps you were heading off on an African safari."

Well, that just did it. Leanne put her hands over her face and shook with laughter. Chet not far behind her managed to say, "Well I would hope not. She'd be dodging bullets from those hunters, thinking she was a leopard." Leanne rolled to the side, grabbed a couch pillow and face planted.

Confused, Rosalie said to Devon, "You told Harold we were having a pajama party. These are my lounging pajamas."

Devon and Chet looked over at a chuckling Harold, who said, "Don't look at me, I didn't buy them for her," and as a saving grace, there was a knock on the door, he jumped up and said, "Dinner's here," and went to answer the door, still chuckling.

The bellhop rolled the dinner cart into the suite. He set the table with the covered plates, popped the cork on a bottle of champagne, and secured it in an ice bucket. He asked if they were in need of anything else, Devon couldn't resist and said, "Maybe a piece of raw meat for the cheetah over there."

Annoyed, Rosalie said, "Bite me, Rock Star."

*****

They dined on filet mignon, baked stuffed shrimp, lemon risotto, and roasted asparagus and toasted the night with champagne. At ten o'clock on the dot, there was a knock on the door, this time Devon said he would answer it. He had arranged to have the twins return with Jenny, the camp director, and the birthday cake he requested. Tomorrow is Leanne's birthday, so he wanted to surprise her. He opened the door to find Luke and Lindsey holding the cake as Jenny lit the candle. They walked into the room singing happy birthday and very carefully set the cake down in front of Leanne. The look on her face was of pure shock, and considering Chet, Rosalie, and Harold weren't aware it was Leanne's birthday they shared the same look but began to sing.

Leanne was speechless. Finally, Lindsey broke the trance and said, "Happy birthday Mommy! Make a wish and blow out the candles."

Leanne looked around at the six faces staring at her and knew she couldn't wish for anything more than what she already had. She was truly blessed.

Chapter 20

Devon, Leanne, Chet, and the twins were on the road early the next morning. The plan was to stop in Provo, Utah which was approximately an eight-hour drive. They would stop by Carla's to pick up the food and then drive straight through to Seattle, which was another 13 hours. Since Leanne wasn't doing any of the driving, she would co-pilot, while Devon and Chet took turns driving and napping. Seven and a half hours later, when they reached the gas station that housed Carla's food shack in the back, they were shocked at what they saw. Cars were parked all over the vacant lot next to the gas station and people were lined up out to the street. Leanne looked around and saw a new sign in front of the gas station welcoming visitors to eat at Carla's Cantina. Chet eased the camper into the gas station and parked it in front of one of the pumps. When they exited the camper, Luis came running out of the office, excited to see them, said, "Hola! I am so happy to see you. We have been expecting you ever since Senora Leanne called to say you were on your way."

Leanne, still in awe of all the people, asked Luis, "Are all of these people here to eat Carla's food?"

Luis beamed and replied, "Si Senora. Ever since Carla put up the new sign and created the webpage you suggested, many people have come to eat her food. It's a good thing she has five sisters to help her because she is very, very busy. Come, come, she will be so excited to see you!"

When Leanne, Devon, Chet, and the twins walked around back, they were shocked to see all of the people sitting at a dozen or more picnic tables. Weaving in and out of the tables were three women in bright colorful dresses, clearing away plates, or serving food. Luis walked them around the tables and into the shack where Carla was at the stove cooking. When she saw them, her hands flew to her mouth and her eyes glistened with tears. She said something in Spanish to the woman at the stove, wiped her hands on her apron and hurried toward them. She hugged Leanne and was chattering away in Spanish. The only word Leanne understood was gracias.

Leanne stepped back and looked at Carla and said, "You did all of this in less than a week? We were just here last week."

Carla was nodding rapidly still speaking Spanish. That is when Luis spoke up and said, "Senora Leanne, she says that none of this would have been possible if it wasn't for you and the money you gave her. She always dreamed of making a cantina and you made her dream come true."

Taken back, Leanne said, "But how did she get everything done so quickly?"

Luis laughed and said, "That is the beauty of a large family and many friends. My brother Pedro made the sign, his son, my nephew Pepito, is of college age and is, how do they say, um…computer-savvy, he did the web page. Carla's sisters came to help with the cooking and serving. Mr. Jenkins down at the hardware store in town made the tables and his wife who is a seamstress, made the table clothes. Shop owners from all over town hung flyers in their windows, and before we knew it, people were lining up for Carla's cooking. It's a miracle, thanks to you Senora."

Carla said something to Luis in Spanish, when she was done Luis turned to them and said, "Carla wishes for you to stay and eat. She is closing the cantina at five p.m. and says we will have a fiesta in your honor. There will be food, drink, music, and much laughter. You can park your camper on the other side of the gas station and spend the night."

Leanne opened her mouth to begin telling Luis that their plan was to make this a quick stop and then get back on the road and drive straight through to Seattle, but Devon interrupted her and said, "I think that sounds like a fine idea. We've already driven close seven hours, if we rest here tonight, we can set out at five a.m. and be back to Seattle before dark."

Chet was all for it and added, "That sounds like a plan to me."

Leanne gave it a moment's thought and said, "Sure, why not, what's one more day." This pleased Luis and Carla very much.

Since it was only two o'clock, Chet decided to take the dogs for a walk and suggested they all walk into town. Luis said it was only a ten-minute walk, and after seven hours in the camper, nobody was complaining. When they got to Main Street, Chet said he was going to head over to the general store and see if he could find some treats for the hounds. Luke and Lindsey asked if they could go too. Chet said, "Sure, I bet from the looks of the place they might just have an old-fashioned soda fountain, and we can get us an ice cream float." Luke and Lindsey were all for that. They agreed to meet back at the general store in an hour.

Leanne and Devon decided to stroll through town and window shop. As they started down the street, Devon's phone rang. He didn't recognize the number, but it had the same area code as Ray's back in Fork Junction, so he answered it, "Hello. Oh yes, hello Doreen. Yes, that would be great. Are you sure Lucy got everything on the wish list? Perfect. Please text me the information, along with Lucy's number, and I will follow up with her, regarding delivery. Thank you, Doreen, I appreciate your help. Yes, I certainly will pass that along to Leanne and Chet. Bye."

When he hung up, Devon turned to Leanne, who had her arms folded over her chest and a suspicious look on her face, he said, "That was Doreen from the motel in Fork Junction."

"Yes, I know who Doreen is. What I don't know is, what you are up to," replied Leanne.

Devon realized with all of the activity at the farm over the weekend, he totally forgot to tell Leanne about the discussion he had with Doreen the morning they left Fork Junction. "Well, that would make sense, considering I forgot to tell you about it until Doreen called. We were so busy at the farm, it slipped my mind," said Devon. "Anyway, when we were at Estelle's for breakfast that morning and I gave her the silly rock, she mentioned that she was going to start praying for the new griddle she saw in the catalogue. When I went into the motel office to settle our bill, I asked Doreen if she could ask Lucy to do some investigating and find out what else Estelle might be looking at in the catalogue. Doreen said that Estelle has been talking about getting new appliances for 30 years, and for 30 years the diner has been the same, with most of the appliances on their last legs."

Leanne smiled slowly and said, "So you thought maybe you could help answer her prayer for a new griddle?"

"Well that was my intention, but apparently Estelle's wish list has been a work in progress for 30 years. She needs just about everything replaced. Dishwasher, oven, refrigerator, griddle, stand mixer, whatever that is, bread proofer, again a mystery, and a deep fryer. Lucy is going to send me the catalogue information and the list, and I, in turn, am going to answer Estelle's prayers, so to speak." Devon replied.

Astonished, Leanne said, "You are going to buy her a whole new kitchen?"

"Well, yes, I suppose I am," replied Devon.

Leanne stepped closer to Devon, wrapped her arms around his neck, and said, "You are a good man Devon Davis," and gave him a kiss.

Devon tapped her nose and said, "I believe someone else has been working her own magic and may have forgotten to mention it."

Leanne replied, "You know, you're right. When we left Carla's after lunch last week, the kids and I took a nap.

Then we got to the hoodoo's and I totally forgot to tell you. When I had gone back to the shack to place the food order for us to pick up on the way back home, I gave Carla $500 that I had brought as my emergency fund and told her to invest in a new sign and menus. Now seeing what she has created and the future success she will have, all because I gave her the money and I believed in her, well, it feels good."

Devon swung an arm over Leanne's shoulders and said, "I may have helped with that a tad. When I went to pay for lunch and the gas, the total was a little over $60, but I gave Luis $200 and told him to give the rest to Carla as a tip."

Leanne smiled up at him and said, "We've met some really wonderful people on this trip. We have seen places we may not have ever made the time to see, and along the way, we have managed to make a difference in people's lives. That feels good. It feels right, like maybe we were meant to take this road trip for a reason."

Devon agreed with Leanne, adding, "Well, for me, the most defining moment of this trip was being at the birth of Leonard and Ambers baby girls, that, I was not expecting to be part of a hoe-down in a barn, but it truly was an amazing moment. A tad bit frightening but amazing. And afterward, when I held those tiny babies in my arms, I was awestruck at the fact that they were each a part of Amber and Leonard. I've never held a baby before. I had no idea that it would be so emotional. They are counting on the adults to make it right in the world for them."

Leanne saw a bench across the street in the park, so she steered them towards it. When they reached it, she said, "Let's sit for a minute. This town is so quaint. I love that all of the storefronts are painted the color of the sunset, like the one we witnessed at the hoodoo's. And the shop keeps leaving the doors open, inviting you to walk in and visit." Leanne leaned her head on Devon's shoulder and asked him, "When we get married, do you want to have a child together?"

He bolted upright, making her head bounce off his shoulder and said, "Are you crazy? I never want to see you in that much pain. Amber was like a wild beast trying to get those babies out of her."

Leanne laughed and said, "It does hurt, but…"

Devon interrupted and said, "Hurt? Bloody hell, it sounded like she was going to split in half. No thank you. I can live without seeing you go through that. Anyway, we have the twins and they are all I need."

Because his horror took over his common sense, he realized that maybe Leanne was asking because she wanted another baby. *Oh boy,* he thought, *I better make this right,* so he said, "But if you are asking because you want to have another baby, then you know I would say yes, and I would prepare myself on a daily basis for the birthing process."

Leanne laughed and said, "Actually, I'm not interested in having more children. As you said, Luke and Lindsey are all we need. However, your reaction to my question was priceless. You can count on me re-enacting it for any and all who ask us that question, because they will trust me."

Devon leaned back and said, "Oh, I have no doubt of that, especially when you get together with the other two cackling hens."

Leanne was about to reply when she was interrupted by an incoming text on her phone. She stood, reached into her back pocket to retrieve her phone, and read the message: *Leanne, it's me, Adele. I wanted to let you know that I received a full price offer on your house, and the buyers are asking to close in two weeks. Also, they would like to know if they could buy it furnished and are willing to throw another $2,000 on top of the offer to cover the furnishings. Let me know if this works for you and I'll draw up the contract and get it over to you tomorrow to sign.*

Devon looked at Leanne and asked, "Is everything okay?'

Leanne turned to him and said, "Yes. That was a text from Adele. She said she has a full price offer on my house and the buyers want to close in two weeks. They would like to pay another $2,000 to buy it furnished."

"Well, that sounds like a good deal. However, the look on your face says otherwise," said Devon.

Distracted, Leanne tapped her finger against the phone. She turned to Devon and said, "I have been kicking around an idea in my head the past few months. I haven't actually wrapped my head around it, but maybe now is the time to."

Devon arched an eyebrow and asked, "Would you like to share this idea?"

Leanne sat back down on the bench, turned to Devon and said, "Okay, so I have been thinking about the cabin."

Devon shifted in his seat and leaned toward her and asked, "The cabin, really?"

"Yes," replied Leanne, "Hear me out then tell me what you think. What if we clean up the cabin and update it? Give it a new coat of paint, and build a wraparound porch, maybe, even a small addition, adding another bathroom, maybe a master suite?"

Intrigued, Devon said, "I'm listening."

Excited, Leanne continued, "Okay, so I was thinking we could turn it into a vacation rental. It would only accommodate small groups, but I thought I could advertise it as a cooking retreat. I would give cooking lessons to newlyweds, the girl's weekends, divorced dads, singles, and families. We could offer a catch and cook session like we did when we ran low on supplies. We could do a Valentine getaway, and I could ask Frieda to come to do a pastry class."

Leanne stopped to take a breath, so Devon, piped in, "Yes, I can see your vision. We could actually do more than a small addition. I say we expand the kitchen out to the old oak tree by the picnic table, a huge country kitchen with a lot of counter space. We could take the three bedrooms downstairs and expand them out to make them larger, adding sitting rooms. We could keep the living room as it is, with the fireplace, and add built-in bookshelves, featuring some cookbooks, and we can add a grand fire pit area off by the garden for happy hours and tasting parties, which will be presented by the guests after their lessons."

Amazed that Devon could take her idea, and turn it into her vision, made her again wonder for the millionth time, how she got so lucky. She turned to him and said, "You don't think it's crazy?"

Devon smiled, kissed her, and said, "On the contrary, I think it's a fabulous idea. But I'm still at a loss of what this has to do with selling your house."

"Well," said Leanne, "I'm thinking that the new furniture I bought for the house is barely used so we can bring it to the cabin. I know we'll need more than that, but I hate to not use it. And with what I make from the sale of the house, which actually is quite a bit more than what I paid for it a year ago, I can put into the cabin."

Devon stood, held out a hand to Leanne, and said, "You know, it might be fun to have some guest chefs. I think we could arrange for Carla and Luis to come and do a class and I bet we could even coax Estelle out of her kitchen with an invitation from Chet to go pick her up and fly her out to the island."

Leanne stopped walking, turned to Devon, and said, "Oh my God. That would be amazing. Carla's Mexican food and Estelle's fried chicken, biscuits and gravy, and those amazing maple bacon pancakes. We could do themed weekends."

Devon took her hand and continued walking towards the General Store, and casually said, "Maybe we could get our man Chet to do a grilling segment, perhaps for the girl's weekend."

Leanne laughed and said, "He certainly is a lady's man. I'll text Adele and tell her to sell the house, but the furniture is not included."

Devon agreed, but he felt he needed to add an additional thought, so he stopped walking and turned to

Leanne and said, "I love this idea. I really think you are onto something, however, there is one thing we might add, when I boarded that plane at SoCal airport, heading to the unknown location of the Claine Enlightenment Retreat, which as we all bloody well know now, did not even come close to being a retreat, but what if we also allotted a few weekends out of the year to host small groups of survivors, say, veterans, cancer survivors or ones of certain tragedies, that could use a break from the heartache for a bit."

Leanne stared at the man before her. A man, who as a teenager, witnessed the brutal murder of his mother at the hands of his own father, a man for over 15 years could not imagine himself worthy of love, who denied himself that simple pleasure of being loved and giving love, a chance at happiness, until he himself ended up with four strangers on Welby Island, all searching for the same goal: happiness. Each and every one of them found it because they trusted each other; they believed in each other, and in the end, they became family with the strongest of bonds, never to be broken. And now, here he is thinking of ways to mend other people's hearts. Surely, they could take their experience and create an ideal setting to bring people together whether it is family or strangers. Again, she wondered how she got so lucky.

Chapter 21

The following morning the clan was on the road at five a.m. The evening before had been full of food, fun, and laughter. Carla and Luis had closed the cantina for the private party, which included not only Carla's five sisters, but their husbands and children, which at last count Devon tallied Carla's side of the family at 25, and Luis's side at 32. Platters of food were set out on a long buffet table, sangria was passed around by the pitcher full and four large coolers were filled with an assortment of soda pop, beers, juices, and water. Piñata's were hung from tree limbs, for the youngsters, who were blindfolded and handed a stick, who eagerly swung at it in the hopes of cracking open the piñata, which in turn would spill its bounty of candies all over the ground. It was an absolutely perfect ending to an amazing road trip. Although the party continued on well past midnight, Leanne and her crew said their goodnights at ten p.m. They knew they had a long day of travel ahead of them and wanted to be on the road at the crack of dawn.

*****

Six hours into the drive, they arrived in Boise, Idaho. They stopped for a quick stretch and to let Bella and Blaze do their business. Leanne had prepared an easy lunch of sandwiches and chips which they ate picnic-style on the side of the road where they had pulled off. A half-hour later, they were back in the camper and on their way. The last leg of the trip from Boise to Seattle was an estimated eight hours, being that it was 11:30 a.m. they expected to be back home a little after 7:30 p.m.

The open road was on their side, they pulled into the RV rental place at 6:30. Leanne had cleaned up the camper, removed all of the linens and towels, and put them in the laundry bin in the bathroom. She loaded all of the stuff from the refrigerator and freezer into a large cooler and boxed up the remaining items from the cabinets. Suitcases were packed and ready to go, so all they needed to do now was load up her SUV and head for Welby Island. Devon opened the passenger side door for her, but she walked past it and around to the driver's side, and said, "Nope, I'm driving. You and Chet have been driving for the past week, and quite honestly, I'm tired of co-piloting, so I will drive us home," she climbed behind the wheel and waited for everyone to settle in and buckle up then she started the car and headed for the marina. They hit a little bit of traffic coming out of the city but made it to the marina in 45 minutes. They piled out of the car and were greeted by Henry, who normally doesn't work nights. As he approached, Chet said, "What are you doing here Henry? You don't work nights."

Henry took a bandana out of his pocket, wiped his brow, and said, "Well, it seems I'm shorthanded these past few days. We had a little incident over at Benny's Friday night."

Chet was helping Devon lift the cooler out of the car; he turned to Henry and asked, "What kind of incident?"

"Well," said Henry, "Ya know that new guy I hired back about a month or so ago, Jeff?"

Chet nodded and said, "Yeah, I reckon I maybe said one or two words to him. Didn't like him much, rubbed me wrong."

Henry replied, "Well you aren't the only one felt that way. Turns out he's been scouting out my customers boats. Taking small items at first, but then he made the mistake of breaking into Godfrey's boat. Ya know the big one with the fancy fishing poles on it? Turns out, he went snooping around and took some valuable coins and some cash that was hidden up on a shelf in a closet. And being the dumb-ass he is, he went into Benny's and started throwing around some big bills, buying rounds of drinks, getting really loud and obnoxious. Well, it didn't take long for the locals here in town to put two and two together, so, Paulie Dobson goes up to him and starts asking all kinds of questions, like, where'd he get those big bills, and why all of a sudden he's buying rounds of drinks for the whole bar when last week Benny had to show him the door because he couldn't pay his tab. Well, Jeff, he didn't take kindly to Paulie asking all these questions, sticking his nose in where it doesn't belong, so he pops him one right in the kisser. Well from there on it turned into a bar room brawl. It took Sheriff Kaye and three deputies to break it up. They dragged Jeff outside, tell him to cool it down, and he goes and pops one of the deputies in the eye. That's when they hauled him off to jail, had his pickup towed and found the coins and the rest of the cash."

Leanne stepped forward and said, "Henry, remember the day I came to the dock and asked for a ride over to Welby Island? I believe it was Jeff's first day."

Henry replied, "Yup, I remember. I asked him to run you out to the island."

Leanne nodded and said, "Well, on the ride over, I tried to make small talk with him, like, where are you from, do you have family in the area and all I got was, here and there. I sat quietly for the rest of the ride. When we reached the bend, and the house came into sight, he let out a whistle and became all chatty, saying, "Wow, is that your house. I bet you have a big family." He helped me off the boat and offered to carry my packages up to the house, but by this time my radar was on high alert, so I politely declined and walked down the dock. When I got to the end, I turned and he was just standing there, staring at the house. He caught me staring at him, so he swiftly untied the boat and took off."

Concerned, Devon walked up and stood next to her and asked, "Why didn't you tell me? I would have gone and had a chat with him."

Leanne put a hand on Devon's arm and said, "You were in LA, and by the time Chet and the kids got home I forgot all about it. But thinking back on it now," she turned to Henry and asked, "He didn't go back out to the island while we were gone, did he?"

Henry shook his head and said, "No ma'am. We've all been taking turns every day going out and checking on your place whiles you been gone. Stan, Pete, Benny Leroy,

Frank and I, one of us went by morning and night, didn't notice nothin' out of the ordinary."

Relieved, Devon said, "Well we certainly would have known if someone tried to break in. We had the alarm engaged, and if it went off, you would be able to hear it in Seattle."

Chet stepped forward, shook Henry's hand, and said, "Thank you kindly for looking after the place. Tomorrow morning, when I bring the youngins' to meet the school bus, I'll stay on and give you a hand for the day."

Henry patted Chet's shoulder and said, "That'd be greatly appreciated. Weathers getting warmer, so we are gettin' busier."

Devon stepped up and said, "Henry, I'd be happy to lend you a hand…"

Both Leanne and Chet said, "HA!" at the same time.

Devon looked over at them and said, "What? I know how to drive a boat and I can certainly tie a knot."

Henry slapped Devon on the back and said, "Son, I can use all the help I can get."

Devon turned to Chet and Leanne and said, "HA!"

Luke and Lindsey were patiently waiting to board the boat. Luke said, "Um, can we go home now?"

Henry helped them load the boat, told Leanne she could leave her car at the marina for as long as she needed and sent them on their way.

Chapter 22

The next morning, Chet and Devon made good on their word. They took the twins over to the marina to catch the bus to school, then stayed and helped Henry until three o'clock when the school bus arrived back at the marina returning the kids. This gave Leanne the whole day to get laundry done, go through the mail and decide what to make for dinner. They had been eating on the road for the past nine days, and although the food was amazing, Leanne felt like she had gained 50 pounds. As she perused through the freezer, she noticed she had a lot of frozen stews and soups and some frozen chicken, however, none of that was going to do. She wanted a light, fresh, and healthy meal. She didn't have any lettuce to make a salad, but she did have the pantry fixings for a corn and black bean salad, along with some red, yellow, and orange sweet peppers that she had roasted and froze a few weeks ago. She decided to call Devon and ask him to stop at the fish market and see what they had in fresh. His phone rang six time's, she left him a message to be sure she didn't miss him before they headed home. Five minutes later, he called her back and said, "Locomotive, your timing is spot on. As you were ringing me, I was hard at work helping to secure the lines of a fishing charter that just returned to the marina. Turns out he's a friend of our man Chet, and he gave him five pounds of fresh out of the sea halibut. I hope that will work for you."

Thrilled, Leanne replied, "Absolutely. After our culinary road trip, I felt like making something light and fresh. I have the makings for a corn and bean salad that will be perfect alongside fresh grilled halibut."

"That sounds perfect," said Devon, "Um, however, you might want to add an unknown home-made dessert to that menu. Frieda is walking across the parking lot as we speak, carrying what looks like a cake box."

"Is she now?" said Leanne with humor in her voice, "She must have been keeping an eye out for Chet to return from our road trip."

"Oh, she most certainly was," replied Devon. "She showed up at the marina at nine a.m. with a bag of piping hot jelly donuts and a thermos of coffee."

Leanne laughed and said, "Well, we better make sure we never put Frieda, Estelle, and Chet in the same room. I'm not sure which one would come out with pie on their face."

Devon laughed and agreed. The bus pulled up so he told Leanne they would be heading back to the island shortly. Leanne hung up and began prepping the salad. Once she had all of the ingredients marinating, she put it in the fridge, took out a pitcher of cold tea, and poured herself a glass. She decided to take it down to the dock and wait for her family to arrive.

As she sat dangling her feet over the edge of the dock, she began to make mental notes on what needed to be done at the cabin. She figured the best place to start would be to go over to the cabin and take inventory of what is there and what they could use. She would need to take some measurements to get an idea of where they could expand. Also, she would call Adele tomorrow and ask her if she could recommend a building or renovating contractor. Better safe than sorry, considering how old the cabin is, and who knows if the plumbing and electrical are up to code. She watched enough renovation shows to know there is always a hidden problem. She tucked away her mental notes as she saw Chet's boat round the bend; well actually, she heard them first. They sounded like they were singing. She stood and shaded her eyes from the sun gleaming off the water and watched as the boat pulled up to the dock. Luke and Lindsey were waving at her, yelling, "Mommy, we're being pirates and Devon taught us a song about beer."

Once the boat was tied to the dock, Devon lifted the twins off the boat. He climbed off after them, turned, and held out a hand to help Chet off. Chet slapped his hand away and said, "Don't you be going on like I'm some old man. You've been the one complaining about how your back aches and your shoulders throb, saying you need some ibuprofen. Man, up son, all ya need is a hot shower and a cold beer."

Leanne stifled a laugh and said, "So I gather the day went well."

Devon kissed her and replied, "I wouldn't actually use the word 'well.' However, it was eye-opening."

Chet handed Leanne a cake box and grabbed the cooler off the dock and said, "Aww, he's been griping all day.

The only time he stopped yapping was when Henry gave him his 15-minute break."

Leanne looked at Devon and asked, "You only got one 15-minute break all day?"

Devon put his arm around her shoulder and followed Chet down the dock and replied, "Well, no, actually we were given a 30-minute lunch break, which is about how long it took me to walk across the street to the pharmacy and buy ibuprofen."

Leanne patted his hand and said, "Then I would take Chet's advice, a hot shower, and a cold beer."

As they climbed the porch stairs Devon said, "How about a cold beer first and then a hot shower."

Leanne guided him to one of the rockers, sat him down, and said, "You sit. I'll bring you a cold beer. And what exactly was that song you taught the twins?"

Devon adjusted himself in the rocker and said, "It's an old pirate song called 'a hundred bottles of beer on the wall.'"

Leanne shook her head and said, "Um, actually, it's a drunken sailor song, that college frat boys now sing," and headed inside to get him a beer.

Chapter 23

The following morning, Leanne got the kids off to school with Chet who was going to give Henry a hand at the marina for a few hours, leaving an aching Devon behind. She cleaned up the kitchen, took a shower, and was ready to start her day. She was just about to pick up her phone to call Adele when Devon walked into the kitchen. She turned to him and said, "Good morning sleepy head. Did I wake you when I took a shower?"

Devon filled his mug with coffee, and said, "No, I was somewhat awake, and if I wasn't so bloody sore, I would have joined you in the shower. Well, at least that was what my brain was thinking, but my aching limbs would have none of it."

Leanne laughed, walked over, kissed him, and said, "I don't think you are cut out for the salty dog life."

Devon sipped his coffee and said, "Well, whatever a salty dog is, and if it works on a dock, then I shall agree with you. What I don't get is, I put an hour in every morning in the gym, lifting weights, running five miles on the treadmill, the rowing machine, and I have never so much as pulled a muscle. I don't know where the bloody hell these other muscles came from. It's like they popped out with every heave-ho of the bloody ropes, or the swabbing of the decks."

Leanne laughed and said, "If you think you'll live, would you be up for a ride over to the cabin? I want to take inventory of what we have, what we can keep, and what has to go. Also, I was just about to call Adele to ask her if she could recommend a local builder or renovator. I think it's best to have a professional assessment of the condition of the cabin. It's old and outdated and could be hiding a lot of unforeseen problems."

Devon agreed, "That's a good idea. Why don't you give Adele a call, I'm going to go for a quick swim, see if I can loosen up these muscles. We can leave in an hour."

Leanne frowned at him and said, "Where are you going for a swim? We haven't opened the pool yet."

"I'm going into the Puget Sound," replied Devon.

"Are you crazy!" said Leanne, "That water has to be thirty degrees."

"Well, actually, I googled it and it should be about 45 degrees, and according to the site I googled about relieving muscle soreness, they recommended ice," replied Devon.

Astonished, Leanne said, "They mean ice packs, not a plunge into freezing water!"

Devon shrugged and said, "At this point, I need a full-body ice down. I'll make it quick. I'm going to jump off the end of the dock and swim to the beach. No worries."

As he turned to leave the kitchen, Leanne put down her coffee mug, and said, "Oh, this I have to see," and followed Devon out the front door.

When they reached the end of the dock, Devon stepped out of his sweatpants and was now standing buck naked on the end of the dock. Flabbergasted, Leanne said, "You're going in bare ass naked?"

Unconcerned, Devon replied, "Well yes, I don't think swimming trunks are a necessity."

"What about a towel? You don't even have a towel for when you get out," said Leanne.

Devon looked at her and said, "Um, yeah, I may have overlooked that small detail. No worries grab my sweatpants and meet me on the beach," and then he proceeded to dive off the dock into the icy waters of the Puget Sound. Leanne watched him hit the cold water and begin to swim toward the beach. She picked up his sweatpants and ran down the dock.

Leanne stood on the beach watching as Devon swiftly walked out of the water. When he reached her, she handed him his sweatpants and said, "You're blue." Devon looked down. "Not there. Your lips, they're blue."

Devon put on his sweatpants, ran his fingers through his hair, and said, "Well that was refreshing and actually quite helpful. I don't feel any aches."

Leanne rolled her eyes and said, "That's because your body is numb from the freezing water."

Devon swung an ice-cold arm around her shoulders and said, "It was invigorating. You should give it a try."

Leanne steered him in the direction of the house and said, "Not a chance, Rock Star."

When they reached the house, Leanne said, "I'm going to call Adele. You go take a hot shower."

Devon spun her around, so she was facing him, pressed up against his bare cold chest, and kissed her lips, long and sweet. She found herself melting into his arms, then remembering the task at hand she placed her hands on his chest and pushed back, and said, "Nice try Romeo, but it's not going to happen. We have work to do, so go get showered and dressed."

Devon relented and let her go, and asked, "What color are my lips now?"

Leanne laughed and said, "Pink."

He tapped her nose and said, "You have the magic touch, you brought me back from the brink of frostbite."

Leanne turned him toward the stairs and gave him a little shove, "Yeah, well, I can't vouch for the other parts of your anatomy, go take a hot shower."

*****

They got to the cabin around ten-thirty a.m. The game plan was to take pictures of every room and tag the items that needed to go. They walked from room to room together. Leanne made notes as Devon stuck a colored sticker on the item that Leanne said was to go. They were finished with the inside and out by noon. Leanne had packed them a picnic lunch, so they sat down at the picnic table to eat. Devon finished his sandwich, wiped his mouth, and said, "So what we have found out today, is, that basically everything in the cabin is junk."

Leanne nodded, took a sip of her water, and said, "Seriously, how did we not notice how bad the furniture was when we stayed here?"

"Perhaps we had more pressing things on our mind," replied Devon.

"True," said Leanne. "Okay, so we could look into donating some of it, or we could make a huge pile and burn it. I have the contractor coming tomorrow. Chet is going to meet him at the marina and bring him out here. Let's get his input and then we can decide. Maybe he can suggest a company that will come haul it away."

Devon stood, gathered their sandwich wrappers and napkins, put them in a plastic garbage bag, and stored them in the cooler. He turned to Leanne and said, "Let's see what this fellow has to say tomorrow and go from there. In the meantime, we can go back to the house, draw up some sketches of what we envision, to give to him."

Leanne stood, closed the cooler, and said, "That's a good idea. Basing our designs around the main structure and building out from there, that will help keep costs down. I've made a rough sketch and have enough notes to get us started." With that said, they closed up the house, got in the golf cart, and headed home.

Chapter 24

The following morning at 11, Devon Leanne and Chet stood in the kitchen at the cabin with Bill Barnes, the contractor that Adele recommended. He took a little over an hour to inspect the whole cabin and the property.

"Well," said Bill, "I'm afraid what I'm gonna tell you, you're not going to like much. It's a total tear-down."

"What!" exclaimed Devon and Leanne in unison.

"Yup, ya got termites eating the beams. Ya got rodents taking up residency in the attic, your electrical and plumbing looks like the work of a handyman, no where's near to code, and ya got a septic tank buried way outback when actually it should be upfront and no farther than ten feet from the house. And from what I can tell from walking out there trying to locate it, you got some leaching going on."

"Leaching? What exactly is leaching?" asked Devon.

"Well," said Bill, "Let's see if I can tell you in layman terms. Ya got poop percolating back there."

Now it was Chet joining Leanne and Devon saying, "What!" With Chet adding, "Percolating, ya mean like coffee?"

Bill took off his hat, scratched his head, and replied, "Well it looks like coffee percolating, but it doesn't smell or taste nothing like it."

Devon turned to Leanne and said, "I'm switching to tea."

Still trying to wrap her head around the thought of poop percolating outback, Leanne ignored Devon and said to Bill, "Okay, so it's safe to assume that poop percolating in the back yard is NOT a good thing, but can it be fixed?"

"Yes ma'am," replied Bill. "We would have to dig up the old tank, get rid of it, and put a new one up in front of the house and connect it to all new leaching fields. But considering what I told you, the EPA will have to come out here and do some sample soil testing. Having some poop in the soil is not altogether a bad thing, it's when it gets into your drinking water then that's when ya got a problem and considering that your water well sits right there between the septic tank and the outhouse, I'm gonna take a gamble and say that there's a good chance your drinking water is contaminated."

Leanne looked over at Devon, who was now wearing a look of complete horror on his face and said, "Don't even go there. Take those thoughts and throw them right out the window. If you so much as mutter one word that you are thinking, I will push you into the septic tank and shut the cover." Devon opened his mouth to respond, but the locomotive said, "Shut it." She turned back to Bill and said, "Okay, so let me get this straight. The house needs to be flattened and the back yard needs to be dug up and checked for percolating poop, and the well water is most likely contaminated with poop."

Bill scratched his head again and said, "Yup, that about covers it. I can write this all up and give you an estimate for the teardown and clean up, and you can give it some thought."

This time Devon did speak, "Oh it's going, all of it. It's going. Next thing you know there will be three-headed chipmunks growing to the size of wild boar running around the island like a bad science project gone awry from percolating poop."

Chet, Leanne, and Bill just stared at him. Devon was having none of this, he continued, "You need to get the head of the EPA out here pronto. I need to know how long that poops been percolating."

Seeing Devon's concern, Bill turned to Leanne and asked, "When's the last time the cabin was occupied?"

Devon didn't give Leanne a chance to answer, he immediately replied, "Last year around this time. There were five of us living here. Oh man, when Rosalie hears about this there's no telling what she'll do. We better call Amber and Leonard and make sure those babies didn't grow a third eye since we left." He was now in a complete panic.

Leanne walked over to Devon, placed her hand on his arm, and said, "Devon, you need to take a deep breath. There is a good chance that the poop percolating started after we left the cabin."

Bill adjusted his hat on head and added, "She's right son, I'm pretty sure you would have noticed some squishy grass over by the outhouse. I'm thinking, with the heavy rains we had over the winter, that may have saturated the ground around the tank and that started the percolating."

Chet, having heard enough said, "Can ya'll call it something else besides percolating? You're ruining my love for coffee."

Leanne needed to reel this in, so she said to Bill, "Can you get someone out here to remove the septic tank and take a look at the soil? That's most important because if the cabin is sitting on a poop minefield, there won't be any further discussion about building anything on this property."

Bill nodded and replied, "Yup, I got just the guy to call. Once I get back to the mainland, I'll give him a ring and see when he's available."

With that settled, they loaded into the golf cart, dropped Chet and Bill off at the dock, and headed home.

Chapter 25

The following morning Leanne came downstairs to find Chet and Devon sitting at the kitchen island. She said good morning and walked over to the coffee pot, only to find it cold and empty. She turned to the two men and asked, "What are you two drinking in those mugs?"

Neither of them looked up from the newspaper they were reading, but said in unison, "Tea."

Frustrated, Leanne said, "Oh for crying out loud, would you two get over it. There will not be poop in your coffee. Get a grip."

Devon put his mug of tea down, looked up at Leanne, and said in all seriousness, "It's not about the coffee, per se, it's more of a visual thing."

"And don't forget about the percolating sound," added Chet with sound effects.

Just then Luke and Lindsey came running into the kitchen, followed closely by Bella and Blaze. Leanne told them to sit at the island as she poured them cereal. Once she set the bowls down in front of them, she walked behind Devon and Chet and muttered, "Looks like I have four children," and proceeded to walk over and make a pot of coffee.

Once Chet and the kids left for school, Leanne cleaned up the kitchen and decided to do some research on the computer. Devon was in the north wing in his office on a call with his manager, Gordy Little. She brought the laptop over to the island counter and booted it up. Once she logged in, she typed 'septic systems.' Even though Bill had given them some details, she wanted to get a better understanding of how they worked. What she read was mostly what Bill had told them, however, what she didn't know was, how expensive they were. $25,000 and that doesn't include getting the existing one dug up and the new one out to the island. She opened her notebook and wrote down the figure and added another $10,000 as a buffer. Next, she googled water wells but considering she didn't know what to look for or even the status of the one at the cabin, she decided to move on to the cabin. Bill told them it was a complete knockdown, and in hindsight, she agreed. She pulled up a website for building your own house, which provided blueprints for various models. Leanne didn't see exactly what she envisioned, so she decided to make her own sketch, using different piece of the other blueprints. She was so absorbed in what she was doing she didn't hear Devon walk up behind her. He looked over her shoulder and said, "Don't you think it's a little premature to be designing houses? We have yet to hear if the lot is even livable, well, for humans, that is."

Leanne stopped what she was doing, turned to Devon, and said, "I was just doing a little research…" but before she could finish, she was interrupted by her ringing cell phone. She answered it and said, "Hello. Oh, hi Bill. Okay, sure, yes that sounds perfect. I'll get a hold of Chet and tell him to meet you guys at the marina at 11:30, and we'll meet you at the cabin. Great, see you then." When she hung up, she turned to Devon and said, "That was Bill. He's bringing the EPA guy out to the island. He said the testing should take about an hour."

"That was quick," replied Devon. "Not that I am complaining, the sooner the better. Will you be okay if they come back with negative results that prevent us from re-building?"

Leanne turned, shut off the laptop, and replied, "Yes. The whole vision was based on building off the existing cabin, but now that we know that we would have to start from the ground up, literally, I think the costs outweigh the reason. For instance, I googled septic tanks, they run about $25,000 installed, but that doesn't include getting the stuff out here to the island. And when it comes time to build, hauling all of the material and laborers out here will be extremely expensive."

Devon sat down next to Leanne and took her hand in his and said," You know you don't have to worry about money. If the land is suitable, and you still want to build then build we shall."

Leanne smiled at him and said, "You would give me the world on a silver platter if I asked, I know that. But this was something I wanted to do with the proceeds from the sale of my house, which would have been possible, if not for the termites, squatting rodents and ancient plumbing and electrical."

"Oh, and let's not forget about the percolating poop," added Devon.

Leanne laughed and said, "Hardly. I'm going to go take a shower and get dressed. Will you be able to go to the cabin with me around 11 o'clock?"

Devon stood, held his handout to Leanne, and said, "Absolutely. The best news of the day would be that the yard didn't start percolating until long after we were gone."

*****

Devon and Leanne arrived at the dock on the beach by the cabin 15 minutes before the others were to arrive. They wanted to be sure they were there in time to drive the men up the path to the cabin. At 12 noon on the dot, Chet's boat motored up to the dock, and to Devon and Leanne's surprise, there were four other men accompanying Chet and Bill. Once the boat was secured, Chet and Bill stepped onto the dock, the other four men proceeded to hand them what looked like golf bags, and a couple of backpacks. Devon squinted into the sun gleaming off the water and said to Leanne, "Do you think, perhaps, the EPA fellows thought there might be a golf course surrounding the percolating poop?"

Leanne, squinting and shading her eyes from the sun, replied, "I'm not sure, but that looks like a lot of stuff for a simple soil test."

All six men began walking down the dock. When they reached Devon and Leanne, Bill stepped forward and said, "Hey there, Devon, Leanne. I'd like you to meet Al Cohen, he is the Seattle EPA office field supervisor, and this is his assistant, Gary Locks. And this is a friend of mine, John Jacobs. He owns a local septic system installation and cleaning company. He wanted to get a look at the present location of the septic system and assess the new location. That there is his son Jed." Hellos and handshakes were given all around.

Leanne looked at the men and all of their baggage then over at the golf cart, she figured they might all fit. Following her sightline, Devon said to the men, "That's a lot of baggage you have there for a simple soil sample test."

John laughed and said, "It isn't a simple test when ya got poop percolating out of the septic tank. Let's go take a look and I'll be able to give you a better idea of what's happening. Normally we would bring out a backhoe, dig a trench around the tank, but with ya'll being out here on the island, we're only going to be able to do a visual by sending a tiny camera on a pole down into the tank, but as I said, let's go see what we got, and I'll know better."

On the ride up the path to the cabin, Al Cohen explained the procedure for soil sample testing. He said they use what they call a long scope drill it will measure the depth of the contamination and suck up a sample. If the septic tank is buried six feet down, then they will start the scope at ten feet and slowly work their way up. That is what makes it such a time-consuming process, plus they have to outline the boundaries and do multiple sampling within those boundaries, depending on the square footage, they could take up to 100 samples.

John Jacobs and his son Jed had a devil of a time trying to find the septic tank cover. The only way to detect where it might possibly be was to follow the percolating poop. They each had on a pair of tall rubber boots, similar to the slogging boots Amber wore the day they went to the beach to find shellfish in the icy Puget Sound. They poked and prodded the earth until they finally found it four feet under near the garden. Once they dug down far enough, they removed what looked like a plastic Frisbee with a handle on it. John lowered the pole with a small camera on the end, into the tank. He knew that most tanks were about six feet deep, so when he hit something solid about three feet down, he was confused. But according to the little camera on the end of the pole, what he saw was a cylinder-shaped plastic container, or as John detected, a plastic rain barrel, meant to catch rainfall for irrigation. He removed his cap, scratched his head, and said, "What the heck? Looks like whoever put this septic system in, did it a long time ago, and did it themselves. This is nowhere near what a septic system should look like. First off, it's too shallow, second, being, it's made out of a plastic rain barrel, and from the looks of it, it's cracked in a dozen spots. I can't even begin to guess how long it's been here, and what concerns me more is how it's hooked up to that house. But here's the good news, the container may only be three feet deep, but there isn't more than two inches of sludge on the bottom, which tells me that house hasn't been lived in for a long time."

Bill stepped forward and said to John, "That was my thinking too. The inside of the cabin is a handyman nightmare. Whoever built it, sure as Sherlock, didn't know what they were doing."

Chet, Devon, and Leanne stood in stunned silence. When Devon finally grasped what Bill and John were saying, he said, "So let me ask you, John, will you be able to remove it and put a new one in, the correct kind, out front where it is supposed to be?"

"I reckon I need to go around front and take a look," said John, he turned to Jed and said, "Grab the pick and shovel and we'll go check it out," and they headed toward the front with Bill following them.

Chet, Devon, and Leanne sat down at the picnic table. Chet was the first to speak, "Sounds like this cabin has been here a lot longer than that big ole house we live in."

"Apparently," replied Devon.

Leanne, however, was thinking more about the big house than the cabin. She turned to Devon and said, "I think we should bring John over to our house. If this cabin needed a septic tank you can bet the big house does too. We know our electrical is run on a battery generator, but I totally overlooked the plumbing. Who knows the last time it was pumped out?"

"Good thinking," said Devon. He turned to Chet and asked, "Do you have anything pressing this afternoon?"

Chet shook his head and said, "Nope. Henry's all set at the marina, he's got Stan lending a hand and he might be bringing on a new guy."

Leanne stood and said, "Okay, it looks like we should be wrapped up here within the next half hour. Devon if you wouldn't mind riding back on the boat, I'll head back to the house and put together something for lunch. Bring everyone to the house and we can go over today's results." With the plan set, Leanne took off in the golf cart.

On the drive back to the house, Leanne was trying to think of what she could whip up for lunch for seven hungry men. She had roasted two chickens last night, with the intention of making a chicken casserole for dinner tonight, she figured she could use them to make sandwiches, and then she remembered that she had all of the frozen Mexican food from Carla, plus the containers of salsa and guacamole. *Perfect,* she thought as she pulled up to the house and parked the golf cart on the back patio, rushed into the house opened the freezer, and took out what she thought would be enough for the guys. She un-wrapped them from their freezer wrapping and re-wrapped them in foil and placed them on two baking sheets. She figured she had about an hour before the men arrived. She turned the oven on to 350 degrees and placed them on the middle rack. She went into the pantry and brought out a bag of store-bought tortilla chips, which she would warm in the oven when the men arrived. She retrieved two large serving platters and two bowls for the salsa and guacamole. She went back into the pantry and retrieved a basket for the chips and some napkins. She pulled out the extension on the kitchen table and set it with napkins, glasses, and silverware. She checked the fridge to see if she had a full pitcher of sweet tea, which she did. She grabbed a couple of lemons from the jar on the counter and sliced them into rounds, removing the pits. She reached up into the cabinet and brought down a glass water pitcher, filled it with filtered water from the refrigerator door, and ice, then placed it in the freezer to chill faster. She estimated she had about 15 minutes before the men walked through the front door, so she cranked the oven up to 400 degrees to ensure that the food was heated through. When the timer dinged, she shut off the oven. She arranged a double layer of chips on a baking sheet and put them in the oven to warm, which was perfect timing as she heard the front door open and the chatter of the men as they entered the kitchen. Devon's nose went on high alert and he said, "It smells like Carla's Cantina in here."

Leanne removed the food from the oven and set it on the counter, leaving the chips in for a few minutes more. She told them to go wash up, lunch was about to be served. When everyone was seated at the table she brought over platters of enchiladas, burritos, tacos, and taquitos, she passed around bowls of salsa and guacamole. She placed the pitchers of sweet tea and water in the center of the table, deciding not to sit and eat with them. She would set aside a plate for herself if anything was leftover. In the meantime, she made herself busy cleaning up the kitchen; it was kind of funny because the room was dead silent, besides the clanking of dishes while she loaded them in the dishwasher.

It wasn't until ten minutes later, that Bill Barnes pushed back from the table and said, "That was the best meal I've had since I don't know when. If my ex-wife could cook like that, I would marry her all over again."

"I can't take credit for it," replied Leanne, "It was made by a wonderful woman named Carla, who cooked in a shack behind a gas station in Provo, Utah," then she proceeded to tell them the story of their road trip, with Devon and Chet adding to the story. She explained how she and Devon had thought up the idea of opening a small vacation rental house with an emphasis on cooking lessons.

When everyone was finished eating and the table was cleared of not one leftover, not even a chip, John pulled out his notebook and said, "Okay, so here's the gist of what I saw as far as the septic system is concerned, it was homemade and installed by, who knows who, but it wasn't done right. It had about two inches of sludge at the bottom, and it was pretty condensed and hard, so my guess is it's been sitting there for a long time. As for the percolating, that looks to be a mixture of dirt and water, don't have nothing to do with that plastic rain barrel contraption."

Al Conquered, "I agree. All of my test samples came back negative for fecal matter."

Relieved, Leanne asked, "So does that mean we can build on the lot?"

"Well," said John, "That's where the not so good news comes in. It looks like whoever put in that contraption, had to put it in the back and far from the house because the island is made up of shale, which prevents being able to dig down deeper than three or four feet. Looks like whoever put that thing in found a soft spot in the yard."

Bill agreed and added, "Yup that be the case, that house there isn't sitting on no footers, just a poured slab of concrete. You would need some heavy-duty machinery brought out here to crush through the layers of shale rock. Me, I'm seeing this beautiful house here, seems you got more than enough room to set up your idea."

Devon looked at Leanne and said, "We could revise our plan, narrow it down to weekend cooking classes and we could set it up in the pool house kitchen. We could limit it to six or eight people with the sleeping quarters upstairs."

Leanne nodded and said, "Okay, let's keep that on the back burner," she turned to John and asked, "Do you think you could locate our septic system and see if everything is in order?" Then turned to Bill and said, "I have to imagine this house was built to code, but would you mind doing a walk through with me, see if you see any red flags?"

"Sure thing Leanne," replied Bill as he followed her down the hall.

They all convened back on the dock a half-hour later. John said the septic system was superior, they should have no issues, however, he suggested it be pumped out considering they had no record of the last time it was done.

Bill said, "I'm thinking whoever built this house wasn't from around here or I would have known about it, being that I've been in the business close to forty years, and that house doesn't look older than five maybe seven years old. Whoever built it, sure knew what they were doing, because it's built to code, if not above, and its sound enough to withstand any major storms we get up in these necks of the woods. Can't say the same about that shack back there in the woods. What do you reckon you'll do with it?"

Without hesitation, both Leann and Devon said, "Burn it."

Bill laughed and said, "That sounds like a good idea, and if you're serious I have just the guy to do it for you, so you don't go burning down the whole island."

Devon and Leanne thanked the men for coming out to the island. They stood on the dock watching, as Chet's boat turned the bend, heading back to the marina.

Chapter 26

The remaining weeks of May flew by. Memorial Day was upon them and along with it came the town parade and picnic. Leanne had closed on her house the previous Thursday, and because she had already signed the contract, not including the furniture, she decided to put it all in storage and figure out what to do with it after the holiday. The whole idea of building onto the cabin and creating a cooking retreat basically went out the window when they found out from Bill Barnes, the contractor that the cabin was in such bad condition it would need to be flattened to the ground. The prospect of rebuilding was not an option due to the island being made of shale rock, so the only thing left to do was to decide what to do with the cabin. To Devon and Leanne, there was some sentimental value, and most likely for Rosalie too, but for Leonard and Amber, they were a whole different story. They fell in love at the cabin, spent their wedding night there, and ultimately conceived their twin daughters, Rose and Annie there, so Devon and Leanne decided to wait until the Labor Day weekend reunion to make any decisions.

The task at hand right now was helping to set up for the town picnic. Leanne was in town a few days ago to close on her house and ran into Pete's wife Eloise, who, without even trying, somehow managed to rope Leanne into joining the set-up committee, which in turn, Leanne volunteered Devon and Chet's help also. So here they were, 8:30 a.m. setting up tables and chairs, securing red, white and blue plastic table clothes onto the tables and placing the centerpieces the elementary school kids, including Luke and Lindsey, made for the picnic. The kids also made flags on sticks, which they were running around town placing on the storefronts.

Leanne and Devon finished setting up the last table. Chet brought over the last tablecloth shook it out and laid it over the table and Leanne secured it with the clips. It was 10:30, so they decided to head back to the island and get changed for the picnic. They had brought over their coolers and chairs earlier and staked out their parade viewing spot.

It took Lindsey close to an hour to figure out what she wanted to wear. Leanne had already laid out a cute red and white striped sundress and white sandals, but according to Lindsey, that would not do. She wanted to wear her pink cowgirl boots and said the dress didn't match. Leanne, wanting to move things along, walked into Lindsey's closet and came out with a cute ruffled denim skirt and a navy-blue T-shirt. Lindsey nix-nayed the T-shirt and went in and got a white frilly blouse with short puffy sleeves, put everything on, and then went to work on her hair. Standing back watching her daughter, Leanne said, "Um, Lindsey, you seem to be going to an awful lot of trouble for a parade and picnic."

Lindsey gave her hair one more brush, placed a silver headband with stars on her head, turned to Leanne and said, "Oh, I'm not doing this for the parade and picnic, I'm doing it to get Johnny Watkins attention. He's the cutest boy in our class."

Astonished, Leanne replied, "You are only seven, which is way too young to try and get a boy's attention."

Lindsey smiled her magical smile, and said, "I'm just testing the waters for when I turn eight in a few weeks," and with that said, she slid off the stool and clomped out of the room in her cowgirl boots.

Leanne followed her daughter down the hall and mumbled to herself, "Oh boy, I'm not ready for this." She would be sure to tell Luke to keep a close eye on his sister.

*****

The parade began three miles down Main Street. First up were high schoolers riding bikes who were tossing candy to all the spectators lined up on the side of the road, followed by the town's fire trucks, sirens and all. There were town council members, the mayor, and various members of the Chamber of Commerce riding in vintage cars. The high school band marched down Main Street playing *Stars and Stripes Forever.* Following close behind, riding on a 25-foot flatbed, was a group of young and old veterans of our country's military, including Chet, all waving small handheld flags. The crowd cheered and saluted them as they passed by. When they reached the end of the parade route, there to greet them was Stan dressed as Uncle Sam. He shook each of their hands thanking them for their service.

As the crowds dispersed, heading to the town green for the picnic and barbeque, Leanne and Devon wandered over to the group of men that Chet was chatting with. As they approached, they recognized Bill Barnes amongst the group, he turned to them and said, "Just the two people I was looking for. I want you to meet a friend of mine."

Leanne and Devon turned towards a very elderly gentleman dressed in his Army uniform, smiling widely at them. He greeted them, "Names Wally Durkin, pleased to meet you both. Bill here's been telling me some about you. Say's you're the folks that bought Welby Island."

Chet joined in and said, "Well let me tell you, Wally, Devon didn't just buy an island, he got himself a hotel size house with it."

Bill turned to Devon and said, "Wally's been living in these parts since he was a boy, knows just about everyone, including who may have built that cabin out on the island."

Interest peeked, Devon asked, "Really?"

Wally adjusted his cane from one hand to the other and replied, "Why don't we make our way over to one of the picnic tables and I can tell you what I know."

Once settled at the table, Leanne pulled out a pitcher of cold tea from the cooler, along with a stack of plastic cups, and poured a cup for each of them. Wally took a long sip and said, "Thank you kindly, Leanne. Okay, I guess I'll start from way back when I was a young boy about four or five. I grew up not far down that road there," pointing at Main Street. "Back then there weren't a lot of houses around, and what there were, spread out by the miles, mostly farming land, with a few local 'purveyors' in between, if you get my drift."

Not having a clue, Devon said, "Well not really."

Wally laughed and said, "Back in the day my folks used the word purveyor, but actually it meant, illegal moonshiners. They would set up their land to look like a cornfield, plant some hops, such as barley and rye, which they would use to turn into a mash or paste. Now you gotta remember, it was illegal to make moonshine, so in the daylight, they look like a farm, but when that sun went down, late into the night, they would boil their mash in homemade stills, consisting of a metal drum with what looks like a big straw connecting to an old fashion plastic rain catcher."

Leanne, Devon, and Chet looked at each other, then over at Bill, who said, "Yup. Just like the one we saw at the cabin."

Wally continued, "Let's see, okay, I was born in 1928, the youngest of three boys, and the prohibition had been going on for some years by then. However, for those moonshiners, business was booming, there wasn't one waterfront from Tacoma to Vancouver that wasn't overrun by loggers. And those loggers, they were meaner than a pit of rattlesnakes. They come in, take over small ports, and next thing you know there be a saloon being built and a house of 'you know what' upstairs."

Confused, Leanne asked, "A house of what?"

Not quite sure how to put it in front of a lady, Wally said, "Um, well, let's see how can I say this…"

Chet turned to Leanne and said, "He's talking about brothels, ya know, ladies of the night kind of places."

Leanne looked at Chet, and then the light bulb went off, "Oh, okay, I get it."

Wally continued, "Anyways, we farmers we kept our distance from the loggers best we could, but they gotta eat and we gotta sell our crops. My brother Joe, he stood six foot four, built like an ox, he was. My pops figures Joe would be the best one to do the deliveries to the port, being this here marina we are sitting at."

"What?" said Devon and Leanne at the same time.

"Yup," said Wally, "This here was one of the biggest stop-gaps for the logs comin' downstream from Vancouver. See where your island is over there, well the stop-gap connected from this port out there to your island. It was constructed out of netting, and as the logs slowed down, they would catch them. Once they had a hundred logs, they would raft them up with rope, make a float, load them up with a few men, and set them downstream to the cutting mill in Tacoma."

Wally stopped to take a gulp of tea and eat some of the cheese and crackers Leanne had set out on the table, and then continued, "About this time, lumber was the most important industry, right behind farming. My brother Joe, he'd make two trips a week down here, once with produce and the second with milk and eggs. We didn't own no cattle, so we just sent what the chickens were laying and what was growing in the fields, tomatoes, corn, squash, and such. Joe would ride the wagon into this here town. There would be the same man from the logger's camp that would meet him. But on this particular day, there was a new man standing at the entrance. He canvassed Joe's wagon, took what he needed, paid Joe, and turned to be on his way, but my brother being who he was, asked, "Where's Manny? I've been coming here for three years and he ain't ever missed a delivery."

The man climbed into his wagon, didn't even look at Joe, and replied, "Manny went up against a thieving rattler and lost," the man snapped the reins and rode off. Joe came back and told my pop's what happened, and my pop never sent him back there again. We stayed away from the logger camps from then on," said Wally.

Wally took another sip of tea and laughed, "Sorry folks, my mind just wandered away from me there. So, you want to know about the shack on your island? Well, here's what I know, and keep in mind it's a rumor, gossip whatever you want to call it, but back in those days, in a small town like this, it was pretty much gospel. So, by now you got all these lumber companies buying up land by the hundred acres. Trains are now coming in from the east, making the transportation of the logs faster. The ports start emptying out and the workers are movin' on, either to work for the mills or the railroad. The ones that couldn't get hired was the rotten apples of the bunch, and they teamed up with the moonshiners. However, prohibition came to an end and the moonshiners weren't making the money they used too, and the government was coming in and taking a piece of whatever little they were making. By now, both my brothers had gone off to the war, being too young yet, left me the job of delivering to the town, even though it was empty of the loggers and being that the ladies of the brothel followed the loggers. The saloon owners, the three brothers Boylan's, were scrambling to find moonshine, but the government was closing in and any monies made were being greatly taxed. The following month when I went back with a delivery, there were only four shops keeps left, and this is where the rumor comes in. Word was that the Boylan brothers hooked up with two of the moonshiners from the Taggert Farm, and they went into hiding on your island. They bartered up and down the river for building supplies. They built the shack and ran an illegal moonshine distillery for close to ten years before the government swooped in and locked them up. The island was eventually purchased in the late 1950s by a wealthy railroad executive by the name of Charles Welby, who is rumored to have kept his mistress and illegitimate children on the island. In 1960, the railroad industry started to take a downward turn, and word is Charles Welby lost everything, including his wife Clarisse, who found out about the mistress and the children the day they showed up on her front doorstep after escaping the island, where Charles Welby left them to die.

Totally absorbed in Wally's story, Leanne sat back and said, "Wow."

Wally nodded and said, "Hold that thought, Leanne, you haven't heard the best part yet. When Clarisse was confronted by the mistress and the three illegitimate children of her husband, she did the unthinkable. She invited them in, cleaned them up and fixed them a proper hot meal then sent them to the carriage house with the housemaid, on the orders to make up the house for her four guests. When her husband arrived home, she greeted him as always, with a glass of his favorite sherry and dinner set out on a silver plate with a matching warming cover. Later that evening, the husband was said to have suffered a fatal heart attack, according to the town doctor, whom Charles Welby's wife had been having an affair with for years and later married after a respectful mourning period. Clarisse and the doctor sent the mistress, who at the time was 17 years of age, off to boarding school in San Francisco, and raised the children, a three-year-old, two-year-old and six-month-old baby.

Leanne looked at Wally when he finished and said, "Double wow."

Totally sucked in by the story, Chet asked, "Where are they now?"

Wally shook his head and said, "Got no idea. Rumor has it that Clarisse and the doctor packed up and headed east. As for the house, the bank took it back and sold it. It's now the Tremont Hotel. As for the island, Charles Welby was said to have paid cash for it, no paper trail to be found."

Leanne looked at Devon and asked, "Isn't that the hotel we stayed in when we got off the island?"

Devon nodded and said, "Yup," which sent shivers down Leanne's spine.

Wally stood and said, "Well, it's been a pleasure meeting you folks, but I best be gettin' goin', my granddaughter is over at the town hall waiting for me. Leanne, Devon, I hope I was of some help solving the mystery of the cabin on Welby island."

Devon stood, shook Wally's hand, and said, "You certainly were. Thank you for taking the time to tell us the story."

Leanne walked around the table and gave Wally a hug and said, "Thank you for your time and for your service. Would you mind if I asked where you served?"

Wally patted Leanne's hand and said, "Two tours in Vietnam. These ninety-two-year-old eyes have seen a lot in their day. Ya'll take care," and with his cane in hand, Wally and Bill walked off toward the town hall.

*****

After a fun-filled day of arts and crafts, horseshoes, potato sack races, and numerous other activities, the finale was upon them, a spectacular firework display that lit up the skies above and the faces of the crowd below. At ten p.m. Leanne, Devon, Chet, and the twins, packed up their chairs and coolers and headed back to the island.

Chapter 27

It was a beautiful early June morning. The twins were on summer break and had started sleeping in later. Devon usually woke with Leanne but tended to take longer to actually rise and shine, however, this morning he walked into the kitchen not long after her. Leanne had made a pot of coffee and was starting to gather the ingredients for waffles, when Devon wrapped his arms around her from behind, kissed her neck, and said, "Good morning beautiful."

Leanne turned and wrapped her arms around his neck and kissed him passionately and murmured, "Morning Romeo."

Devon laughed and said, "Well I can see someone has their dial on playful."

Leanne gave him a little shove and said, "Hey, you started it last night. However, I do feel rather light on my feet this morning." Getting a better look at Devon she asked, "Um, why are you wearing just a towel wrapped around your waist?"

Devon smiled wickedly and replied, "Would you like to see what's under this towel?"

"No. The kids may come down those stairs any minute," she replied.

Devon started to undo the knot and said, "Are you sure?"

"Are you crazy," said a flustered Leanne, "Please go put some…" she didn't finish her sentence, just closed her eyes and squealed as Devon dropped the towel, exposing his swim trunks. Peeking through her fingers she sighed with relief, and then realizing, swim trunks go with swimming, she said, "Wait. Don't tell me you are planning on diving off the dock into that freezing water again?"

Devon tapped her nose and said, "Bingo. That is precisely what I intend to do. You should join me. It's invigorating, good for the soul, and starts the day off on a positive note."

Leanne turned back to her mixing bowl and said, "Not one word you just said makes any sense. Jumping off a dock into freezing water is far from invigorating; it can stop the soul in its track and as for the positive note, it says you're a nut job."

Devon laughed and said, "You're just a chicken with no sense of adventure." He knew if he pushed the right button, she just might take him up on his dare and join him.

Leanne put down the egg she was about to crack, turned and looked Devon in the eye, and said, "Excuse me? Did you just call me a chicken?"

"Well, not exactly," said Devon, "I was actually saying that you are tad bit frightened to go on an adventure."

As Devon headed out of the kitchen, Leanne wiped her hands on the dishtowel, untied her apron and marched after him, and said, "A tad bit frightened, huh? I'll show you I can be adventurous. Just you wait right there while I go change."

Pleased he hit the right button, he knew he was pressing his luck as he called after her and said, "It's a clothing-optional adventure." He got no response.

Five minutes later Leanne came downstairs wearing a one-piece black swimsuit, carrying a towel, she marched right past Devon, out the front door and down the steps. When they reached the dock, they saw Chet pulling up in his boat. He was an early riser and always headed over to the mainland on the weekends to get the newspaper, or so he says that is the reason. But every weekend he comes home with a brown bag of fresh jelly donuts, which leads to the assumption that he goes to Frieda's bakery to help her with the five-thirty a.m. rush of fishermen, heading out for their morning catch. Though Chet never said as much, Devon and Leanne surmised that was the situation, hence the bag of jelly donuts and flour all over his shirt.

He was just tying the boat to the dock as Leanne and Devon approached. He looked them up and down and said, "What's with you two? Why are you wearing swimsuits?"

"Devon thinks I'm too chicken to jump into the water. Thinks I'm not adventurous enough. Well I'm going to show him," replied Leanne.

"Leanne, don't be telling me you're going to follow this fool into that ice-cold water," said Chet, "You gotta be part polar bear to do that."

Leanne flexed her shoulders, rubbed her hands together, and said to Chet, "I have no intention of following Devon into the ice-cold water," and with that said she took a running leap off the dock. When she surfaced, she let out a loud, "WAHOO," yelling to Devon to not be chicken, so he dove in. Once he surfaced, he swam over to her and kissed her trembling lips and said, "Let's get moving. I'll race you to the beach." That day Devon learned one more fascinating attribute about his future bride. She's an ace swimmer. She beat him by two body lengths.

When she climbed out of the water, Chet held up a towel for her. She dried her hair, shook the water out of her ears, wrapped herself in the towel, and with a winning smile on her face, waited for Devon.

Winded, Devon walked up the beach and took the towel from Chet, dried his hair and body, then wrapped the towel around his waist. Leanne walked up to him, poked him in the chest, and said, "Don't ever press the buttons of a girl who grew up swimming in Lake Michigan, makes the Puget Sound feel like a hot tub."

Devon wrapped an arm around her shoulder and said, "Well played."

Chet laughed and said to Devon, "She got you good, son," chuckling the whole way up to the house.

*****

Luke and Lindsey must have been woken by the smell of the bacon cooking because not long after Leanne put it in the frying pan, they came running down the stairs and into the kitchen with Bella and Blaze right behind them. They hopped up on the stools at the kitchen island next to

Chet. Devon walked behind them, tapped them each on the head, and said, "Good morning Tickle Terrors."

Both replied in unison, "Morning Devon, morning Mommy, morning Chet."

Chet poured each of them a glass of juice and said, "So Pint Size, what's the plan for your birthday next weekend? Ya know that's only seven days away."

Leanne arranged waffles, bacon, toast and the jelly donuts Chet brought home from the bakery on a platter and laid it on the island, then passed around plates and napkins. Chet helped the kids load up their plates with a waffle and two pieces of bacon. He poured syrup into little puddles on the side of the plate, just the way they liked it. Once they were all settled, Luke said, "Well, Lindsey and I were talking and since we had so much fun at the parade and picnic last Saturday, we were wondering if we could have a party here with our friends?"

Surprised, Leanne said, "Are you sure you don't want to go into the city? Go to the Wharf and the Space Needle."

Lindsey finished chewing and said, "No, we want a party. Everyone thinks it's cool that we live on an island."

"Well, how many friends were you thinking of inviting?" asked Leanne.

This time Luke answered, "Our whole class."

"But not Seth or Evan or Tabitha," added Lindsey.

Leanne looked at Lindsey and said, "You can't invite the whole class and leave those three out, it's not nice. Why don't you want to invite them?"

Lindsey, the more vocal of the twins said, "Well, Seth is a bully, he picks on all of the girls and Evan snorts milk out of his nose when he laughs, and Tabitha has a crush on Luke, but Luke likes Susie Jones, but Susie Jones doesn't know that Luke likes her, but Tabitha does, so she's mean to Susie."

All eyes went to Luke. He continued to shovel waffle into his mouth, keeping his eyes down. Leanne decided to let that go for now. She turned to Devon and asked, "What do you think? Could we throw a party here next weekend?"

"I don't see why not," replied Devon. "As a matter of fact, I was thinking maybe something along the lines of a pizza-movie party. We have that humongous theatre room, and it just so happens that I know someone, who knows someone who can get me a copy of the not yet released Prince of Putterly Pond."

"NO WAY!" yelled Luke and Lindsey at the same time. Then Luke said, "That's like the best movie ever. All the kids were talking about it last weekend, saying they can't wait to see it. That would be way cool Devon."

Lindsey asked, "Can you really get it, Devon? Like for sure?"

Devon smiled and said, "Yup. As I said, I know someone who knows someone. I'm going to Los Angeles Monday, so I'll pick it up then." Devon didn't dare tell them that the Queen is played by none other than his good friend Renay Zimmer.

"Well," said Leanne, "It looks like it's a pizza-movie party. I'll make invitations on the computer and email them to your class list. I'm inviting everyone. Not leaving anyone out. Got it?"

"Okay," said the twins. They hopped off their stools and ran over and hugged Devon, "Thank you, Devon," then ran outside to play.

Chapter 28

Leanne sent out an email invite to Luke and Lindsey's whole class, being 22 kids. They go to a very small school, only having one class for each grade level. She thought with it being summer break and such short notice that she may hear back from maybe a handful. However, that was not the case; all but two kids were able to come.

Chet made arrangements with Henry to help shuttle the families to the island. He would also pick up the pizzas from Franks Pizzeria and the cupcakes that Leanne ordered from Frieda. Devon was in charge of setting up the games that Luke and Lindsey wanted, being the potato sack race, ball and bucket game, a ginormous tic-tac-toe inflatable game, and of course, the tried and true, pin the tail on the donkey set up on an easel. Actually, it was an easy party to pull together. Leanne had it all planned, out the kids would play games when they arrived at 11 a.m. at 12 noon they would have pizza, start the movie at one, which will be over by three, then cupcakes and presents and wrap it up by four. Easy-peasy…she hoped. She knew that at least one parent would be accompanying their child to the island but imagine her surprise when she received the RSVP's asking if the whole family could attend. She had heard from Frieda that the party was the talk of the town, some eager to see the island with the huge house, and others were eager to see Devon, which she was sure to warn him about. He was unconcerned, he had been to numerous school functions for the twins and there was never a scene.

At precisely 11 o'clock, the first of six boats made its way around the bend, toward the dock. Luke, Lindsey, Devon, and Leanne waited for the arrivals and helped offload the passengers.

The kids were running around on the front lawn, it was organized chaos. Leanne had set up an adult section on the front porch where most of the parents were congregated, except for the three moms who volunteered to help Devon with the lawn games, which required a lot of eye batting, arm touching and giggles. At one point when she made eye contact with Devon, he mouthed the word "HELP."

Two of the other mothers that Leanne was friendly with from volunteering at the school, offered their assistance in the kitchen, which Leanne was thrilled to have since easy-peasy went out the window the minute the first boat arrived. They worked on heating up the pizzas while Leanne went outside and announced pizza was on its way. She had set up numerous picnic blankets under the big tree on the side of the yard, coolers were filled with juices and waters, and two long tables held paper plates, napkins, and assorted individual chip bags. The moms came out carrying boxes of pizza and lined them up on the table, Leanne turned and yelled, "Pizza, come and get it," which set off a stampede to the table. Chet worked on getting the kids in a line while Devon took the opportunity to escape his 'helpers' and stood next to Leanne with an arm draped over her shoulder, watching Luke as he ate his pizza on a blanket wedged between two girls, both vying for his attention. He looked like a deer in headlights.

Devon said, "He's quite the lady's man."

Leanne nodded, and thought to herself, *This is only the beginning of a very long road for him and girls*. She may be biased, but Luke is a really, really cute kid, with his messy blond hair, big beautiful blue eyes, and a heart of gold. Leanne gently nudged Devon with her elbow and said, "He might need some man to man advice on how to handle it. You did pretty well with your three mommy helpers earlier."

Devon scoffed and said, "Hardly. I tried to send you an SOS, which apparently you ignored,"

Leanne laughed and said, "Pizza to the rescue. Why don't you go get the movie set up, and I'll get this moving along?"

Devon grabbed a piece of pizza from the box, tapped Leanne on the nose, and said, "I'll go rescue Luke and take him with me."

"Good idea," replied Leanne.

*****

Devon and Chet were cleaning up the front yard, preparing for Leanne to set out the cupcakes. The movie, which was being attended by not only the kids, but all of the parents who were also eager to see it, was just about to end. Leanne was scurrying around the kitchen when

Devon walked in and said, "Um, Leanne, you might want to come out front."

As she began arranging the cupcakes on a platter, she replied, "Give me five minutes."

Devon walked over to her, took the cupcake out of her hand, and said, "I think you need to come out front now."

Leanne looked up at him and didn't like the look on his face. The last time she saw that look, Blair and Micah had emerged from the woods at the cabin. She wiped her hands on the dishtowel and followed Devon down the hall and out the front door. She stood silent for a few seconds, and when it finally registered, she said very slowly, "You have got to be kidding me. He can't possibly have balls big enough to show up here, nonetheless with her on his arm?"

Devon continued to keep his grip on her arm, but he could feel the locomotive start her engine, he cautiously asked, "That definitely isn't Allie. Who is she?"

Without looking at him, staring straight ahead watching as Blake walked up the lawn, and said, "No, that is not Allie. That is Penny Fucking Perkins." Devon lost his grip on her arm when she yanked it away and headed down the stairs to where Chet was standing with Blake and Penny Fucking Perkins. He knew this was not going to go well as he headed down the stairs behind her.

Leanne walked up to Blake and said, "What the hell are you doing here?"

"Nice to see you too Leanne," replied a smirking Blake.

Not in the mood for his bullshit, she asked again, "What are you doing here, and how did you find me?"

Blake smiled and said, "It was easy. I have your address, but apparently, you don't live there anymore according to the woman who answered the door. She told me she heard you moved out to the island. So, I went to the marina and asked a guy named Henry if he knew you and he said he did and offered us a ride out here to the twin's birthday party, which is the exact reason I came to Seattle."

Leanne glared at him and said, "You were not invited to the twin's birthday party, nor was your latest conquest." Looking at Penny Fucking Perkins, she said, "Geeze Penny, if you wanted him way back when you could have had him and saved me a whole lot of trouble. Maybe you could have said so over one of our mandatory coffee meetings back in kindergarten."

Penny made an attempt to touch Leanne's arm, but she stepped back, so Penny said, "Oh Leanne, I would never have thought of taking Blake away from you when you were married. But when he told me about your breakdown and how you went away to get help, and then you came back and stole those kids from him, well then, of course, I needed to be there for him."

Ut oh, last time Devon saw that look on Leanne's face, she was ready to steamroll over Blair. He moved next to her and put a securing arm over her shoulder and whispered in her ear, "Count to ten."

Leanne mentally counted to ten, then to 20, then 30, took a deep breath and said very firmly, "Today is about Luke and Lindsey. They are in watching a movie with 20 of their classmates and will be coming outside soon for cupcakes and to open their presents. You have two choices, you head back to that dock, and Chet will take you back to the mainland, or you go into the house and wait for the party to be over and all of the guests to leave and then you can be with the kids. But I will not have you ruining their day. Do you hear me?"

In his full arrogance, Blake replied, "My being here won't ruin their day. It will be the best present they get. Their daddy," shooting a look at Devon.

"Make your choice. Now," said Leanne.

Penny put her arm through Blake's and said, "Come on honey-bunny, let's go inside and wait. Once the party is over the kids will be so happy to see you."

Blake relented and walked past Leanne and followed Chet up the stairs and into the house. Devon turned to Leanne and said, "Hold it together for the kids. Take a deep breath and calm yourself. We'll go inside, get the cupcakes then come back outside get everything set up. The kids will be out from the movie in a few minutes. We'll get through this. Once all of the guests are gone, then we will deal with Blake. Okay?"

Leanne took a really deep breath, held it then slowly exhaled and said, "Okay. I'm good. Thank you, Devon."

Devon put his arm around her and said, "For what?"

"For keeping me from strangling Blake and throwing his body in the Puget Sound," replied Leanne.

Devon laughed and said, "Well that could have mucked things up a bit because then we would have had to dispose of Penny Fucking Perkins, and quite honestly, I think she is going to be punished quite enough once Blake tires of her. Who knows, she might end up doing your dirty work for you."

Leanne laughed, leaned into him, and said, "I wish," when they heard the kids laughing and saw them running their way, they hurried inside to get the cupcakes.

*****

The last of the party guests boarded the boat at four o'clock. Chet had called ahead to Henry and asked that he send someone to cover for him since he wanted to stay on the island in case he was needed to swiftly remove Blake and Penny Fucking Perkins. He had stashed them out of sight in the pool house, offered them coffee, which they declined. However, a little later when he returned to check on them, he found that they had made themselves right at home. They had the TV on and had helped themselves to a bottle of red wine from the wine rack behind the bar. Annoyed Chet said, "Well, I see ya'll made yourselves right at home. I guess down there in L.A. they don't have no manners."

Blake didn't bother to look away from the TV, but replied, "Don't fret old man. I'm sure that Brit that Leanne has latched onto won't miss a bottle of wine."

It would have been a good idea if Blake had turned to speak to Chet, then he would have seen Devon standing right behind him. Devon walked over, picked up the remote control and turned off the TV. Then he proceeded to remove the bottle of wine from the table and placed it on the bar. He turned to Blake and said very calmly, "The twins are in the kitchen. Go see them. You have 20 minutes and then you will be on your way. Do I make myself clear?"

Blake stood with his wine glass in his hand, brought it to his lips and proceeded to finish the glass, put the glass down on the table, walked over to Devon, poked him in the chest and said, "You don't get to tell me how long I can spend with my kids. I'm their father, not you."

Devon, removed Blake's finger from his chest, giving it a little bend backward and replied, "Well, see, that's where you're wrong. You are in our house, uninvited nonetheless, so I can and have told you how long you are allowed to stay. However, if you prefer, I can flatten you right here and now and drag your bloody ass to the dock and throw you on the boat, your choice."

Blake huffed and pushed past Devon, telling Penny Fucking Perkins to "Come." They walked across the patio and entered through the kitchen door, followed closely by Devon and Chet. The twins were sitting at the island telling Leanne all about the movie. Leanne turned and looked at Blake as he entered the kitchen, as did the twins. Neither one moved. Blake walked over to them and grabbed them in a group hug and said, "Happy birthday kiddos!" When he let them out of the embrace, Luke and Lindsey both turned and looked at Leanne with questioning eyes.

Knowing she had to do the right thing, rather than what she really wanted to do, she turned on a 1,000-watt smile and said, "Surprise! Daddy's here." Lindsey and Luke looked very confused, so she added, "Why don't you take Daddy into the living room and show him all the presents you got today."

They both hopped off their stools, Lindsey took Blake's hand and said, "Come on Daddy, we got some really cool stuff."

Luke, however, was eyeing Penny Fucking Perkins, and finally said, "I know you. You're the PTA lady from our school in California."

Blake stopped Lindsey from pulling him, turned to Luke and said, "This is my friend Ms. Perkins, and yes she was the PTA president at your old school. But now she works for my company overseeing some important charities."

Lindsey walked over to Penny Fucking Perkins and said, "Are you banging Daddy like Allie?"

Holy shit, Leanne needed to put an end to this acquisition and said, "How about we stay right here and have a cupcake. I'm sure Daddy brought you a present."

"Ooh, I would love one of your cupcakes Leanne. You always made the best for the bake sales," said Penny Fucking Perkins.

Leanne ignored Penny Fucking Perkins and went to the refrigerator and brought out a box of cupcakes, got a large plate down from the cabinet, placed six cupcakes on it and set it in the middle of the island, with a pile of napkins next to it. She looked at Blake and said, "So what did you get the kids for their birthday?"

Luke and Lindsey turned to him with eager eyes and big smiles. He looked down at them and said, "Well, it's really hard picking out presents for seven-year-olds, so…"

Leanne interrupted and said, "They're eight Blake."

Blake shot her a look, and said, "Whatever," then turned back to the kids and said, "Well, since I wasn't sure what to get you, I decided on these," he took the two envelopes that Penny Fucking Perkins pulled from her purse and handed the pink one to Lindsey and the blue one to Luke.

Lindsey and Luke tore open their envelopes and each held up a brand new hundred-dollar bill. Confused, Lindsey looked at Luke, then turned to Blake and said, "Daddy, do you want us to keep two secrets?"

Well, that did it. Devon and Chet just lost it and headed out the back door laughing. Leanne tried her hardest to hold it in, but excused herself and hurried out the back door, following Devon and Chet. When she got to the patio, she was wiping away tears of laughter from her cheeks. Once she composed herself, she said to Devon and Chet, "That child has no filter. I need to work with her on that."

Devon said, "That was priceless. It was worth having them arrive uninvited."

Still laughing, Chet said, "How about when she asked Penny Fucking Perkins if she was banging daddy like Allie."

Well, that just set them off again. Finally, Leanne said, "Okay. Let's pull it together so we can get them off this island. Chet, do you want to call Henry and have someone come get them?"

"Nah, I'll take them myself. How about I stop at Pete's and pick up some steaks for dinner and we'll cookout tonight?"

Leanne said, "That sounds perfect."

Devon added, "I'm going to ride over with you, just for the fun of it," then they headed back inside.

Chapter 29

Leanne was sitting at the kitchen island browsing the internet on her laptop when Devon walked in sleepy-eyed and bare-chested. He kissed the top of her head as he walked towards the coffee pot. Once there, he poured himself a cup of coffee, turned, and asked Leanne, "Would you like a refill?"

Leanne looked at her empty mug and said, "Yes please."

Devon filled her mug, and then looking over her shoulder asked, "What are you looking for?"

Leanne took a sip of her hot coffee and replied, "A few things actually. We're in the last week of June; we need to think about getting our marriage license. It says on the website that you need a driver's license or birth certificate and there is only a three-day waiting period from application to receiving the license, which gives us some time. However, I think we should work on the details of the reception."

Devon sat down next to her and said, "As I recall, you were interested in a Hawaiian Luau theme, correct?"

Leanne nodded and said, "Yeah, but now that I've done my research, I'm thinking it's just too much work and a bit over the top."

Devon said, "I could make some phone calls, see about getting some fire eaters and hula girls flown over from Hawaii."

Leanne looked over at him and said, "You have a connection to fire eaters and hula girls?"

"Well, not directly," replied Devon, "But I could call Guy Grant and ask him for some recommendations. He did a movie a few years back that was filmed in Hawaii and they used fire eaters and hula girls."

Leanne gave it a moment's thought and then said, "You know what, let's go with a beachy theme with a simple buffet-style reception. I was thinking you and I could wear casual summer attire, maybe khaki shorts and a white shirt for you, and barefoot, definitely barefoot. And I could wear a…"

"Wait, back up a moment," said Devon, "Why definitely barefoot?"

Leanne looked down at his naked toes and answered, "Because your toes give me butterflies."

Devon raised an eyebrow and said, "Excuse me?"

Leanne laughed and said, "Remember back at the cabin, the day you and I were setting off to find the gurus hidey-hole?"

"Yes, I remember quite well," said Devon, "But what does that have to do with my toes?"

Leanne continued, "Well, I'll tell you. You came into the kitchen wearing only a pair of jeans, I looked at you and said, "I hope you plan on wearing a shirt," and then I looked down at your bare feet and I got this fluttering in my belly."

"Aahhh," said Devon, "Hence the butterflies."

"Exactly," said Leanne.

Devon added, "I believe that was the same morning you tried to stop me from having a cup of coffee, said you would put it in a thermos, and I told you…"

"You don't want to go traipsing through the woods with me having no coffee in my system. It would be worse than any bear you'll run up against," mocked Leanne in her best British accent.

"Well yes, something to that effect," replied Devon. "But let's get back to the barefoot wedding. Are you sure you don't want all the bells and whistles?"

Leanne looked at him, and said, "I'm marrying you. Those are all the bells and whistles I need. But, if you would like a big traditional wedding, then we can have one."

Devon laughed and said, "Oh, no thank you. I'd be happy eloping and having a very, very long honeymoon."

"I bet you would," said Leanne. "Okay, since I have your attention, let's work out a few details. First, the marriage license," looking at the calendar on her phone, she said, "What about July 14th. We can go into Seattle get the license and maybe we can ask Chet if…"

"Ask me what," said Chet as he walked into the kitchen, and being that it was Saturday morning, carrying a bag of jelly donuts from Frieda's bakery.

Leanne turned to him and said, "Good morning Chet. Devon and I were just talking about getting our marriage license. We have to start planning for the wedding and reunion Labor Day weekend. We were thinking about July 14th to go to Seattle to get our license and I was about to say to Devon, that maybe you would be willing to watch the twins so we could have an overnight getaway."

Chet put the bag of donuts on the counter, poured a cup of coffee and said, "Sure thing Leanne. That sounds like a plan."

Devon hadn't said a word, so Leanne asked him, "Does that work for you?" Lost in thought Devon, didn't answer, so Leanne asked again, "Devon, does that work for you?"

Devon snapped out of it and said, "Sure."

Not convinced, Leanne said, "If you would prefer to go another day that would be fine by me."

Devon got up, kissed Leanne's head, and said, "No. That sounds perfect," then walked over to the coffee pot and refilled his mug.

Leanne knew something was off but decided to let it go, so she turned to Chet and said, "We're thinking of a casual beachy theme wedding. I'll talk to the caterer we used for Amber's wedding about the buffet items. I was thinking fresh shellfish, salmon, and halibut, and then have a grilled meat station which I was thinking maybe Pete could recommend a couple of people to man the grills since he and Eloise will be attending as guests."

"I'm sure he can send PJ and Scotty. I'll ask him tomorrow when I go to the mainland," replied Chet.

Leanne closed her laptop and said, "You know what, I think I'll go take a shower and when the kids wake up, I'll take them over, I feel like getting off the island for a bit.

I'll pop into Pete's and talk to him and Eloise," then she got up and left the kitchen.

Chet turned to Devon and said, "What's with you? Cat got your tongue."

Devon looked at Chet and said, "What does that even mean?" and walked out the back door.

Chapter 30

Today is the marriage license day. Leanne was packing a few things in her overnight bag when Devon walked into the room and asked, "Are you almost ready?"

"Yes, just have to add my stuff from the bathroom," replied Leanne. Once everything was packed, Devon grabbed the bag off the bed, and they headed downstairs.

Chet and the twins were sitting at the kitchen island eating cereal. Leanne opened the refrigerator and said to Chet, "I marinated some chicken for dinner tonight and there are zucchini and squash in the vegetable drawer."

Chet stood up and walked to the sink, rinsed his cereal bowl, and put it in the dishwasher. He turned to Leanne and said, "Stop fussing Leanne, we'll be fine. As a matter of fact, we have plans for today. Don't we kiddo's?"

Luke nodded with a mouthful of cereal and Lindsey excitedly said, "Yup. When we bring you over to the mainland, were going to Frieda's and she's going to teach us how to make donuts. And then we're going to Benny's for lunch."

Devon raised an eyebrow at Chet and asked, "You're taking them to a bar?"

Chet scoffed and said, "Benny's ain't just a bar. It just so happens he has the best burgers this side of Washington State. Won best burger four years in a row at the county fair over in Wakefield."

"And today's Wednesday, you get a free milkshake with your burger," added Lindsey.

Luke finished his bowl of cereal and carried it to the sink, as did Lindsey. Luke turned to Chet and said, "I'm ready, let's go. I'm hungry for some donuts,"

Leanne looked at him and said, "You just finished a bowl of cereal."

Chet laughed and said, "That was his second bowl."

Leanne shook her head, told the twins to go wait out front, they would be right out. She turned to Chet and said, "You have our cell numbers, and I left the hotel number by the laptop on the counter."

"Stop your worrying Leanne," said Chet, "We'll be just fine. Now let's get going. We got places to go and people to see," and they headed for the door.

*****

Leanne and Devon arrived at the County Government office at nine a.m. They wanted to get there early so they could spend the rest of the day sightseeing. When they opened the door to the licensing office, they were shocked to see it packed with people. They were asked to sign in and told to take a seat, that the wait was approximately an hour. They scanned the room and spotted two chairs in the corner. When they sat down, Leanne said, "This place

214

reminds me of that so-called airport we flew out of in LA to Welby Island."

Devon replied, "When my limo pulled up in front of it, I remember thinking, this has to be some sort of a joke. But when I walked inside and you were the only one there, I must say, I was quite relieved. I'm not fond of large airports as is, but it's much worse if I'm recognized."

A half-hour later, the girl from behind the counter called out, "Leanne Dougherty and Devon Davis." The room went dead silent. Devon was hoping the baseball cap and sunglasses he was wearing was enough coverage, but apparently, having his name yelled across the crowded room, gave him away. Before he knew what was happening, people were pulling out their cell phones and snapping pictures of him and asking for selfies. Leanne made her way to the front counter and asked the girl, "Do you have an office or conference room we could use?"

The young clerk just nodded with her star-struck eyes glued to Devon. Leanne knew the young clerk was going to be of no help, so she made her way through the group of people surrounding Devon, grabbed his arm and tugged him towards an open door leading to a conference room. Once there, she shut the door and said, "What the hell?"

Devon shrugged and said, "Welcome to my world."

Just then a man opened the door and walked in. He told them that his name was Franklin Ford, and that he would be taking their application, adding, "I'm the office supervisor. I apologize for the commotion out there; apparently, Stacey didn't connect the dots until it was too late. Anyway, I'm told you are here for a marriage license."

Leanne leaned forward and said, "Yes. We're planning on getting married Labor Day weekend."

Franklin was filling out a form, without looking up, he said, "The way it works is, you submit the application, and then there is a three-day waiting period. We can mail the license to you or you can come in and pick it up, your choice. Once you have the certificate it's valid for 60 days, you don't use it, you lose it. I'll need to see your driver licenses." Both Leanne and Devon handed him their license. When he was done entering Leanne's information, he handed hers back to her. As he began to enter Devon's information, he looked up at Devon and said, "Happy Birthday."

Devon had been saying a silent prayer that the guy wouldn't make the connection, but he wasn't that lucky. The worst part was the look on Leanne's face. He opened his mouth to say something but the look she shot him said "LATER." Franklin went to hand Devon back his license, but Leanne snatched it out of his hand and stuck it in her purse. When the application was finished and signed, Franklin let them out the back door that led to an empty alley, as to avoid the waiting room. Once in the alley, Leanne swung around and unloaded on Devon, "Are you fucking kidding me? This whole time you knew you were coming here on your birthday and you didn't think I would find out. Do you know I have laid awake every night these past two weeks wondering if your reaction at the kitchen island when I picked July 14th was because you were getting cold feet? I thought maybe it was a game you were playing, 'Oh I'll keep pressuring her for a wedding date, and then I'll tell her I was just kidding.' I have been a wreck."

"Leanne…" Devon began, but the locomotive had started her engine and was full steam ahead.

"Don't you Leanne me," she said.

Devon grabbed her by the shoulders and said, "Stop. You need to hear me out."

Leanne was so frigging mad, she knew it was best to count to ten and hold her tongue, so she huffed, crossed her arms over her chest, and stared daggers at him.

"You're right. I did react when you picked July 14th, but it had nothing to do with getting our marriage license. I don't know if I can explain this properly, but for some reason when you said the date out loud, I drifted back to my childhood. Back to my sixteenth birthday and I shut down. I don't know why it hit me so hard, but I promise you, with all my heart, that I love you. I could never, not love you. The only thing I want in this life is to marry you. Please believe me."

Leanne swiped at the tear that slid down her cheek and said, "If you love me so much, then how come you couldn't trust me enough to tell me? You could have turned to me any given night as we lay side by side and told me. You know I would have understood. No questions asked. But instead you shut me out, leaving me to imagine the worse, that you don't really love me and maybe you were having doubts about us."

Devon pulled her into his chest and held her tight. He waited a few minutes until he was able to speak and finally said, "Leanne, you are my world. Without you I am an empty shell. There has never been a doubt cross my mind.

I am so sorry for causing you heartache. That was never my intention."

Leanne clung to him, then took a deep breath and let go, backed up a pace, holding Devon's hands she said, "Devon, that day on the picnic table at the cabin when you told your story, my heart broke into a million pieces for you. I have never once asked you when your birthday is, even after you surprised me in Denver for mine, and when we celebrated Chet's on the island with all of his friends, and then just last month, the party at the house for the twins. I was waiting for you to tell me when you were ready. But now that I do know, thanks to Franklin Ford, why don't we do this, why don't you pick a date, any date, that would bring you joy to say, 'I'm me, I'm alive' and we will make that your official re-birthday. Nobody needs to know, just you and me. Okay?"

Devon smiled slowly and said, "I know the exact date that my heart opened and let me love. It was the day you, Luke, and Lindsey arrived on the island with Chet. I can't really explain the feeling, but it was like I was looking at my future and my life was just beginning."

Leanne smiled and said, "That was August 30th. So, from this point on, that will be your re-birthday," she reached up and kissed him with all the love she felt for him.

When they parted, Devon said, "Thank you. Thank you for understanding and thank you for loving me."

Leanne took his hand and started walking down the alley and said, "Yeah, well it's a good thing I can count to ten. I was ready to kick your ass back there in that office."

Devon laughed and said, "The look on your face said as much. Now let's go enjoy the day. Today is just about you and me," and they headed for the wharf.

Chapter 31

It was mid-August, two weeks before the reunion and wedding. The guest list had grown to just under 75 people, including Devon's bandmates and their families, along with his manager Gordy Little and his wife. Guy and Renay happen to be filming on location in Vancouver and will fly in by helicopter Saturday and stay the night. Leanne and Devon didn't want their wedding to cause any chaos or concerns for the locals, so they were heading over to the mainland to have a meeting with the town council. When they walked into town hall they were greeted by the whole town, all familiar faces. Devon looked at Leanne and said, "This is not what I was expecting. This can't be good if the whole bloody town is here."

Concerned, Leanne turned to Chet and said, "Do you have any idea what's going on?"

"Let's go take a seat, you'll find out soon enough," replied Chet.

They made their way through the crowd and took three open seats upfront. Chet's cronies, Leroy and Stan are on the council, along with Henry, Pete, and Adele. Leroy being the President called the meeting to order and asked Adele to read the minutes from the last meeting. Once that was done, Leroy turned to the crowd and said, "The request for a special meeting came from Devon and Leanne, so I will turn the floor over to them."

Leanne looked at Devon, who in turn looked at Chet. Chet stood and said, "Okay folks, Devon and Leanne wanted to come to talk to ya'll about their upcoming wedding on Labor Day weekend. They got concerns about turning the town into a circus because of the celebrities they got coming. Maybe ya'll can help them out a little, Leanne, why don't you tell these folks what's on your mind."

Leanne looked at Devon who was now wearing an ear to ear grin, as he whispered, "Good luck."

Leanne stood and moved to the center of the room, turned to the council, and said, "Hello." She turned back to the town's people and said, "Well, umm, I guess I'll start by saying, thank you all for coming. Devon and I thought we may have been meeting with just the council, but I guess not. As Chet said, Devon and I are concerned with some of the people that will be attending our wedding, which may attract attention if word gets out beyond Swallow Bend. And for those of you that don't know Devon, well, he's um, popular," Chet snorted out a laugh, but Leanne ignored him and continued, "As are the guests from Los Angeles. We have taken precautions in advance to hire more security, which we hope will just blend in, rather than stand out. We don't have enough room at the house on the island to accommodate all of them, so they are going to need to travel in from Seattle, and hopefully won't be followed by paparazzi. We know this is going to be an inconvenience for all of you on a busy holiday weekend, but…"

Eloise, God bless her cotton socks, stood up and said, "Leanne, honey, what can we do to help?" The whole room murmured in consent.

Not expecting that response, Leanne said, "Well, I'm not quite sure. Maybe if any of you know of someplace discreet to put them up near here, it would be better than Seattle."

Adele said, "Leanne, I got three big houses for sale up on Sky Harbor Road, all furnished, but empty. Each house has six bedrooms and bathrooms. They all used to be summer rentals, but the families want to sell them. I'd be happy to talk to the owners and ask for permission to use them. I know all of them and I'm sure they would be happy to have your guests stay there."

Then Joanie Stevens, the school principal, stood and said, "I got three vans and a school bus you could use to shuttle them back and forth. Nobody's going to be looking for fancy Hollywood stars in a town school bus," which got a laugh from the crowd.

JR, the owner of the local auto body and gas station in town said, "I can lend ya'll a few fellas' to drive them."

Henry stood and said, "I've got a friend down in Tacoma that can send up some of his crew to lend a hand getting everyone to and from the island, since I won't be working that day. I've already talked to him, and I'll be sure to talk to my guys, about no star gawking."

The last person to stand was Katie Clark, fresh out of college. She worked as a reporter at the local paper The Swallow Bend Gazette. She said, "I have an uncle that works at the Seattle Times. I can talk to him and see if any paparazzi are sniffing around. Maybe he can throw them off the scent with a misprint of where you are getting married, let's say, on a yacht off the coast of San Francisco." The whole room went dead quiet. Katie looked around the room and said, "What? Sometimes reporters get it wrong."

This time Devon stood and said to Katie, "You are brilliant! Can you come over to the island tomorrow and we'll call my manager, Gordy Little, and you two can talk. And Miss Smarty Pants, you have just earned yourself an exclusive on the wedding. How are you with a camera?"

Katie was speechless she just stood there gawking at Devon until her mother Nelly Clark elbowed her. She snapped out of it and said, "Um, I majored in journalism and minored in photography. So, I'm pretty good."

"Fabulous," said Devon, "You have just been hired as our official wedding photographer."

This time Katie was able to speak and said, "Really! Oh, thank you Mr. Davis, I won't let you down."

Leanne snickered at the title of Mr. Davis, but Devon ignored her and said to Katie, "I'm sure you won't. Come out to the island at noon tomorrow."

When the meeting was over, everyone went about their business. Leanne, Devon, and Chet stood in the middle of the room, and Leanne asked, "What just happened here?"

Chet hooked arms with both of them and steered them toward the door, and said, "Me and Annie, we moved here the day we got married. I wasn't around much in those days, the Army owned me for another year, so I was always flying off to where they told me to go. But Annie, she set us up real nice here. We had us a three-bedroom cottage over on Creekside Lane, painted yellow, with a white picket fence and a big front porch with a swing, just like the one I courted her on at her momma and daddy's house. Built it herself she did. When my time was up with the Army, I came home, ain't ever imagined this beautiful house with the swing. Inside was set as pretty as a magazine picture, even had my own bark-o-lounger in front of the TV. My Annie, she had an eye for decorating and a green thumb to boot. She had the prettiest garden, won a blue ribbon ten years in a row from the Botanical Garden Club. When we weren't here, we were traveling seeing the sights. We would go north to Canada, south to San Francisco, and east to Yellowstone. Yup, we had some good adventures. Now I know it sounds like we didn't work, footloose and fancy-free, but we did. My Annie, she was a schoolteacher over at that same school those kids of yours go to. Me, well, I did a little bit of this and that, but I guess you could say my strong suit be, knowing what was coming next. For instance, when the railroad was the hot ticket, I bought a small piece of it when I was 16 years old, used all my odd job money. When I joined the Army, I bought a little piece of a company that was making airplanes call Grundell Aerospace. When I settled back here with Annie, I got a call from an army buddy of mine, wanted me to invest in something called a com-pu-ter. Well, I had no idea what that was or what I was getting into, but he assured me that it was a good investment. So, I thought, *What the heck, why not.*"

Leanne stopped him right there, and asked, "Are you telling us, you were an original investor in Micro Comp?"

Chet shook his head and said, "Naw, not an original investor, but a few years after. Now, my buddy, he's the original investor. Anyways, me and Annie, we settled here in Swallow Bend and never left. These folks, they've been really good to me and Annie. When she got sick, they circled around us like a den of momma bears. It took five years for my Annie to go home to the Lord, and when she did, these folks here, they hung onto me and propped me up, never lettin' go. And they'll do that for you too, don't you worry none."

Leanne and Devon walked with Chet in silence, absorbing all he said. They reached Frieda's Bakery, where the twins were hanging out while they were at the meeting. They walked into the sweet aroma of pastries and donuts and were surprised to see Luke and Lindsey waiting on tables, while Frieda handled the counter. Even when they saw them walk in, Luke and Lindsey didn't abandon their jobs. When Luke's table got up to pay their check, he cleared the table of the dishes, came back with a rag to wipe the table, then walked over to them and said, "Welcome to Frieda's, can I interest you in the pastry of the day, apricot-brie? I highly recommend it."

Devon looked at him and said, "Who are you and what have you done with Luke?"

Lindsey heard Devon so she came over and said, "That is Luke silly. We're working and that is what Frieda told us to say, but he did forget to ask you if you wanted coffee first. Coffee is always first, says Frieda."

"Well, okay then," said Devon, "I will have coffee and the pastry of the day."

"Make that two," said Chet.

"I will have the same," said Leanne.

Luke wrote down the order and headed to the counter to give Frieda the ticket, then put three coffee mugs on a tray and carried them over to the table. Frieda followed behind him carrying the coffee pot and filled Devon, Leanne, and Chet's mugs and sat for a minute. Luke brought over the pastries and asked if they needed anything else.

Frieda turned to Leanne and said, "Those two have been such a big help. I got bombarded and without Chet's help, I was all alone."

Luke overheard and said, "When we first got here it was empty, then a few minutes later, the door opened and all of these people came in, so Lindsey and I had to help. It was really cool."

"And fun," said Lindsey, who was clearing the table next to them.

Frieda stood, smiled at the twins, and said, "I don't know what I would have done without you two. However, I think the rush is over now, so why don't you each go pick out a donut or a muffin and come sit with your family."

Frieda returned twenty minutes later and handed each twin a ten-dollar bill and thanked them for all of their help. Then she turned to Chet and handed him a bag of jelly donuts, placed a hand on his shoulder and whispered to him, "Don't worry, they didn't replace you," and with a wink and a smile she went back to the counter.

They left Frieda's and headed for the marina. The twins ran ahead of them, thrilled to have earned ten dollars. Devon turned to Chet and said, "Speaking of money, let's get back to these investments of yours that you say you only dabbled in. What kind of return have they brought you?"

Chet kept walking and casually said, "Well it's been a while since I dabbled, but last I checked my bank statement, it was around six."

Leanne looked at him and said, "Six thousand?"

Chet kept walking and said, "Nope."

"It can't possibly be only six hundred dollars," said Devon.

"Nope," said Chet.

Then Leanne asked, "Six hundred thousand?"

"Nope," said Chet.

Both Leanne and Devon stopped walking, looked at each other and said at the same time, "Six million?"

Chet kept walking and replied, "That sounds about right."

Stunned, Leanne, and Devon both shouted, "What!"

Chet stopped walking and turned to Leanne and Devon and said, "Since my Annie died I ain't had anything to do with it, so it just sits in the bank collecting interest. But lately, I've been giving some thought to spending some of it."

"On anything in particular?" asked Devon.

"Well," said Chet, "I was going to wait to talk to ya'll when Amber, Leonard, and Rosalie got here, but since you two are pecking at me like a pair of woodpeckers, and I know it ain't gonna stop till I tell you, I might as well run it past you first."

Concerned, Leanne asked, "Run what by us?"

Chet shuffled his feet, looking at the ground he said, "Well I've been thinking on an idea, and it has to do with the cabin. Now I know it's yours, and if what I have in mind don't suit you, then you just say so." Leanne and Devon stayed silent, so he continued, "I was thinking after hearing what Bill Barnes said about the place needing to be flattened, and then the good news that there ain't any percolating poop, that I could use some of that money to build a park. Nothing fancy, just lots of flowers like my Annie used to grow, some picnic tables, maybe a barbecue and some sort of bathroom, a place where the people of the town could come over and have a picnic and use the beach."

Unable to speak, Leanne brought her clasped hands to her lips as a tear slid down her cheek. Devon cleared his throat and said, "Sir, I think that is a marvelous idea. It is not my land; it is our land and it would be my pleasure to be a part of creating such a special place in honor of Annie. I know Leanne, Amber, Leonard, and Rosalie would be too."

Chet said, "I've been saving all my money in hopes of doing something special to honor her memory. And those town folks back there at the meeting they loved Annie a whole lot, so it just seems like a good idea. I don't need your money, but I could sure use your help to make my vision come true."

Having composed herself Leanne walked over to Chet and wrapped him in a hug and said, "We'll make the park all that you imagine and more, and I know Annie will be guiding us every step of the way from up above."

Chet nodded at Leanne and headed for the marina, trying to contain his emotions. Leanne and Devon followed close behind.

Chapter 32

The weekend started off with making final arrangements for the upcoming wedding next Saturday. Leanne had made a spreadsheet of what was done and what was left to do. She printed three copies from the printer in her home office off the master bedroom. Actually, it was one of the two ginormous walk-in closets, but considering neither, she nor Devon, had enough clothes to fill one closet, they turned the second one into an office for Leanne. She highlighted what wasn't done yet and headed downstairs to the kitchen, which she surprisingly found empty. She knew that Chet left early to help Frieda at the bakery and then he was hoping to meet up with Bill Barnes to discuss plans to tear down the cabin. But it was close to noon so she thought she would find the other three natives restless and hungry. She looked out the back door, but nobody was out there, so she walked through the kitchen and down the hall to the front door and stepped out on the porch. From there she saw Devon, Luke, and Lindsey way down at the end of the dock, all three dangling their feet over the edge, with Bella and Blaze laying close by. Curious, she walked down the front steps and headed towards the dock, when she reached them, she said, "What's going on?"

Luke looked up at her and said, "Not much, we're just plating."

"Yeah," said Lindsey, "We're complating."

Confused, Leanne looked over at Devon, who laughed and said, "Well actually, the word is contemplating."

"What exactly are you contemplating?" asked Leanne.

"The water," said the twins.

Still confused, Leanne shot Devon a look, he explained, "I happened to mention the word contemplating, and the little inquiring minds wanted to know what it meant, so I looked it up on my phone. The definition is, *to look thoughtfully for a long time at,* and since we only have the water to look at, that is what we are contemplating."

Leanne shook her head and said, "Whatever. But why are you even down here on the dock?"

"Well, I got a text from Chet saying he was heading back to the island, and he was bringing a surprise. So, we decided to come down here and wait for him," said Devon.

Leanne laughed and said, "Well I could have saved you a whole lot of contemplating. Chet called earlier and asked if I needed anything before he headed back to the island, and I asked him if he would stop by the fish market and see what they got in fresh today. He asked if I wanted anything particular and I told him to surprise me. So, there's your surprise. When you're all done contemplating, come up to the house for lunch," shaking her head she headed up the dock towards the house.

As she was about to pull open the screen door, she heard a commotion coming from behind her. She turned to see Chet pulling up to the dock and he wasn't alone. She walked to the edge of the porch and shaded her eyes, and said, "No. It can't be." She slowly descended the stairs and began to walk across the lawn. She got halfway down the dock when Amber came running at her, she took a few quick steps back but there was nothing to grab onto, and, BAM, they went off the dock and into the Puget Sound.

Leanne and Amber swam to the beach. Once out of the water they collapsed on the sand. Amber turned to Leanne and asked, "Why does that keep happening?"

Leanne still trying to catch her breath said, "Maybe because every time you see me you come at me like the bull eyeing the matador. I swear Country Girl I didn't have more than three seconds to process what was going to happen before you were on me. You run like greased lightning."

Amber stood up and held out a hand to Leanne and helped her up and said, "I'm so sorry Leanne. I guess I got so excited when I saw you, I just took off."

Leanne tried to straighten her crooked T-shirt and ran both hands through her soaking wet hair, then turned to Amber and said, "Forget that. What are you doing here? You weren't supposed to arrive until Wednesday."

Amber shook the water out of her ears and tried to wring out her sundress the best she could and replied, "Well, Rosalie and I got to talking and we thought we would come out a few days early to help you with the wedding plans and spend a little girl time."

And right on cue, Rosalie stepped off the dock and onto the beach, laughing she said, "Locomotive, she took you down like a freight train...again."

Leanne took Ambers hand and grabbed Rosalie's and said, "Come on, let's go get changed and then we can catch up," they headed up the beach and across the lawn, with Chet, Devon, Leonard, Harold, Luke, Lindsey and hounds following behind them.

Once Leanne and Amber changed, they came back downstairs to find everyone gathered in the kitchen. Devon and Harold were making sandwiches, while Chet poured sweet tea into glasses, and Rosalie and Leonard were setting the table. The twins sat at the island waiting patiently. Devon placed two salami and cheese on white bread, no crusts, no condiments, as requested, in front of them. Leanne walked over to Devon and asked, "What can I do to help?"

Devon handed the kids each a napkin and replied, "Not a thing. We have it all under control. Why don't you go sit down with the other hens, Oh, and here's a piece of advice," he tapped her on the nose and said, "Stay the bloody hell away from any body of water while Amber is around."

Leanne laughed and said, "Good advice."

Over lunch, they talked about the surprise visit. Amber said that Kate and Lee insisted that she and Leonard go ahead early and that they would bring the babies on Wednesday. Leonard's father, John Mathers had offered to fly the whole Quinn clan to Seattle on his private plane. However, he and Ellen weren't arriving until Saturday and Leonard's grandparents weren't coming because they were in Iceland.

When everyone was finished eating, Leanne decided it would be the perfect time to talk about the cabin. She told them about the plans to expand it and make it into a small vacation rental, until they learned from Bill Barnes that the place was infested with termites and rodents and the electrical was a fire hazard.

Rosalie, being Rosalie said, "If you had asked me a year and a half ago, I would say burn it down, can't say my opinions changed much."

"Well," said Amber, "I never really hated the cabin. I think I was more disappointed as to why I ended up there. But meeting ya'll," she turned and took Leonard's hand, "And meeting my prince charming, that's what matters, not the four walls of the cabin."

Surprised to hear that, Leanne said to Amber, "I thought you two would be against tearing it down, being that you met there, got engaged there, and most likely conceived Rose and Annie there."

"Well," said Amber, "If truth be told, deciding to stay at the cabin on our wedding night wasn't such a good idea after all."

Astonished, Devon looked at her and said, "What? You bloody well begged me, even though I told you numerous times it wasn't such a good idea."

Amber shrugged and said, "Well, in hindsight, maybe I should have listened to you. But anyway, I'm pretty sure that is not where our babies were made. So, I'd be fine with you bulldozing it to the ground."

All eyes turned to Leonard, who had suddenly become very interested in his napkin. Rosalie eyed him and said, "Spill it, Brainiac."

Leonard shot Amber a look, who in turn shook her head. Leonard looked at Rosalie and said, "Um, well, there really isn't anything to tell."

"Ha!" said Rosalie. "Your cheeks turn pink when you lie."

Coming to Leonard's rescue, Amber said, "Stop interrogating him Rosalie and I'll tell you."

All heads shot left to Amber. She shifted in her seat, straightened and began, "Okay, so after we left ya'll we were heading straight to the cabin, that was until we saw the lounge chairs you had set up on the beach for us. I thought how romantic it would be to take a moonlight swim…" Leonard made a noise that sounded like he was choking. All heads turned his way. Amber ignored him and continued, "Well it took a little convincing to get Leonard to agree, but once he did, we dropped our clothes like a too-big pair of pants and ran for the water, and that's where it all began."

Curious as to where this was going, the table sat in complete silence, so Amber clamored on, "Well, ya see, when we were running down the beach to the water, I must have stepped on a shell, because I cut my foot. It wasn't anything awful, that didn't happen until I sat in the sand to check it out. Before I knew what was happening, these teeny tiny little crawly things were biting my hiney and crawling all over me." Leonard began to squirm in his seat. Amber continued, "Well, when I started hollerin' and jumping around like a flea on a cat, Leonard picked me up and ran for the water. Let me tell you, that water was no warmer than the day we went shell fishing, but it did add some relief to the bites all over me. When we were numb and it was safe to say that the bugs were off me, we headed back up to the beach chairs and that's when I noticed the crab that had latched on to Mr. Herman."

Confused, Chet said, "Country Girl, what in the blazin' tarnation's you talkin' about? There wasn't anybody over there with you."

Leonard coughed, took a sip of his tea, and was squirming in his seat. All heads turned to him and Rosalie asked, "Leonard, what the hell is she talking about?"

Leonard shook his head and said, "I can't think about it. She'll tell you."

All heads turned back to Amber, she looked at them and said, "Don't ya'll have a name for your private parts?"

Giving that a moment's thought, Devon, Leanne, Rosalie, Harold and Chet said in unison, "No."

Shocked, Amber said, "Well you should. We call Leonard's Mr. Herman."

That did it. Leonard pushed back from the table, stood up, and began gathering plates. And then the lightbulb went off and Rosalie said, "Are you telling us that you stepped on a shell, cut your foot, sat on a pile of bugs and then a crab clamped onto Leonard's manhood?"

"Yup, pretty much," replied Amber, "And it doesn't end there. When we finally get to the cabin, we had to use the champagne as an antiseptic, and when we were out back pouring it on our…you know what areas, out of nowhere comes this big ole bat, flew right out of the trees and started attacking Leonard. Well, I was having none of that, so I ran inside grabbed that old broom in the laundry room and I beat that thing silly, or so I thought. It wasn't until Leonard and I made a run for it that it got back up and chased us to the back door."

Flabbergasted, Devon said, "Why in the world didn't you come back here?"

This time Leonard answered, "Because it wouldn't let us out of the cabin."

"What do you mean it wouldn't let you out of the cabin?" asked Devon.

"It sat on the golf cart and wouldn't move," replied Amber, "We tried six times and finally gave up at four a.m. So, we went to bed, but that didn't go so well either. The minute we shut off the light all we heard was, scratch, scratch, scratch."

"I swear that bat was trying to get in," said Leonard.

"Leonard, honey, I told you, the bat never moved from the golf cart and what we were hearing was coming from up above. We were in Leanne's old room," she said to the five pairs of eyes staring at her.

"So let me get this straight," said Rosalie, "You left us after the reception, drove to the cabin, decided to take a romantic bare ass naked swim, but instead, cut your foot on a shell, got bitten by bugs on said bare ass, Leonard had a crab attached to his ding-dong, and a bat attacked you and held you hostage in the cabin."

Amber took a sip of her tea and said, "Yup, that about sums it up. And when the sun started to rise, that bat flew off and we high tailed it back here. We didn't want to wake anyone…"

"Or have to tell our story," Leonard added.

Amber continued, "So we went to the end of the dock and waited for Chet because we know he goes over to the mainland early every day."

"So that's what you fool kids were doing out there. You told me you were too excited to stay on the island, wanted to get a jump on your honeymoon in Hawaii, so I gave you a ride over and told them all back at the house what you told me," said Chet.

Amber said, "Well that part was true. But that was after we hit the hospital in Seattle. I needed a tetanus shot, and a couple of stitches on my toe, but Leonard, he just needed a butterfly bandage and some ice for the swelling. Back to your question Leanne, about us conceiving at the cabin, that's a big fat no. My guess is four days later, in a king-size bed, in a Hawaiian Villa overlooking the Pacific Ocean, is when it happened or any day thereafter."

Speechless during Amber's whole story, Leanne gathered her thoughts and said, "So when we saw you in February and you told us about christening the cabin inside and out, you made that up?"

"Yup," said Amber, "And Leonard and I made a pact to never mention what happened. No offense Leanne, but we're talking about Mr. and Mrs. Herman here. There was no way I was gonna let Momma and Daddy, nonetheless, Hannah, Bailey Jr. or Petey, know what happened. I would never have heard the end of it, and I'll ask ya'll to keep it to yourselves, thank you very much."

Leanne crossed her heart and said, "I won't say a word, I promise. However, after hearing that story, I don't think you are going to like my suggestion."

"Well," said Amber, "As long as it doesn't have to do with sand ants, crabs…"

"Or bats," said Leonard.

"No, it doesn't involve any of those things, but it does involve us taking a ride over to the cabin," said Leanne.

Concerned, Amber and Rosalie looked at each other, Rosalie asked, "What's on your mind, Leanne?"

"Actually, Chet came up with an idea. We've been kicking around what to do with the cabin, but we would like it to be a group decision and it would be best to take a ride over there to visualize it," Leanne replied.

Rosalie said, "I'm game. Harold?"

"Sweet Rosalie, you know I would follow you to the moon if you asked," said Harold and kissed her hand.

"We're in Leanne," said Amber and Leonard.

So, they cleaned up the kitchen from lunch, loaded into the golf cart with the kids and dogs, and headed to the cabin.

Chapter 33

Harold and the twins had never been to the cabin, so Leanne didn't know what kind of reaction to expect when they emerged from the woods on the golf cart. Harold let out a big whistle and said, "My darlin' Rosalie, I cannot see you staying in a place like this. If I had any notion that this is where you were going, there's no way I would have signed you up. That brochure the Claine's sent me, it had a picture of Devon's house on it, for Pete's sake. I was duped; those Claine's they were scammers, that's for sure."

Rosalie patted his hand and said, "Don't worry about it. I survived, and truth be told, after all was said and done, you actually accomplished what you set out to do, and I know that came from your heart. But Harold..."

"Yes Rosalie," said Harold.

"If you ever try something like that again, I will suffocate you with a pillow in your sleep," said Rosalie as she got out of the golf cart.

Luke and Lindsey just stared at the house. Finally, Luke asked, "Mommy is that the dictionary you painted on the house?"

Leanne didn't want to give them too much information, so she replied, "It is. We got a little bored and thought it would be fun to paint our feelings on the cabin."

Lindsey took a few steps closer and read these five letters out loud BITCH, she turned to Leanne and asked, "What does that spell?"

Leanne shot a look at Rosalie, who in turn said, "Don't look at me."

"You wrote it," Leanne countered.

"They're not my kids," Rosalie volleyed back.

"Oh for crying out loud," said Amber, "I'll answer her," she walked over to Lindsey and bent down to her height and said, "Now Lindsey, you asked a question and you deserve an answer, so I'm not going to sugar coat this, and one day you might want to use this word, but it's not a nice word, so keep that in mind, okay?" Lindsey nodded, so Amber continued, "The letters you just spelled say 'Bitch.' It's a bad word for someone that's not very nice."

Lindsey gave that a moment's thought then asked Amber, "Well if someone is not very nice, then why is it a bad word?"

The group behind Amber snickered, Amber turned and shot them her best stink eye, then turned back to Lindsey and said, "Well, it's like this, there are clean words to say someone is not nice, like, she's mean, and then there are dirty words that mean the same thing, like a bitch."

Lindsey gave that some more thought, and then she said, "Oh, I get it. Like Tabitha is mean to Susie, so she's a dirty bitch."

A gasp came from the group. Amber stood up and said to Leanne, "Is this what I have to look forward to with the twins in a few years?"

Leanne nodded and said, "Yup. Boys are so much easier. Girls, well they beat to a whole different drummer," pointing her chin at Lindsey.

Devon decided this would be a good time to rescue Amber, so he said, "Okay, let's move this along and talk about why we brought you over here. As we told you, Leanne and I were thinking of turning the cabin into a vacation rental. However, after further research, we found out that the cabin is in very poor condition and must be flattened. That brings us to Chet's idea." Devon turned to Chet and said, "Why don't you tell them what your idea is."

Taking a few moments to look around at the surrounding, Chet finally said, "Well I got to telling Devon and Leanne about a thought I had. We didn't want to make any decisions until we ran it by you folks, but I was thinking maybe we could tear down the cabin, clean up the property, and turn it into a park. We could plant some pretty flowers; add a few picnic tables and maybe a grill or two. It could be a place the town's people can come to have some fun and enjoy the beach."

Excitedly, Amber said, "Oh Chet that sounds like a great idea."

Devon turned to Amber and said, "You haven't heard the best part yet." Then he turned to Chet and said, "I suggest you sit down at the picnic table before you tell her the next part or else there is a good chance you'll end up on your backside."

Knowing what Devon was saying was true, Chet walked over and sat down at the table, the others followed. Leonard steered Amber to the other side of the table away from Chet. Once everyone was situated, Chet began, "So anyway, my Annie, she loved her flower gardens. She had what they call a 'green thumb.' Everything she planted bloomed into amazing beauties. So, I was thinking we could fill this whole area here with some wildflowers, over there we could make some flower beds, maybe a birdbath or two. My Annie loved her birds. And then over there, can be the picnic area. If what Bill told us is right, then there should be a big slab of concrete under that cabin. We could build a few brick barbecues, add a half dozen or so picnic tables. That's pretty much my vision. Those town folks, they've been really good to me since my Annie died, and just as good to us before the good Lord took her home, so I'd like to do something special for them. Show them my gratitude."

Since Amber was busy swiping at her tears, Leonard spoke, "Chet I think that sounds like an awesome idea. Amber and I will pitch in to help pay for it."

"Us too," boomed Harold.

Chet cleared his throat and said, "Thank you kindly. But that won't be necessary."

All eyes shot to Devon, he shrugged, raised his eyebrows and said, "Don't look at me. He won't take a nickel from us either."

Concerned, Rosalie said to Chet, "Please don't take this the wrong way, but do you have enough money to pay for this? It could cost thousands of dollars to just flatten the cabin. We would be more than willing to help out financially."

"That's mighty kind of you Rosalie, of all of you, but I have been saving for a few years and have enough to cover the costs," said Chet.

Again, all eyes shot to Devon, and this time he said to Chet, "Oh bloody hell, just tell them, they're family."

"Tell them what?" Rosalie shot back.

Chet looked around the table; Devon was right, these people were his family, so he said, "I ain't keeping no big secret. It's just money that I got in the bank from some investments I've made over the years."

Suspicious Rosalie asked, "How much money?"

"Well now, I haven't checked my account interest lately, but the last amount was a little over six million."

"Six million!" exclaimed Rosalie, Harold, Amber, and Leonard all at the same time.

"As I said, I've made a few investments over the years. But anyhow, that's not the point of this trip to the cabin. Now that ya'll know I got money to pay for it, how about we start kickin' around some ideas," said Chet.

Lindsey and Luke had just come back from exploring the cabin, so Lindsey said, "I have an idea. We can make a fairy garden. Fairies like flowers."

"Well ain't that a coincidence Pint Size, my Annie, she loved fairies too. Me, I thought she might be slipping a little when I see her out there yapping away to the flowers, but she insisted it was those fairies she was talking to."

Wide eyed, Lindsey said, "Oh they're for real Chet. But they only come to people who believe, just like Santa."

"Okay then, we'll build us a fairy garden. When we get back to the house, we'll get on that thing your momma is always stuck like glue to, and we'll look up favorite fairy flowers. Sound like a plan?" asked Chet.

Lindsey smiled from ear to ear and said, "Yup. Sounds like a plan."

Luke added, "We saw four big trees on the other side of the cabin. Maybe we could put up a tire swing. That would be really cool."

The momentum was contagious, Amber piped in, "Oooh, I know, we could build a playground with a carousel made with unicorns instead of horses."

"That's a great idea, Amber," shouted Lindsey, "Unicorns and fairies are best of friends."

While everyone was talking fairies and unicorns, Rosalie got up and walked to the edge of the woods, where the path leads down to the beach. She stood there for a few minutes then turned around and went back to the table and said, "What do you think about this idea? I saw it done on one of my property listings on the beach a few years back. The cabin is made of wood planks. We could remove them by hand, have them cut to size, sanded and weather treated and lay them down as a path from the beach to the park. It would sure make the trek a lot easier."

"Rosalie, that is a fabulous idea," said Leanne, "We could have the path cleared and widened and add landscaping lights to illuminate it in the evening."

Harold put his hand on Chet's shoulder and said, "Well Chet, it looks like you are going to create a magical place in honor of your Annie. I'm thinking she'd be mighty pleased."

Chet nodded but didn't speak, though his eyes glistened with tears as he looked at the faces of his newfound family. Amber walked over to Chet and sat down next to him and said, "Ya know Chet, we didn't name our Annie just after Leanne, we also did it to honor your Annie too, who may not be sitting down here with us today, but don't you worry, she is all around us. I can feel her embrace."

Leanne said, "Funny you should say that Amber, a few minutes ago I felt a breeze on the back of my neck, but the air is still as a statue."

"Okay, you two are freaking me out," said Rosalie, "Because when I turned to walk to the edge of the woods earlier, I swear I felt someone holding my hand. It was light as a feather and cool to the touch."

The group sat there at the picnic table, absorbing what Amber, Leanne, and Rosalie just said, and out of nowhere, a red cardinal flew out of the trees and landed on the end of the table right next to Chet. In stunned silence, the group watched as the bird tilted its head and looked directly at Chet and a few seconds later it fluffed its feathers and took flight. Everyone sat there with wide eyes and gaping mouths, all but Chet, who was smiling as a tear slid down his cheek. They all sat like that for a few minutes until Luke broke the silence and said, "That was way cool."

Amber found her voice and said, "Ya'll, that was a sign from up above. When you see a cardinal that means a departed loved one is close by. I, for one, believe that was Chet's Annie. Did you see the way that bird looked at him? I swear it smiled at him."

Feeling a tad bit freaked out himself, Devon stood and said. "Well, on that note, I think it's time we head back to the house."

Leanne agreed and said, "Okay, let's head back and write some notes on the ideas we had here today, and work on a design."

Chet stood, and as they were walking to the golf cart, he turned to all of them and said, "I'd like to call it: "Annie's Place," with the saying, "Made with Love-Meant for Joy."

They all agreed the name was perfect and the sign would say just what Chet said. They climbed into the golf cart and headed home.

Chapter 34

It was Wednesday morning and the rest of the Quinn clan was arriving that afternoon. Devon made arrangements to have a limo pick them up at the airport and bring them to the marina, but Amber was eager to see the twins, so she and Leanne took Leanne's SUV and would drive back with Kate, Lee and the babies. Leonard stayed back on the island so there would be room for the car seats. He was out front down on the water's edge looking for crabs with Chet, Luke, and Lindsey when Henry motored up to the dock. Chet shaded his eyes to get a better look, and once he noticed it was Henry, he started down the dock. When he reached Henry, he saw that he was not alone; there was a young guy with him, maybe about Devon's age. Henry threw Chet the rope and Chet tied him to the dock. When they stepped off the boat and onto the dock Chet said, "Hey there Henry, what brings you out this way?"

"Mornin' Chet," replied Henry, "Couple things. Leanne placed an order with Pete for his barbecue package. Must be for that big crowd you got comin' in this afternoon."

Chet laughed and said, "That be the Quinn clan. You know them from last year this time when Amber and Leonard got married."

"Yup, remember them well. Good people," said Henry, "Also wanted to let Devon know that I got a few more men coming on board to help with the transfers on Saturday." Turning to the young man he said, "Chet this is Kenny, I hired him last week. Mostly doing wash downs, but he'll be helping out this week running back and forth anything ya'll might need, and then he'll be on shuttle duty come Saturday."

Chet turned to Kenny, held out his hand, and said, "Pleased to meet ya son. Grateful for the extra hands, we got a crowd coming, some local, some not so local."

Kenny shook Chet's hand and said, "Happy to oblige sir. You need anything, you just holler."

Henry patted Kenny on the back and said, "Son, why don't you roll that there cooler up to the house. That's Devon standing on the front porch. Tell him it's the order from Pete's."

Kenny lifted the cooler from the boat to the dock, struggling slightly with the weight, set it down, and wheeled it up the dock towards the house."

When Kenny returned, he and Henry got back in the boat. Chet untied the lines and tossed them to Henry, who said, "See ya bright and early tomorrow morning."

"As always," replied Chet.

Henry chuckled and said out loud to himself, "Seven a.m. every day, like clockwork," and they motored off.

Chapter 35

"Hey, it's me," said the caller.

"Why are you calling me? I told you text messages only," said the voice on the other end.

"Listen, I think we got a problem," said the caller. "They got a whole bunch of people coming out to the island this afternoon. The old man called them the Quinn clan. Then they have a whole bunch more coming to some shindig on the island this weekend."

"Hmmm…" said the voice, "Looks like a change of plans. We're going to have to move it up. We need to get him alone before Saturday."

"How are we going to move it up when the dang island is filling up? I think we have to scratch the plan for this weekend and do it next weekend," said the caller.

"NO! We stick to the plan," shouted the voice. "You find a way between now and Saturday to get him. That is why I sent you there."

"Okay. Okay, chill, I think I have an idea. I'll get back to you," said the caller.

"You better and next time text me, no calling," said the voice and hung up.

Chapter 36
Reunion/Wedding Weekend

Chet was up at the crack of dawn Friday morning. He figured he could put in a few hours helping Frieda at the bakery, then stop by the caterers to confirm that they had everything they needed for the reception tomorrow after Leanne and Devon say their 'I Do's' on the beach. When he entered the kitchen, he saw Kate sitting at the kitchen island. He didn't want to startle her, so he cleared his throat and said, "Good morning Kate."

Kate looked up, smiled at Chet, and said, "And good morning to you. What has you up this early?"

"Not early for me. This is my usual wake up time. I like to get up and listen to the nothingness," replied Chet, "Helps me get my thoughts together for the day ahead. And now I can ask the same of you. What brings you down here so early?"

Kate laughed and said, "Like you, not early for me. I'm married to a farmer who's up every morning at the first crow of the rooster, but we come out here to the island and he sleeps like a rock and snores like a chainsaw. But I'm with you, nothing like the morning quiet to start the day off on the right foot."

Chet poured himself a cup of coffee and asked Kate if she would like a refill. She looked at her empty mug and said, "Yes please."

After he filled her mug he asked, "What's that you're working on there?"

"Well actually, it's a list for some items I need from the market. I was going to ask you if you wouldn't mind picking them up for me while you're in town. I would go over with you, but the market doesn't open for another two hours and there is nothing I need right away," said Kate.

"Sure thing Kate," replied Chet. "What do you say we take our coffee and go sit on the front porch? Ain't nothing more peaceful than a setting moon and a rising sun."

"That sounds like the perfect way to start the day," replied Kate, and they headed out of the kitchen and down the hall to the front door. Once seated in their rockers, they sat in silence just staring out at the Puget Sound; the only noise to be heard was the chatter of the morning swallows and the lapping of the calm water onto the beach. Kate released a heavy sigh and said, "I could sure get used to this. I've been living on a farm my entire life. I never even knew about this side of the country. It truly is a wonder, isn't it?"

"Yup, it sure is," said Chet. "As I told you, I was born over in Derby, nearby your place, but we left there when I was three. My daddy, he was a good man, always providing for Momma, me, and my baby sister Lila, a year younger than me. But it always meant following the next big trend. If it wasn't mining for gold, it was working on the railroad. That's how we ended up in Seattle and once I set my eyes on this here side of the country, I knew I was home."

"Do you have any family close by?" asked Kate.

Chet ran his fingers through his snow-white hair and said, "Nope, didn't have much kin to start with. My baby sister died at the age of four from scarlet fever. Ten years later, my momma caught pneumonia and passed on. From then on it was just me and my daddy. We stayed put in Seattle where I went on to finish high school. Six months after I graduated, my daddy died of a heart attack on the job, which left me with two choices: live on my own or join the military. I chose the military, which turned out to be a good choice. I came back to Seattle in between tours and met my Annie. She was working at a new coffee shop that just opened up. It was love at first sight, well for me at least," laughed Chet. "She was new to town, the family just moved here from Montana. I courted her for three months before I had to leave for my tour. Longest year of my life, but when I got back, she was still here waiting for me, so I asked her to marry me and we moved down here to Swallow Bend and never left."

Kate smiled over at Chet and said, "I'm not sure if it's the sun rising, or how you light up when you talk about Annie, but it seems a little bit brighter out here. I think I really would have liked her."

Chet nodded, after a minute he said, "I know she would have loved all of you. Leanne, Devon, Rosalie, Amber, and Leonard, coming into my life as they did, I got to believe it was a gift from Annie. I think she's trying to tell me to live my life again. And those two kiddos, Luke and Lindsey, well they keep me young."

Kate laid her hand on top of Chet's and said, "Well from what I know about all of you, I'd say Annie gave you all a gift, and I think she would be disappointed if you didn't take advantage of it. So, it may be about time you make your move with Frieda, the baker I have heard so much about."

Chet turned, looked at her and finally said, "Hmm, I think you just might be right. To be honest with you, all these years I thought I would be dishonoring Annie's memory, but now that I've said it out loud, I think she orchestrated the whole thing. That'd be just her way."

Kate smiled and said, "Well, what are you waiting for. Get over to that mainland and tell her that you want her to be your plus one for the wedding tomorrow."

They both stood and started inside Chet turned to Kate and said, "Thank you, Kate. I appreciate you lending me an ear."

"Thank you, Chet, for suggesting we come out here to bring the sun up. It makes thinking about getting on that plane back to the farm a whole lot harder," laughed Kate.

Chet said, "Well let's go get me that list of yours and I'll be on my way to the mainland."

Chapter 37

Chet had just rounded the bend from the house and was heading to the marina when he spotted a boat sitting idle. He motored over to it and yelled out, "Are you broke down? Do you need some help?"

The person on board stood, wiped his hands on the rag he was holding, turned towards Chet and said, "Oh, hey there Chet. Not quite sure what's wrong with her, but I can't seem to get her started."

"Well Kenny, why don't you tie me up to your boat and I'll climb aboard and take a look," said Chet.

Kenny took the rope from Chet and tied it to his boat. Once Chet crossed over to Kenny's boat he stepped back to where the engine was and got down on his knees to take a look. While he was occupied, Kenny poured the chloroform onto the rag and swiftly put it over Chet's face from behind. Chet struggled, but he was in an awkward position and couldn't get his feet under him, and within less than a minute he was out cold. Kenny had to work fast. He grabbed the ropes he brought and secured Chet's feet and tied his hands behind his back. He grabbed another piece of rope and jumped onto Chet's boat, he tied the rope to the stick shift, started the boat, turned it facing out to sea, put it in neutral, taped the ransom note to the steering wheel then got back on his boat, untied the lines and yanked the rope in his hand attached to Chet's gear shift, and Chet's boat took off like an arrow from a bow. He quickly got behind the wheel of his boat, started the engines, and headed for the designated meeting place. He grabbed his phone and sent the text, "Got him, on my way."

Chapter 38

It was an unusually hot day on the island. A heatwave had crept in over the past two days, but relief was on its way in the form of thunderstorms overnight, but for now, everyone was gathered out by the pool. The kids were playing a game of Marco-polo while the adults were lounging around in various forms, all but Kate and Leanne, who were in the kitchen putting together some cold salads to go with the chicken that was marinating for dinner. Devon came in carrying an empty pitcher of sweet tea; he placed the pitcher on the counter and said to Kate, "Kate, what time did Chet leave this morning?"

Kate stopped what she was doing, turned to Devon, wiping her hands on her apron, and said, "It was close to seven, maybe a quarter of. I had made a grocery list and asked him to pick up a few things for me at the grocer's."

"Hmm," said Devon, he turned to Leanne and said, "Was he running any errands for you?"

Leanne put the salad in the refrigerator and, "Nope. But he could be helping Frieda; she is making our wedding cake after all."

"No, she closes at three every day. He wouldn't still be there," said Devon.

"Well, it's just after two-thirty," said, Leanne as she glanced at the clock on the microwave, shocked she said, "What the...how did it get to be four o'clock already?"

Slightly concerned, Devon said, "I'll give Frieda a call and see if he is with her."

Then Kate said, "Now, I'm not one for gossip, but this morning Chet and I had coffee out on the front porch while the sun rose and we got to talking about Frieda, and I told him it was time to make his move and ask her to be his plus one at your wedding. Maybe he was working up his nerve and stayed after she closed to talk to her."

Devon dialed Frieda's number and said to Kate, "Possibly." Once Frieda answered Devon turned his attention to the phone, "Good afternoon Frieda. It's Devon. I'm good thank you, I was wondering if Chet was still there with you?" Devon slowly turned and locked eyes with Leanne and said to Frieda, "So you haven't seen him all day. No, no nothing's wrong. Apparently, he must have gotten tied up somewhere else. I'll give Henry a call. I will, and if you hear from him, please have him call me. Yes, yes, thank you, Frieda."

Devon hung up and was about to dial Henry when Amber walked into the kitchen and said, "Woo wee it's a scorcher out there," she looked at Leanne's face and said, "What is it? What's the matter?"

Kate walked over and put her arm around Amber and said, "Nothing honey. Chet's just running a little bit late, that's all,"

The back door swung open and Rosalie came in and said to Devon, "Hey Rock Star, I thought you were whipping up a batch of your famous margaritas..." She stopped mid-sentence, looked around the room and landed on Devon and asked, "What's going on? I don't like that look on your face. Last time I saw that look the gurus emerged from the woods."

Devon scrolled through his phone until he found Henry's number, and said to Rosalie, "It's probably nothing, but Chet seems to be running a little bit late, so I'm getting ready to give Henry a call to see if he's on his way."

Leanne walked over and stood next to Rosalie as Devon dialed, all four women were staring at him. When Henry picked up, Devon said, "Hi Henry, it's Devon, I was wondering if Chet was on his way back to the island yet. Oh, you haven't. Um, well could you do me a favor, could you gather Stan, Frank, Pete, Leroy and Benny and come out here to the island? Yes now, if possible? Well, we're not quite sure, but Chet left just shy of seven a.m. this morning and he's not back yet. I contacted Frieda, but he never arrived there this morning. True, you would have seen him if he came into the marina. Okay, thanks. See you soon." Devon hung up and turned to the four women staring at him with concern in their eyes.

Just then Leonard walked in carrying Annie on his hip and said, "Hey Amber, I thought you were getting juice bottles for the girls? What's the matter? You guys don't look so good."

Kate walked over to Leonard and took Annie from him and said, "Why don't ya'll go out on the front porch. I'll take the babies, Luke and Lindsey over to Hannah's side of the house and fix them grilled cheese sandwiches and they can watch a movie and have a sleepover."

Leanne nodded and said, "Thank you, Kate. I can't let the twins hear anything about this. I'll run upstairs and grab their pajamas and toothbrushes."

"Don't you worry darling, I'll get them. We'll keep them occupied. Now go outside and wait for Henry," said Kate.

Amber went over to Leonard and took his hand and said, "Come on, let's go outside and Devon will fill us in," and they headed out of the kitchen followed by Leanne, Devon, and Rosalie.

Once on the front porch, Rosalie turned to Devon and said, "What's going on? I don't like this feeling I have in my gut right now."

Leanne took Rosalie's hand and said, "Let's walk down to the dock. Devon will fill us in. Chet's friends from town are heading over."

When they got to the dock, they saw Bella and Blaze sitting up on alert at the end. Devon whistled to them, but they didn't flinch. Devon turned and looked at Leanne, who was now wearing a mask of panic on her face. She said to Devon, "Fill us in."

Devon took a deep breath and said, "Okay, this is all I know right now. According to Kate, she and Chet had coffee on the porch early this morning. She had made a grocery list and asked Chet to stop at the market for her. Chet left here just before seven this morning and it is now going on four-thirty and he is not back yet. I called Frieda, but she said he never showed up there this morning, she thought maybe he stayed on the island to help us. So, I then called Henry and he hasn't seen him all day either."

"Are you saying he's missing?" asked Rosalie.

"I'm not sure," replied Devon, "I've asked Henry, Stan, Frank, Leroy, Pete, and Benny to come out to the island. They should be here in about ten minutes."

"Don't you think we should call the police?" asked a teary-eyed Amber. "He's been gone for almost nine hours. What if his boat broke down and he's out there drifting to Hawaii? We need to call the Coast Guard." Leonard wrapped his arms around Amber and pulled her close. She rested her head on his chest and let the tears flow.

Trying to stay calm, Leanne said, "Let's see what Henry has to say and then we can call whomever we need."

Rosalie, never at a loss for words, walked away from the others, and headed down the dock to where Bella and Blaze were sitting. The others followed in silence.

Exactly ten minutes later Henry pulled up to the dock with Stan, Frank, Leroy, Pete, and Benny. Once secured, the men stepped off the boat and onto the dock. With concern in his eyes, Henry said, "What's going on Devon? You've got us all a little worried."

Leanne said to Devon, "I'm going to run ahead and see if the house is empty. Bring everyone up and meet me in the library."

"We'll come with you," said Rosalie, taking Amber and Leanne's hands, "I want to let Harold know what's going on."

Devon explained to the men what he knew as they walked up to the house. Once everyone was settled in the library, Devon began, "So I've told you everything I know. Now we need to figure out what to do from here."

"We should call the Sheriff is what we should do," said Stan.

"Let's put our heads together for a minute first," said Henry. "Did Chet mention to any of you that he might be going somewhere today?"

"Well if he was going somewhere, he'd need his boat to get over to the marina," said Leroy.

"Maybe he wasn't heading to the marina, maybe he went north or south, may be needed to pick something up in Tacoma," said Pete.

"Naw," said Henry, "If he was going to Tacoma he would have come to the marina then taken his truck."

"Was his truck at the marina?" asked Devon.

"Not sure," said Henry. "Didn't think to look."

"We're wasting precious daylight, I say we head back to the mainland and pull together a search party," said Benny.

"And call the sheriff," added Stan for the second time.

Devon looked at Benny and said, "You're right. Let's head over to…"

Devon was cut off by the ringing of Henry's cell phone. Henry flipped it open and said, "Hey Charlie. What's that? Slow down, I can't understand you. Where? Okay, can you tow it in? Okay. How far out are you? Okay, I'll see you at the marina soon. Thanks, Charlie." Henry hung up and looked around the room at the worried faces of Chet's friends and family and said, "That was Charlie Walker. He and his son Earl were out fishing up north off the cliffs near Edgewater, said they ran across a boat just bobbing on the current. Didn't look like no one was in it, so they took a closer look, and well, it looks like its Chet's, and they said it's been rigged to drive its self."

"What?" said Rosalie, "How do you rig a boat to drive by its self?"

"Hold on Rosalie," said Henry, "There's more. Charlie says there was a note taped to the steering wheel."

Cautiously, Devon asked, "What kind of note?"

Henry took off his cap, ran his fingers through his hair, and said, "A ransom note." The room let out a collective gasp. The questions started flying from everyone's mouth at the same time. Henry put up his hands and said, "Hold up, hold up, we got more questions than we do answers, let's head back to the mainland and get the sheriff. Charlie and Earl hitched a tow line to the boat, said they're about 40 minutes out."

Devon and Leonard headed over to the marina with Henry and the others. Leanne, Amber and Rosalie stayed on the island with nothing else to do but worry. Devon promised to call them once Charlie arrived with Chet's boat and the ransom note.

*****

Two hours later, at seven p.m. Leanne's cell phone rang. She, Rosalie, Harold, Amber, Kate, and Lee were gathered at the kitchen table. She answered the phone, put it on the speaker, and said, "We're all here, Amber, Rosalie, Harold, Kate, and Lee."

"Good," said Devon. "So, this is what we know thus far. The sheriff is with us and he's debating whether or not to call the FBI. Benny, Leonard, and I would like him to hold off until sun-up tomorrow. But right now, we know he was abducted, and the ransom note is asking for five million dollars by noon tomorrow. I've called Gordy and told him to stay put in LA in case I need him to transfer some money. Everyone in town knows what's going on, so we are going to form a search party and head in different directions and knock on doors. Leonard and I are going to stay the night at Henry's and work on getting the money. Leonard spoke to his father who wants to bring us the money first thing in the morning, which looks like it may be our fastest option. The note also said they would contact me with the drop location, which will hopefully give the sheriff and the FBI time to get to the location and hide. I am to go alone or the deals off. So, with that said, I know you are all sick with worry, but you have to trust us to do what we can over here. Leanne, I'm really sorry about our wedding, but as soon as we have Chet home safe and sound, we will get married, I promise."

Leanne said, "Devon that truly is my least concern right now. All I want is for you and Chet to come home safe. Please don't do anything foolish."

Devon let out what sounded like a laugh, but with a hint of anger, and said, "I can't make you any promises. Once I find out who is behind this and have laid their hands on Chet, they might well wish they had re-thought their plan. Listen, I have to go. I'll call you later tonight. I love you."

"I love you too," said Leanne, and hung up the phone.

Kate laid her hand over Leanne's and said, "The kids are all fed, and settled in over with Hannah and Jenna.

Why don't we pull together some dinner? If we keep our hands busy, it will help to keep our minds busy too."

Leanne smiled and said, "That sounds like a good idea. I always seem to bring my troubled thoughts with me into the kitchen, and for some reason, it always makes me feel better. Harold or Lee could one of you get the grill started. The wood and the kindling are already stacked in it, and the lighter is in the basket on the shelf next to the grill."

"Sure, thing Leanne," said Harold and Lee at the same time, and to Leanne's ears they sounded just like Chet.

Rosalie got up from the table and went to the refrigerator and brought out a bottle of Chardonnay, grabbed four glasses off the wine glass rack, and put them on the island. She poured a glass for each of them and said, "We need to have a glass of wine, take a deep breath and release the tension, or we will be no good to anyone, especially Chet. Kate's right lets have dinner and we can kick this shit show around. We need to put the worry on burner number two and turn on the thinking burner. I'll take care of setting the table and Harold and I will clean up."

Harold walked in and said, "Grills fired up Leanne, needs about 15 minutes before its ready." Rosalie walked over to the counter and poured Harold a glass of red wine from an open bottle, handed it to him and added a kiss to his cheek.

Leanne smiled and said, "Good thing Devon didn't see that PDA (public display of affection) or he would have had a comment or two or three or four."

"Ha! I would tell him, I'm like a fine wine, I mellow with age," Rosalie countered, which sent a well-needed round of laughter through the kitchen.

Kate handed Harold a beer and asked, "Would you mind bringing this out to Lee? I know that face he's wearing. The slight burrow of his brow means he's thinking and he's worried."

After Harold left the kitchen, Amber picked up her glass of wine, took a sip, then set it by a plate on the table Rosalie was setting and said, "I'm going to go check on the girls and update Hannah, Clay, Petey, Jenna, and Bailey Jr. on what we know. And Momma, if you and Daddy don't mind watching the girls, I'd like to sleep over here tonight with Rosalie and Leanne."

"Not at all Baby Girl," said Kate, "Those two angels are good as gold. When you were gone earlier this week, we put them to bed and didn't hear a peep from them from seven to seven. I think you three need to stick together, ya'll need each other right now, and it wouldn't hurt to ask the good Lord for some guidance."

"I love you Momma, and don't you worry I've been praying and promising," Amber kissed Kates cheek and headed towards the back door.

Chapter 39

Rosalie spent most of the night tossing and turning. Finally, at six a.m. she gave up and quietly got out of bed so she wouldn't wake Harold, which wasn't likely since he slept like a rock. She grabbed her robe and put on her slippers and headed downstairs to the kitchen. When she walked in, she found Kate and Leanne sitting at the kitchen island, they both looked over at her, and Rosalie asked, "Can't sleep either?" Both women nodded. Rosalie poured herself a cup of coffee and sat down next to Leanne. They sat in silence for a while until the back door opened and in walked Amber.

"Where in the world have you been at this hour, Baby Girl?" Kate asked.

Amber walked over to the island and said, "I couldn't sleep a wink. Every time I closed my eyes, I saw Chet's face and heard him telling me, *you're braver than you know,* and I keep repeating those words in my head hoping he can hear me."

Leanne took Ambers' hand and said, "I keep praying he's not hurt. I know it's eating us all up. When Devon called late last night and said the FBI is now involved, it made me feel slightly better. John and Ellen Mathers are flying in early this morning with the money and a trap is being planned to hopefully catch the person or people behind the kidnapping."

Rosalie turned in her chair and looked at Leanne, Kate, and Amber and said, "Somethings been scratching at the back of my brain as I laid awake these past few hours, and I can't figure it out. So, let me ask you. Why Chet? I keep coming back to, because whoever kidnapped him, knows that Devon would do whatever it takes to protect that man, and the only people that know how strong that bond is are us, and the townspeople, right?" The three women nodded. "Okay so with that said, I just realized what it was scratching at me, it's the ransom amount, five million. It seems awful high which leads me back to the fact that Devon would do anything or pay anything to protect Chet..." Rosalie stopped talking, stood up and walked around the island so that she was facing all three women, because she had just put two and two together. "Remember the day we confronted the gurus and Devon asked me to come up with a number to buy the house? Well I threw him a low ball of two point five million, but..." Right then and there the light bulb went on for Amber and Leanne and they both said in unison, "Blair."

"Holy shit," said Leanne. "How did we not see that from the beginning? I need to call Devon and let him know."

"Wait, wait a sec," said Amber. "Give me a minute," as she paced back and forth, she stopped, looked at Leanne and Rosalie, and said, "I know where he is. I know where they have Chet. He's at the...cabin."

"Oh my God Amber, how did you know?" Leanne asked.

This time Kate answered, "She's got a sixth sense, so I would go with her instinct."

Leanne stood up and said, "Let's go get dressed and head over there."

Amber said, "Leanne, we should call the sheriff. Whoever has Chet could be armed and dangerous."

"No time," said Leanne, as she grabbed a rolling pin from a drawer, "Grab your weapon of choice, and let's get a move on." All three women ran upstairs to get dressed, within ten minutes they were back downstairs and heading for the golf cart. Leanne handed Kate her cell phone and told her, "Call Devon and if you can't reach him call Henry, tell them to meet us at the cabin."

On the ride over to the cabin, Leanne said, "Okay, we need a game plan. Amber, what's your weapon?" Amber lifted the cast iron skillet she grabbed from the stovetop. Leanne approved. She asked Rosalie, "What's your weapon?" Rosalie held up a can of hairspray. Leanne said, "What the hell Rosalie, how is hairspray a weapon?"

"I figured it's like mace, I can spray it in their face," said Rosalie.

"Good thinking Rosalie," said Amber, "That stuff can burn the eyeballs right out of their socket."

They didn't see any boats tied to the dock as they approached the path from the beach to the cabin. They jumped out of the golf cart and started the trek up the path. "Okay," said Leanne, "The plan is to get to the edge of the woods and spread out. If it's all quiet then we regroup and head to the perimeter of the cabin. Rosalie, you and the can of hairspray, take the living room window. Amber, you and your cast iron skillet and me and my rolling pin will take the back porch. Rosalie, you peek in the window, if you see anybody in there... Oh crap, duck!" They ran behind a tree as the back door of the cabin swung open and a guy came out. He wasn't very big, and he didn't look like a thug. He was on his phone, they could hear him shouting, "Where the hell are you? No, this was not the plan, leaving me here to babysit the old man, and you ain't packed us hardly any food in that cooler, and not one beer. No Cece, you listen to me, you need to come pick me up before the drop. Once we have the money, we can hit the highway. I'll loosen the old man's ropes just enough that it takes him an hour to wiggle free. No! Don't you hang up on me Cece, Cece, don't you dare!" said the guy with the phone as he kicked the picnic table, he then headed back inside.

Leanne turned to Amber and Rosalie and whispered, "Let's make our way around the front, and see if we can get a window open. But one of us has to stay here as a lookout."

"I'll do it," said Amber. "If something fishy happens I'll give you an owl hoot, like this, whoo, whoo."

"Hey, that was pretty good Amber," said Leanne, "Okay, come on Rosalie, let's go," but before they could get two feet, the back door swung open again and out came the man, pushing Chet in front of him. His feet and hands were bound by rope, which made it difficult to walk. Once he got him down the stairs, the guy turned Chet towards the outhouse and said, "Don't try any funny business or I'll tie you to a tree."

As Chet continued to slowly shuffle towards the outhouse, the guy gave him a 'move it along' shove and Chet tripped and went straight down, face first. And like a bolt of lightning, Amber ran across the yard and rammed headfirst into the guy, taking him down in one of her Bailey Jr tackles. From then on it was total chaos, Amber was wrestling with the guy on the ground, Rosalie was spraying him in the face with hair spray, and then Leanne clobbered him with her rolling pin and knocked him out cold. Once the dust settled, they got Chet untied and used the ropes to tie up the guy.

Chet was standing up, rubbing his wrists and said, "What the heck? Where did you three come from? All I saw out of the corner of my eye was this streak of blond hair come charging my way."

Amber was brushing herself off and said, "And all I saw was red when he pushed you down. Nobody and I mean nobody messes with my family," she walked over and wrapped Chet in a big hug.

Chet turned to Rosalie and said, "Then I see Firecracker here, wildly spraying something in his face like it's a nest of bees."

"Hairspray, my weapon of choice," said Rosalie, "His eyelashes will be stuck together for a week."

Then Chet turned to Leanne and said, "Then you come along with what looks like a rolling pin and ring his bell. I thought I was watching Charlie Angel's."

Just then, Devon and Leonard came busting out of the woods, with Henry and the sheriff right behind them. When they reached Leanne, Chet, Rosalie, and Amber, and some guy lying on the ground tied up, they just stared speechless at the scene in front of them.

It wasn't until Henry and the sheriff turned the guy over, who was now moaning, asking, "What happened?" did they recognize him.

Henry said, "That's Kenny, the guy I just hired last week."

Chet said, "Yeah, that's him. I left the house yesterday morning, close to seven, came around the bend and seen a boat broke down. I pulled up next to it, asked if he needed help and he says the engine just died. So, I roped up to him, climbed on board to take a look, next thing I know, I'm tied up and being dragged out here."

The sheriff and Henry each took hold of one of Kenny's arms and hoisted him up to his feet. The sheriff handcuffed Kenny and removed the ropes the women had used to tie him up with. The sheriff turned to Chet, Devon, and Leonard and said, "Henry and I will take him in if ya'll want to go back to the house with the women. Chet you can come in later to give me a statement."

"Nope, I got a wedding to perform later, so I'd much rather come with you now," said Chet.

"But Chet, you must be hungrier than a stray cat," said Amber.

"Don't you be worrying Country Girl, I'm hitching a ride with these fella's and heading straight to Frieda's for some jelly donuts," replied Chet.

"Chet, you went down like a redwood in the forest, are you sure you're not hurt?" asked Rosalie.

"Firecracker, I've dove into enough foxholes to know how to get my hands under me," said Chet.

"Leonard and I need to come back with you to meet his father. Now that we have Chet back, we don't need the money, but we still have a date with whoever is behind this kidnapping at noon," said Devon.

Rosalie stepped forward and said to Devon, "We figured out who hatched this plan. That's how we knew to come to the cabin to look for Chet. We were all up pretty early this morning, sitting around the kitchen island trying to figure things out, and I mentioned that something was scratching at the back of my mind, it wasn't until I said it out loud that it registered."

"And what, may I ask, was scratching, as you say, at the back of your mind?" asked Devon.

"The money," replied Rosalie, "Or I should say, the amount of the ransom. Think about it, Rock Star, where have you heard that figure before, five million?"

The silence lingered for a minute then the light bulbs went on and Chet, Devon, and Leonard all said in unison, "Blair."

"Bingo," said Rosalie.

"But wait a minute," said Chet, "This fella here kept calling someone all in a snit about being left here on the island, but he called her CeCe."

"That's true. We heard him talking to her too," said Amber, "And he was not a happy camper."

Everyone turned and looked at Kenny, and then Devon asked him, "So Kenny, mind telling us who CeCe is?"

"Don't ya'll be looking at me, I'll never rat her out. She's my girl and I won't be turning on her," said a defiant Kenny.

"Okay then," said Devon, "How about you just tell us what CeCe looks like."

Kenny's face lit up and he said, "She's smoking hot. Met her at a festival in Aberdeen, she was line dancing and I couldn't take my eyes off her sweet swaying ass. Woo, wee she is something else."

This time it was Leanne who asked a question, "Kenny, speaking of eyes, what color are CeCe's.?"

"They are the bluest of blue. One look at those eyes and I was a goner."

Devon, Leanne, Chet, Rosalie, Leonard and Amber looked at each other and said, "Blair."

"I don't know who ya'll are talking about, but my girl's name is CeCe," said an annoyed Kenny.

Devon turned to the others and said, "Well, this just made things a whole lot more interesting. The drop is scheduled for noon. Leonard and I took a ride out to Old Pump Road and saw the drop location, which is an old logging weigh station. The FBI will be staking out the perimeter, which is heavily wooded. Per the person that text me from Chet's phone last night, said to come alone, drop the bags with the money in the abandoned parking lot, turn around and drive back the way I came. No funny business or Chet would be a dead man."

Now, this conversation caught Kenny's attention. He started to pull away from the sheriff's grip, yelling, "That's not true! Cece said the drop was going to be down at the seawall in Cliff Haven. She's coming to pick me up by boat and we were going to head down there. Once we had the money, we were going to Portland then flying to Hawaii."

Devon looked at Leanne, and then Leanne turned to Kenny and said, "Kenny, by any chance did CeCe ever mention the name, Micah?"

"No. Why should she? She said she only had eyes for me," said a pouting Kenny.

"Oh boy, she got you good Kenny. Micah is Blair's husband. Together they have spent a lot of time in Hawaii. She's probably ditching you and heading to Hawaii, letting you take the rap for the kidnapping," said Rosalie.

"That's a lie!" Kenny shot back, "Cece said she's never been married. Said once we get the money, we're going to Hawaii to get hitched, said that would be our honeymoon."

Chet stepped forward and said, "Son, you got duped. Blair is a mean slithering snake. She'd cut you lose faster than a cobra's bite. Be best for you to cooperate with the sheriff and the FBI, tell them all you know."

"You're lying, all of you! I know CeCe, she loves me, she wouldn't do none of what you're sayin'," Kenny shouted at the group.

"Okay Son, don't say I didn't warn ya. Now can we please go, I'm starving, and I have a gal I need to see about being my plus one. So, let's shake a leg," said Chet.

The plan was Devon, Chet and Leonard would head back to the mainland and let the FBI know what was going on. Leanne, Rosalie and Amber would head back to the house and let everyone know Chet was safe, then Henry would pick them up at 11 o'clock and bring them to the mainland, so they would be there in plenty of time to watch the sheriff haul Blair's ass into jail, if things went as planned.

Chapter 40

When Leanne, Rosalie, and Amber returned home they filled everyone in on the morning's adventure and the rescue of Chet. After they took showers and got dressed, Kate insisted that they eat some of the coffee cake she made earlier that morning, before heading over to the mainland. As Leanne reached for a second piece, she said out loud, but was more or less talking to herself, "How in the world am I going to be ready for my wedding by three o'clock?"

Kate refilled her coffee mug and said, "Don't you worry about it, sweetie. Lee, Harold, and I have it all under control, with a little help from Devon." He pushed the time out to five o'clock; Stan and Leroy were spreading the word through town. "The out of town guests are arriving around two and Adele and Pete are looking after them, getting them settled in the rental houses. Eloise is working with the caterers on that end and we have it covered on this end. The only thing you'll have to do is slip into your wedding dress and say, 'I do.'"

Astonished, Leanne said, "How did he manage to arrange all these details while worrying sick about Chet?"

"He's Devon," said Rosalie and Amber at the same time.

Amber added, "I can't wait to see your dress. Did you go the full length or tea length?"

"Well," said Leanne, "Actually, I don't have a wedding dress. Devon and I decided that we wanted our wedding to be beach casual, so I bought a sundress in Seattle a while back. Devon is wearing khaki shorts, with a white T-shirt, and at my request, we will both be barefoot."

"Why barefoot?" asked Amber.

"Because Devon has the sexiest toes ever," replied Leanne.

"What isn't sexy about that man?" added Rosalie.

"Huh," said Amber, "I'll have to check his toes out. But for now, we better get down to the dock. Henry will be here in five minutes."

Just as they got to the end of the dock, they saw Henry motoring around the bend. He pulled up and secured a line and the three women climbed on board. Once settled Henry turned the boat and headed for the marina. Leanne asked him, "So, what's the latest Henry?"

"Well," answered Henry, "Chet ate six jelly donuts at Frieda's, and now he's with the sheriff answering questions. Kenny's locked up and madder than a rabid raccoon. Leonard's parents just arrived about an hour ago and were relieved to hear that Chet was rescued, though John Mather's wasn't comfortable lugging around five million dollars, so an FBI agent took him and Ellen to Seattle to put it in the bank."

Rosalie said, "Well, I am more than ready to see the look on Blair's face when she finds out she's busted." Leanne and Amber agreed.

Leanne added, "I think the real show is going to be when they bring her into the station, and she sees all of us waiting for her, and Kenny locked up. I sure hope they can find out where Micah is and lock his ass up too if he had something to do with this."

"I don't know Leanne," said Amber, "My intuition has been pecking at me ever since we mentioned Micah to Kenny. I'm thinking the gurus may have parted ways. That day we confronted them; Micah was too scared to have the police involved. I don't think he would go along with this hair brain scheme of Blair's."

"Yeah, I'm with Amber," said Rosalie, "I'm thinking she ditched him for a younger trained monkey."

Leanne gave that some thought and said, "Possibly. We shall soon find out."

When they got to the marina, Devon and Leonard were waiting for them. Leanne stepped onto the dock and walked over to him and said, "Now listen to me Devon, don't go doing something stupid, like trying to take down Blair. Do exactly what the FBI instructed you to do. Drop the duffel bags, turn around, and come back here. We're getting married in five and a half hours, and I'll need you standing next to me. Understood?" said Leanne.

Devon kissed her and said, "I promise. It takes about 30 minutes to get to the spot on Old Pump Road and another 30 to get back, so I will be back here at half-past 12, count on it." He tapped her nose and got into Leanne's SUV and drove off.

Rosalie and Amber walked over to Leanne and each took a hand as they watched Devon drive away. They didn't speak a word, they didn't have to, they were each silently praying.

*****

True to his word, Devon was back and parked at the marina at 12:29 p.m. When Leanne saw him all of the anxiety and tension drained from her body. She slowly walked towards him and straight into his waiting arms. The stress of Chet's kidnapping had taken its toll and the mere fact that this could happen to them, to anyone close to them, was a new reality. They stood there in each other's arms for what felt like an eternity, until the sheriff called out from his office across the street, "They got her, bringing her in now."

Word travels fast in Swallow Bend, by the time the FBI van pulled up in front of the sheriff's office, Main Street was lined with friends and neighbors that know and love Chet. Leanne, Devon, Rosalie, Chet, Amber, and Leonard were front and center. The rear door of the van opened and a very angry, handcuffed Blair, emerged. It took her a minute to register where she was, and who the six people standing in front of her were, but once it did register, she went bat shit crazy. She was trying to free herself from the grips of the two agents holding her arms, as she wildly kicked her feet; she began screaming, "I hate you. All of you! You are nothing but pathetic losers. I should've killed the old man, and burnt down that house, my house, that you stole from me, with all of you in it."

"That's enough," said one of the agents holding her arm, "You just added threatening to kill to your charges," as he steered Blair into the sheriff's office and her waiting jail cell.

Devon turned to the other's and said, "Well she didn't seem very pleased to see us," which brought on a round of laughter. "What do you say we head back to the island? I, for one, have some very important business to tend to. I am about to marry the woman of my dreams," he wrapped his arm around a smiling Leanne, and they headed for Chet's boat.

Chapter 41
The Wedding

The guests were gathered on the front lawn down by the beach. They stood in two rows to form an aisle, as they watched Leonard walk Leanne down to the beach. Devon was standing in the sand, barefoot, with Luke and Lindsey each holding his hands. Rosalie, Harold, and Amber stood next to Chet, watching a radiant Leanne walk towards them. She was wearing a simple floral sundress, and her hair fell to her shoulders in soft curls. But it was the smile on her face and the look in her eyes that told the story, a love story, of second chances and true love. The sight of Devon standing there holding the hands of her children, waiting for her, filled her with a tsunami of emotions. As she reached Devon and the twins, Leonard leaned over and kissed her cheek and then went to stand next to Amber. Chet stepped forward and said to all of the guests, "Please hold hands and form a circle around Devon, Leanne, Luke, and Lindsey." Once the circle was complete, Chet began, "All of you are here to witness the blessing of the unity of marriage between Devon and Leanne. You have formed a complete circle in honor of your love and friendship for them, and for this, I know they are truly grateful. And now it's time to get this show on the road. 'Do you, Devon, take this amazing gal, Leanne, to be your wife?'"

With his gaze latched onto Leanne's eyes, he said, "I most certainly do,"

"Good answer Son," said Chet, which got a chuckle from the circle. "Now Leanne, do you take this man, Devon, with a heart as big as this here country, to be your husband?"

Without hesitation Leanne said, "With all of my heart, I do."

Chet turned to Luke and Lindsey and said, "Rings please."

Luke handed the ring he was holding to Leanne for Devon, and Lindsey handed Devon the ring she was holding for Leanne and watched as Devon slid the ring onto Leanne's finger and Leanne slid the ring onto Devon's finger. Chet took each of their hands in his and said, "It is with my greatest pride and joy, that I now pronounce you man and wife…" and there was no need to finish the sentence with 'you may now kiss the bride' because Devon and Leanne were way ahead of him.

Epilogue

The next day, Henry and the sheriff came out to the island with an update on Blair and Kenny. The FBI had transferred them to Seattle last night, and from what the sheriff witnessed, as they loaded them into the van, they were none too happy with each other. The sheriff said, "While they were in their separate cells they were screaming back and forth at each other, pointing the finger. However, come to find out, after the fingerprints came back, Kenny was clean as a whistle, not so much as a parking ticket. His last known address was Aberdeen, Texas just as he said. Blair, on the other hand, was not so squeaky clean. She has a long history, starting with her real name, Cecelia Welby." Turns out her mother was the teenage mistress of Charles Welby, the man they had heard about from Wally at the Memorial Day picnic. "According to Blair, she did some research a few years back and made the connection. She tried to inherit the island, but since her mother told her that he wasn't her father and showed her a birth certificate that said, 'father unknown,' Blair didn't have any proof that Charles Welby was her father, so she had no claim. However, she was granted the right to build on the island and that's how the big house came to be five years ago. The FBI is heading to Aberdeen, Texas to talk to the mother, at Blair's childhood home."

"As for the husband Micah, his whereabouts are unknown, and Blair is not too keen on talking about him. Says he emptied their bank account, left her an envelope with a $1,000 and a one-way plane ticket from Hawaii to Texas. The FBI will be sniffing after his trail, because if his rap sheet is anything like Blair's, who spent years swindling and stealing all across the country, then they'll be looking to find him."

The sheriff stood and said, "Well that's all I got for now. I learn anything more, I'll be sure to update you. And congratulations on your wedding, sorry I had to miss it."

Leanne and Devon walked the sheriff and Henry back to the dock and thanked them for coming out to the island. Devon untied the lines and gave them a push-off. He stepped back to Leanne, put his arm around her shoulder, and said, "Well that was quite a lot to digest."

"Oh, I'm sure that's not the last of it. I bet once the FBI start turning over rocks, they'll find a whole bunch more on Blair and Micah," said Leanne.

"I have no doubt, Mrs. Davis," said Devon.

"Me either, Mr. Davis," said Leanne, and they turned and headed up the dock towards the big house.

THE END

Annie's Place